# KINGDOM COME

Other Books by Laura Chester:
*Nightlatch*, prose poems, The Tribal Press, 1974
*Primagravida*, nonfiction, Christopher's Books, 1975
*Chunk Off & Float*, poetry, Cold Mountain Press, 1978
*Watermark*, a novel, The Figures, 1978
*Proud & Ashamed*, poetry, Christopher's Books, 1978
*My Pleasure*, voice pieces, The Figures, 1980
*Lupus Novice*, nonfiction, Station Hill Press, 1987, new edition 1999
*Free Rein*, prose poems, Burning Deck Press, 1988
*In the Zone*, selected writing, Black Sparrow Press, 1988
*The Stone Baby*, a novel, Black Sparrow Press, 1989
*Bitches Ride Alone*, short stories, Black Sparrow Press, 1991
*The Story of the Lake,* a novel, Faber & Faber, 1995
*All in All*, prose poems, Quale, 2000
*Holy Personal*, nonfiction, Indiana University Press, 2000

Editor of the Anthologies:
*Rising Tides, 20th Century American Women Poets*, Simon & Schuster, 1973
*Deep Down, New Sensual Writing by Women,* Faber & Faber, 1988
*Cradle & All, Women Writers on Pregnancy and Birth*, Faber & Faber, 1989
*The Unmade Bed, Sensual Writing on Married Love*, HarperCollins 1992

# KINGDOM COME

a novel by

## LAURA CHESTER

CREATIVE ARTS BOOK COMPANY
Berkeley, California
2000

Creative Arts Book Company
833 Bancroft Way
Berkeley, California 94710
(800) 848-7789

ISBN 0-88739-359-4  Paper
ISBN 0-88739-360-8  Cloth
Library of Congress Catalog Number
Printed in the United States of America

ACKNOWLEDGMENTS:

I would like to thank Dick Jimenez and Sidney Franklin of the Crown C
Ranch; as well as Mary, Norman and Ruth Hale of the Hale Ranch; Bob, Lloyd
and Lisa Sharp of the San Rafael Cattle Company; Mike Elliston of the P.O.
Ranch; Carew Papritz, Margie Buyer and Charlie Davis of the Poco Toro
Ranch; Loreto Mendez and Earl Niichel of the Whispering Rose Ranch; Gooch
and Katie Goodwin, Helen Ashburn of La Frontera; Louise Timken of the Vaca
Ranch; "Pancho" Francisco Cordova and George Lorta of the Circle Z Ranch;
Joker Mendoza, Nancy McQuiston, Harvey Whelan, Marcia Burden, Jim
Pickerel, as well as Dan and Melody Skiver of Arizona Trail Tours, and Jimmy
Lewis, for their stories, recipes, friendship and support, which have nurtured
this book and helped bring it to life.

Special thanks to my husband, Mason Rose, for his constancy, understanding
and continual encouragement, not to mention his superior knowledge of the
computer which was often a source of aggravation to me. With special love for
my two sons, Clovis and Ayler, and with great appreciation to the friends and
family members, who have helped me in numerous ways: Jill Johnson, Helen
Chester, Anne Fredericks, Francine Segan, Sherril Jaffe, Chris Tomasino and
Summer Brenner. I am grateful to you, as always.

The quote on Eros, was written and recorded by Thomas Moore, *On
Creativity*, published by "Sounds True," Boulder, Colorado, copyright © 1994,
reprinted with the author's permission. A special nod to *La Dame Aux
Camilias*, by Alexandre Dumas.

The description of the gilded mirrors was inspired by the work of Anne
Fredericks. The song lyrics and music were adapted from the song, "Bethel," by
Robin Young, printed with his permission.

Parts of this novel were first published by David Berg-Seiter on the internet lit-
erary magazine, *Web del Sol*, and by Mark Begley in *Wake Up Heavy*, #3. In
addition, the section that begins: "On the hottest, most sweltering day of the
year," was published by *Wake Up Heavy* as a limited broadside. P.O. Box 4668
Fresno, CA. 93744

*to my brother*
*David William Chester*

We don't know who Eros is. All we know is that he beckons us, he entices us, he leads us to places that we don't know, but it turns out that these places are the places we sought from the very beginning. He leads us to our own hearts. He leads us to a new world, that we didn't know existed, but later discover is our own world. So it is important, it is essential in living the creative life, to be led, to be taken to those places that are full of mystery, and find there the world that we were hoping to live all our lives. We didn't know where we were headed, but because we live creatively, we find our way to that very place that we have longed for.

Thomas Moore

eacon hill has always seemed like a little toy town to me, trapped within the larger city, like a privileged child kept home from school, a well-protected place with old-fashioned streetlamps and valuable charm, the askew brick sidewalks making the winter even more treacherous. Of course, there was Charles Street with its coffee and ice cream, realtors and restaurants — it had drawn me at first, until I wearied of the static antique displays, the stylized wooden spoons. It carried me no further than a stage set. There was no place to park.

At the time we purchased our Pinckney Street townhouse, eternally deprived of light, I agreed with my husband — it was perfect, our dream, everything we needed to be happy. I believed that painting the plaster walls "museum white," installing track lighting, and stripping the windows of the unnecessary curtains would give us the brightness we thought we could have, but the brain cannot be fooled. There must be some part of the brain that is always on the lookout for the real thing, until it is sated, until it has had its luminous fill.

Gradually I became used to my own grey mood, as one finally accepts winter in Boston, but I came to resent the encroaching ivy that did so well even without the sun. It seemed to be omnivorous, ripping at the slates of the roof, which were already feeble, digging its nails into the mortar of the house. I feared the ivy would cover the windows, block out what little light we had, but in the midst of this dread, which was more like suspension really — the mood of half-sleep accepted by the resigned insomniac, neither clear nor stormy, but overcast — in the midst of this daze came clarity, the floodlit unveiling that awakens every nerve.

I find it almost uncanny that my marriage ended on Valentine's Day — blood red might have been the appropriate palette, but I still remember the scene in black and white, which is true of most shocking things. The black headboard, his Italian sheets illuminated by the steel-grey sidelights.

Caught up by the romantic impulse of the day, I bought a bottle of Merlot, quickly purchased for the charming stag on the label, a heart-shaped anthurium, because it looked like it might last forever — I recall that bucket of them now as obscene — their pistils erect as cat parts, spiked —

I had lived for eighteen years in the shade, and suddenly felt the need for a stronger light, the purity of air at a certain altitude, no buildings to obstruct the view, the far far-reaching atmosphere, circling, coursing with tremendous cloud, the dramatic slant of sunshine breaking through a storm front pushed north from Mexico. I wanted to claim this last frontier of open range, the San Rafael, surrounded by mountains — pronghorn grazing in the distance, harrier hawks swooping over golden undulations, the cottonwood that ran along the streambed of the Santa Cruz, the wandering Hereford who stood by the roadside, mother and son, listening to the metal *zing* of the cattle guard as I drove past, heading for La Querencia, setting up a trail of road dust on the way to my Aunt Carla's.

# Part One

# BEACON HILL

IT WAS THE WORST CHRISTMAS of my life for several reasons. Even I could no longer believe that the proper holiday trimmings would create a harmonious family feeling, or that swags of evergreen down the banister would bring us all together. I had hung our Christmas cards on long red ribbons around the living room doorway, just as Granny Hawkins used to do. I had polished the brass angel candleholders and set up the crèche in the hallway, but the greater my effort, the more snide my children became. Even Jovey was being resistant. Night after night Jen stayed up late with her Boston friends, and we got to enjoy her exhaustion.

Buying a tree with Jack was like buying anything with Jack. It was his decision, because he was the one with the taste. It wasn't done in a joyful mood, because he couldn't see spending an entire Saturday morning walking around some lot. I wanted to take my time, inhaling the scent of fresh-cut evergreen, selecting the most balanced tree, just the right height for our living room, but before I'd made one circle around, he already had our tree bound and paid for.

"It'll be perfect," he assured me. "Blue spruce— they're the best. Did you pick anything out for yourself yet this year?"

I had fallen into the habit of choosing my own Christmas present, and I'd found a blue mosaic frame — very lovely, not too expensive. I had the shopkeeper wrap it up, so that Jack wouldn't even see what it was he was giving before he gave it — *He'd* be the one who would be surprised.

Now I understood why my mother had said — *Make something for me. Anything you make yourself I will like.* I had said the same thing to my children, and still had a box of those treasures: a little clay owl glazed an earthy umber, a collage of ripped magazine paper with a hand-written poem, colorful crayon swirls all blackened out with poster paint, scratched with a pin to make a picture.

As an eight-year-old I used a similar pin to make a house and family on the varnished piano bench. I liked how the shellac scratched so easily off — but that particular artwork did not please my father, who could only see I'd wrecked a piece of furniture.

Jack carried the tree home, and together we got it mounted in its metal holder. When it had been screwed in tight at the proper angle, he sawed off the lowest limbs, all the while swearing at the punishing needles. That was his contribution. Then the phone rang, and off he went to scrub the resin from his hands. Soon I could hear the beep of his computer starting up, and there I was with a heavy heart, contemplating the three cardboard boxes full of ornaments. What was I trying to provide?

I shut my eyes and thought about Sam riding out across the San Rafael, pulling a cedar tree home behind his quarter horse. He was wearing a lined canvas jacket, brown fleece gloves, and despite the immense loneliness of the ranch in December, the mountains, the distance, the singular man, there was something so tranquil — the soft, silent snow coming out of the sky, making its quiet covering — that it made me feel cozy, close.

That particular Christmas, ten years ago, Jack had been doing a big job in Chicago, so I'd taken the kids out to Aunt Carla's ranch. It was wonderful seeing Sam again. We had ridden out together like a happy family, singing, joking, and I almost fell back in love with him, though we kept ourselves in check.

Sam and Pedro were both there in the living room when my aunt brought out her box of Christmas tree ornaments. We all took turns unwrapping them from ancient tissue paper. The kids claimed favorites, a purple carousel with a pinwheel that whirled from the heat of a hot bulb, a wooden baby angel on a rocking horse, a guitar with actual strings, and a small glass bird with clip-on feet — it had lost its whiskery tail. There were ornaments shaped like fruit and bells and a homemade, starched, lace star. We used large colored lights that glowed like a honey hive, and at the very end, we threw threads of metal tinsel on every limb and then marveled at our creation.

I remember enjoying both children back then, loving the quietness of our evenings on the ranch without the telephone constantly ringing. We all sat around the kitchen table together making paper chains out of red and green construction paper, cutting snowflakes that unfolded, linking one to the next, getting out a deck of cards for Hearts or Fish or Concentration. Sam taught Jen how to braid a *riata,* and she was fascinated, eager and helpful. Now everything to her was a chore.

That evening I'd steamed asparagus tips, stir-fried shallots and crimini mushrooms to toss over a bed of linguini, no cream, since Jen was not eating milk products. It seemed like a miracle when the four of us could sit down in the kitchen together and actually share a meal. I had placed a wreath in the center of the tablecloth with four red candles. The candles stood at varying heights and looked a bit like the members of our family sitting around the table.

"Do you know what linguini means in Italian?" I asked. No one answered. No one seemed to hear. "Sparrow's tongue," I told them, "because the cut is about that width."

"Gross," Jen said, looking down at her plate.

"Well, it's delicious," Jack said. "That's all that matters. Your mother is a fabulous cook. Please don't sing at the table."

"I'm not singing. I'm humming."

Jack ate quickly. Didn't he realize we were all together at last, eating together for the first time in months? Jovey didn't have much of an appetite, because he'd just eaten a bagel with cream cheese, and Jen was picking out the asparagus spear by spear, as if the pasta had a contaminating sauce. She had always liked plates with divided sections as a child, airplane trays with foiled containers.

"Pee stinkers, *yum,*" Jovey announced, describing the pencil-thin asparagus.

"Just wait til you're on institutional food," his sister warned. "You'll have to watch out or you'll get really fat, with a ton of pimples."

"*Ooo*, scary."

"Are we going to the Brickers' Saturday night?" I asked. "We were all invited."

"No way," Jen answered. "I'm not going over there. Mr. Bricker's a lech."

"Elbows," Jack warned, and Jovey lifted them off the table with exaggerated slowness.

"He's always staring at her boobs," Jovey explained.

"Give it a break." Jen slugged him, before covering her chest with crossed arms, while Jack glanced sideways, as if he hadn't noticed her *boobs* before.

The phone rang and all three of them suppressed the urge to jump up and run for it. It was a family rule that we didn't answer the phone during dinner, letting it go on the machine. "I wish we could do something as a family for once."

"We're doing something right now," Jen responded.

"But what about Christmas Eve?"

"Mother was hoping we'd go to the candlelight service."

Both children groaned, and I could have joined them, because I had promised Donna that we would go with her to Midnight Mass — I wanted to do something different — but we'd probably honor Granny's wish and go to the local Presbyterian Church, for as Jack explained, she was getting so old, this might be her very last Christmas.

I asked Jovey if he would give us a concert after dinner, but he was noncommittal. Then Jack began to clear the table, loading the dishwasher, setting a good example, but sometimes I thought he was almost too efficient.

"I made gingerbread men for dessert," nodding to the tray of sprinkles and silver balls, hoping the kids would help me decorate.

Jen reminded me that they were not twelve years old, and Jovey started eating his gingerman naked. Jack didn't bother with an excuse, but sprang for the stairs as soon as the phone rang again. Apparently dinner was over.

"Does Buster want a cookie?" I asked the pug. He cocked his head as I picked up the tray and slid the bottles of sprinkles and red hots and silver balls into the trash — *Gone forever.*

"*Ooo,* Mom's going off the deep end."

Jen jogged upstairs to the living room, while Jovey and I followed. I knew I was nagging, but I couldn't seem to help myself. I had been waiting for this moment for so long, both of them home to help me. "When are we going to decorate the tree? Would you rather not have a tree?"

"We *like* having a tree, Mom."

"It's just all this family stuff gets on our nerves," Jen put in. "There's so much pressure. We just want to relax. Christmas is such a big hype anyway, and you always overdo it."

"We could do things differently next year. We could take our money and go to Price Chopper and buy food for people who really need it."

"Fine," Jen responded, "but next year I'm going to Sun Valley with Marni's family."

"I'll help you string the lights, Mom," Jovey said, "but then I've got to go over to Copley — I'm going to meet some guys. Could we do the tree tomorrow maybe?" I knew that would never happen.

Seeing the expression on my face, he stopped for a second, came over and hugged me.

"Will you at least get under here and water this thing? It's dying of thirst."

"It's already dead, Mom," he said.

INSTINCTIVELY, I GRAVITATED to the North End when I wanted to lift my mood. Even a decaf-cappuccino seemed to boost my spirits, and I loved to listen to the old men bantering on the sidewalks, picking up phrases I actually knew and saying my standard, "*Buon giorno.*" I had an on-going flirtation with an Italian grocer on Hanover Street, where I went to buy pasta. This stocky little man always lit up when he saw me, and told me how he made his tomato sauce from scratch, how he loved the smell of garlic on the breath of a woman — inhaling the arousing aroma from his fingers. Then he'd feed me an herbed olive on a plastic spoon, or stuff a half-loaf of bread into my bag.

Jackson, on the other hand, didn't like the smell of cooking coming up from the basement kitchen into the rest of the house. He asked me to keep the door shut. I didn't understand how anyone could dislike the smell of simmering stock, or roasted winter squash sliced up with apples and onions.

My mother's family was originally from Italy, but everyone said I resembled the Weston side. No matter, that night, I would pour boiling water on dried porcine mushrooms and think of the fresh variety in the markets of Gubbio, how fragrant the air was with white acacia all along the road. This little bag of brittle mushrooms with the life sucked out of them, made me realize how we were all in this transient state. I would pour boiling water and they would spring back to life, releasing the earthy essence of Umbria.

Sprinkled on top of *polenta gratinati* — the recipe said to stir for a full forty minutes, never changing directions, but I wondered what would happen, if I did switch hemispheres. It was a dish that could be exhausting to make, for as the mixture became thicker, it became more difficult to work. Traditionally, it was always made by a man, but Jackson would never have the patience for polenta — I couldn't think of a single forty-minute period when he wouldn't be interrupted by the phone.

Boston's Public Gardens were dismal in December, but I was somewhat cheered by the well-lit charms of Charles Street. Stopping to consider a bunch of dark green holly, which I could place in the niche halfway up the front hall stairs — I turned and grabbed a handful of white narcissus instead.

I would grate up four different kinds of cheese — fontina, tallegio, emmenthal, parmesan, transforming that corn meal baby mush into a delectable treat. I was bolstered by my plans for a comfortable evening, armed with my supplies and the white fragrant flowers.

Jack always appreciated my cooking. It didn't seem fair that he never gained weight. I had begun to gain slowly, about a pound a year, ever since we gave up cigarettes. Right on schedule, my eyes also started to go bad. I first noticed it trying to thread a needle — a simple task, but no matter how I poked the thread or held the needle, I could not make that slit of an opening come into focus. Normally, during the day, I could read the paper or a hardback book, but maps and medicine bottles began to be a problem, and it became even more annoying in a restaurant when the list of entrées danced upon the page and I had next to zero visibility.

I bought my first pair of reading glasses at the Galleria behind Thomas Graves Landing. Jovey was with me, and he helped me pick them out. He always had a great sense of style, a trait he did not inherit from me. I kept my new glasses on the windowsill next to my bed, where I could easily reach them. But one evening, reading under the intense lamplight, I could see the skin around my eye reflected from the inside of my glasses as I glanced up. The lens had a magnifying effect, so that I perceived the mammalian coating of down that covered my skin, the coarser brown hairs of my eyebrow, and the dramatic indentations around my eye, crevassing in all directions.

The following morning, well-rested, cold water splashed on my face, my reading glasses put away in their hard little coffin container,

I looked relatively youthful. I knew time wasn't standing still, that my years of radiance were numbered, but I would make the best of it.

Still, I began to observe teenage girls with their medicinally pure faces. It seemed as if life had not touched them. Concern and laughter, sorrow and tears had not left their mark. No wonder Jack wasn't showing much interest — everything had to be exquisite for him to take any pleasure in it.

Jen, our eighteen-year-old daughter, now a sophomore at Skidmore, had that bone-hard quality of skin particular to athletic girls. But her legs were slim, not overly muscular, like most of the other PE majors. Her short brown hair was boyish, styled, flecked with golden highlights, which lent a certain warmth, but her blue-green eyes had the cold defiant quality of a hard-cut gem. They always held me at a distance.

Donna Marie, my Sicilian friend, called Jen — "That little snot. I just don't get it — whose genes are in her?"

Jen also had a peculiar hooked nose, which she had inherited from Granny Hawkins. Jack insisted it was Jen's most interesting feature, it kept her from looking preppy, his unspoken complaint about my looks, but Jack was the only true preppy in the house. I could hardly imagine Jovey fitting into that mold.

Coming home that night with my cone of flowers and full shopping bag, slightly winded from the climb up Pinckney, I flung my hat and gloves down on the wheelback chair in the entrance. Jen had left a note saying she had gone to Marni's for the evening. The house was quiet. I suspected nothing wrong, though the red light on the answering machine was pulsing for attention. It was only Jack, saying he couldn't make it home for dinner either, which was a disappointment after all the shopping I'd done. He certainly sounded cheerful for an overworked man under so much pressure, but intensity was what he craved. I often joked that his profession was like a lover on the side — it obsessed him — all those phone calls.

Jack was one of the top partners at an interior decorating firm that primarily did commercial buildings. He had to get the new executive suite model ready before Latish would give the go-ahead. Jackson had good taste given a generous budget, preferring chrome and polished wood, a mixture of the modern, softened by natural warmth, grey or wheat-colored carpets with geometric flecks. You usually didn't notice his curtains or upholstery, though the overall effect was serene. His work gave the impression of wealth in the New World, successful restraint. I'd gotten used to his crazy schedule. Jovey filled in, keeping me company on those quiet evenings. The two of us played Ping-Pong or watched old movies. He could still give his mother a generous hug, but then he'd dash upstairs to grab his electric guitar, distorting the distortions of Pearl Jam.

It had been a real shock, bending down to kiss Jovey a few nights ago, smelling tobacco on his skin. I asked him if he had any cigarettes, and he pulled a flattened pack of unfiltered Camels from his back pocket— at least he didn't lie. I carried them into the bathroom with two fingers, doused them with water and threw them away, but even after that minimal contact, I could sense the aura of tobacco all over me, as if I'd been dipped in a room full of smoke. I could not wash my hands of it. And what was worse, it elicited this gut-level craving, desire mixed up with repugnance.

Knowing that I had the house to myself, I felt a keen sense of liberation. I thought about igniting the dry birch logs in the unusable fireplace. The library was still cozy with its red bookshelves and low lamplight. I poured myself a glass of wine, put on my favorite Callas *Traviata,* and settled back, waiting for Jovey to arrive. He'd be going away to school after Christmas. We were pulling him out of public school, because he had started to go "down the tubes," one of his own expressions.

It had begun in freshman year, with the sleaze look, which drove Jack mad, though Jovey was a teenager and needed to express himself. But when we found out that he wasn't doing his homework, playing computer games instead of learning how to type, getting D's and F's when he should have been on honor roll, and finally, when he was caught smoking dope, we had all agreed on Underledge, Jackson's alma mater, one of the few all-boys schools left on the east coast. It was only an hour and a half north of Boston, and he could come home easily. It was going to be an adjustment for me too.

"Mom," he had said the other evening, putting an arm around my shoulder, "you're going to have to find a few new hobbies when I go."

I laughed at his concern, though I dreaded his departure, and had to keep this feeling at bay. I had been a mother for eighteen years, and it was hard to imagine that daily role ending. What would replace it, hobbies?

I decided to forget the polenta, and began to whip up a simple frittata instead, grating zucchini, salting it up to get rid of the excess moisture, pressing it down with the heel of my hand. Nothing drove Jack crazier than seeing one of his birch cabinet doors left open, or God forbid, a drawer. *Would you like me to shut this? Does this want to be closed?* If a counter wasn't kept perfectly clean, it was an insult to his eye. At least his orderliness kept my bad habits in check, though I often felt smudged around the edges compared to him, as if my clothes didn't quite fit me. All I wanted to do was to enjoy our house, while Jack wanted it orderly, like an office.

Even I was impressed by the amount of mess I could create making a cup of green *salsa verde* — pulverizing parsley and cilantro in the Cuisinart, adding shallots, garlic, extra green olive oil, a tablespoon of capers, the grated peel of a lemon, kosher salt, and then to finish it off, a good dash of mango vinegar, and a bit of Mrs. Renfro's hot green chili sauce — the perfect zippy accompaniment to the zucchini frittata.

I looked around the kitchen — it was dark outside. My pug was still out in the garden, patiently waiting, but when I let him in, he scolded me for a good three minutes until I let him lick the last of the bowl. I felt chilly, and went back upstairs for a sweater. But by the time I reached my bedroom, I had forgotten what I'd come for.

Suddenly I felt the need for more color in my life. Why not

paint those window sashes turquoise? Why not crunchy chartreuse curtains in the living room? Wouldn't that be different? Wouldn't that get Granny Hawkins gawking? I wanted to auction off her heavy, antique furniture. It had never been our style anyway, but we'd inherited some of the best pieces, when she moved from her mausoleum of a house into a Back Bay apartment. Jackson thought we had to use the furniture at least until she died. He hated for his mother to disapprove of anything or to accuse him of being ungrateful.

But what about a great big saddlebag armchair, a coffee table you could put your feet on, rather than those hinged mahogany sections that folded up and down. What purpose did they serve? Exit the obsidian mantle and cream woodwork, the tedious Oriental. Perhaps I *did* need a project for when Jovey left home. I wanted a deep, soft, real feather sofa, not *nole me tangere* white. I wanted Buster to be able to leap up beside me, to sleep at my feet with his comforting little sounds.

Originally, I had only used "my room" as a place for projects, but now I slept there too, not out of hostility, or even lack of interest, for Jackson was a good-looking man — five feet eleven inches, one hundred and eighty-five pounds. He was so attractive, both men and women often turned on the street to stare at him. I especially liked gazing at his body when he stepped from the shower — his fleshy, firm shoulders, his muscular calves. I liked the lemony scent of his spicy cologne, the silky starched feel of his cotton shirts, always impeccable. But here, in my own room, I could drop my sweatpants right on the rug without suffering looks of disapproval.

Jackson's blue-green eyes often drew women in. They thought he meant more than he did. I always knew a crush was in the making when I heard a woman say that he looked *just* like some old high school sweetheart, sure thing. He looked like a northern Italian, as if he'd leapt from some icy mountain pool, but he was not one bit Italian. He was English and Scottish, and had a short temper that was well repressed by what he considered to be his Bostonian good manners. His anger had to leak out somewhere, over little insignificant things. *Would you like me to clear this? Does this want to be cleaned?*

I had come to accept his sensate nature. Aesthetics were everything to him. One has to take a person as he is — there is no real changing a husband. Jack had much to recommend him. He was extremely successful, but also a man of culture. He appreciated art, and would go with me to the opera. He was also a reader, and we both enjoyed movies. We considered ourselves lucky, happily married. We were. But lately, he had become more and more isolate. When I came up to his study, he was always on the phone. He would wave me away with the flick of his hand, which I found insulting, for I'd always honored his need for privacy before. He believed that in his line, work never stopped. If you wanted to be good at anything, you couldn't just do it eight hours a day — you had to do it full time, you had to sleep with it.

Maybe that's when I began to stay in my own room. But then, maybe it was just an early phase of menopause, this shifting from fertility to absurdity. I was certainly more at the mercy of the moon, and I did get weirdly hot at odd moments, especially at night. Jackson also said that I'd begun to make noises. I could hardly imagine myself snoring. Maybe he was confusing me with Buster downstairs in his oval, wicker basket, ripping through the night with those labored inhalations, all that oxygen traveling through various contortions on its way to his strong little lungs.

Often I couldn't get to sleep, and had to go through my late night ritual of a lavender bath, toast with marmalade, and a glass of warm milk, followed by two or three chapters. This would usually put me to sleep, but it kept Jackson awake.

Tonight my windowseat bed was unmade as usual. The feather puff looked as if I had kicked it back, and the pillows were scattered, "my rat's nest." Hearing a little twittering sound, I was drawn to the glassed-in porch of my studio beyond, remembering at that moment that I'd forgotten to put the birds back. Turning on the light, I saw the male hopping about on top of the cage, cocking his head, and then on my desk, in a tall pub glass with its wide mouth narrowing toward the bottom, was the female, trapped by her own descent, her head turned backward, her wings neatly closed. She had drowned in two inches of water.

Pulling her out by the tail felt as crude as any death forces one to be. Her eyes were still open but they had lost their luster. Her feathers still had that lovely mottling of browns. What would he do without her?

I thought of how Buster had mourned Prissy-Marie, our other pug, when she'd been hit by a car on West Cedar. He had gone into a deep dog depression. I knew that animals felt things very strongly — it was as if they were made up of little fibers of feeling. Every memory was recorded not as thought, but emotion. I was sure Buster even responded to his food that way — it made him happy, dancing, or with a sniff, it did not. He responded to human beings in a similar manner, immediately sensing if there was warmth and kindness, or hostility. It is hard to fool dogs or children.

My main concern now was that Jackson would be upset. He had given me the birds for my birthday, and this would be taken as another sign of my carelessness. He claimed I was hard on equipment. I broke the CD player by forcing it. I dropped the ceramic knife, chipping the blade, I bumped off the glass ball at the bottom of the banister, carrying down one of my hand-carved mirrors. I spilled food and stained material, ninety-dollar-a-yard material. And now I had let my bird die. But at that moment, Jovey banged in the front door, dropping his backpack on the black and white tiles, calling upstairs, "I'm home!"

BILL BRICKER, MY GARDENING FRIEND and next-door neighbor, had once been in charge of a major advertising firm. He was now in charge of his wife's Lhasa apso. He got all bundled up in scarf and gloves and walked the full eight feet over to our house. "I feel like a fruit taking this dog for a walk." He shuffled in, collapsing in an armchair. "I'm too old for this. I can't have another baby."

"It'll keep you young." I tried to cheer him up, though I didn't exactly envy his position, fifty-eight, with a thirty-four-year-old wife. Roberta was a fashion model but she was losing the *feed me* figure he'd married.

"You should never listen to what the French say."

"And what do the French say?" I played along.

"Half the man's age plus seven years." He glanced up with an ambiguous scowl, as if expecting to get a reaction, but I was lost in my own equation.

Buster was always riled by the arrival of Wally, the Lhasa apso, who had a tremendous amount of sexual energy, given his moppy, too-precious appearance. Bill and I sat there in the tidy tan and white living room, before the loathsome Sheraton coffee table with the silver nut tray and antique porcelains, and watched the two male dogs go at it. When he put his feet up on the hinged front section, I said, "Will you do me a favor and break that thing?" His response, poor dear, was to put his feet back down, thinking it a reprimand.

Wally forgot about preliminaries and immediately wormed his way under Buster's box-like carriage and began by licking his distended parts. Buster seemed to oblige him with some disgruntlement, like a child who's getting a good scrub. "I don't want another baby," Bill went on. "I've already done that." Admittedly, he'd *done that* with

30

another wife, back when he owned a respectable spaniel. Bill seemed mesmerized by the dogs' antics. "I'm even losing my sex drive," he admitted. "That shouldn't happen with a young, beautiful wife."

Bill was frank about a lot of things, and that endeared him to me. I could commiserate, for I could hardly remember the last time I had felt turned on, with the exception of about one ten-minute stretch right before my period. Sneezing was the closest I'd come to orgasm lately.

"I wanted to take her to Venice, just the two of us, but she thinks that Venice is polluted. So we're going to some island to sit in the sand. She wants the baby, *in utero*, to hear the sound of the waves."

"Yes?" I responded, thinking it a nice idea, the heartbeat of the mother beside the heartbeat of the ocean.

Bill had enough unearned income to do anything he wanted, but I pictured him like a horse that had fallen down and gotten all tangled up in his reins. Why didn't he go off to Venice alone if he wanted? What was holding him on Beacon Hill? What code of rigidity kept us buckled in place while our dogs did unspeakable things?

Wally ran Buster in circles, and then managed to tackle him from behind for a ten-minute dry hump. Finally, I thought to invite Bill downstairs for a cup of hot chocolate. We could put the dogs outside in the winter garden, where they couldn't do too much damage.

Over the years Bill had helped me bring my garden to life, planting white "Triumphater" bulbs, an elegant, tall tulip with spiky blooms. He had suggested the foxglove with their choir of bells, pale pink and towering yellow, as well as a trinity of laurel with their crisp, three-dimensional blooms, and then cascades of bleeding hearts. Their fairy-tale quality appealed to me, though I had yet to recall that story Aunt Carla once told, slowly taking the heart, bit by bit, apart.

I had begun an army of lilies of the valley like some holy crusade. Amazing how quickly they multiplied. No real trees towered here — everything was on a more minimal scale — woodruff, vinca, white epidimedium, planted in clumps of three, covering the earth around the original walkway, which ended in a pleasing circle. The bronze statue of a girl stood naked there, about four feet high, hugging herself in such a way that she appeared to be modest or chilled.

I liked to indulge Bill because he was miserable, and because he thought everything I did was superb. The hot chocolate I made was the best in the world — the flower arrangement in the hallway, so beautiful — the mirrors I carved belonged in a museum. He insisted I looked at least two years younger than I actually was, maybe even more with make-up.

"I can just see my life repeating," he went on. He had already wiped sand from numerous hotdogs, blown up a thousand plastic inner tubes, and kissed a million poor ole bruises, but he couldn't bear the thought of being a bad father, either. Bill had a very strict moral code, very upright, very Protestant ethic — that seemed to be part of the problem.

I wondered how Bill would respond if I told him about the candles. I'd come home and found candles all over Jack's bedroom. Jack claimed there had been a power outage while I was skiing with the kids in Vermont. I checked, and it was true, but still, I could hardly see why Jack would put sixteen candles all around the room.

I couldn't imagine Jack having an affair. He wasn't the type. In fact, my friend Donna liked to say that he seemed pathologically monogamous. I was the one who lay around imagining romantic scenes, not that I'd have the nerve for it. Only in my dreams did I get that full complete feeling of crazy kissing, where I could feel the muscles in my lover's arms, his shoulders, his long dark hair in my hands, but on waking my arms were locked in an embrace, holding nothing, just this empty hole.

I was longing for something I had known in the past, before car trips with kids squashed in the back of the Audi, Buster placed squarely in the middle like a demilitarized zone, before the supposedly simple Sunday breakfasts with homemade sour-cream waffles and hand-squeezed orange juice, before the decoration and upkeep of our perfect townhouse, before we ever had our remarkable children, before we'd even met. But I was a child myself back then. Those feelings could hardly be valid.

"Did I tell you the doctor thinks it's going to be twins? Because of the medication. For God sakes — *Twins!*"

"Well, they can take turns pushing your wheelchair," I smiled, offering my hand. He took it in a friendly way, giving it a swing before letting it drop, sensing it was time to go. I knew he'd be crazy about the baby, or babies, if that were the case. Maybe I was only imagining Jackson's transgressions. Maybe it didn't mean anything. But the truth was, I knew one thing for certain, that everything *did* mean something, and that it all led up to some big unknown, which was the one thing that kept me going.

DURING THE SUMMER MONTHS, while they were still small, I'd take Jen and Jovey off to New Hampshire for a couple of weeks to visit my Dad in his ramshackle colonial — a house that Jack had trouble visiting, because there was so much that needed repair, so much to put in order. He complained that the dishes rattled on the shelves when you walked across the kitchen floor.

While we were away, he would hire a crew of painters to go over everything in the Beacon Hill house, removing the imprints of our daily presences — little hands dragged over woodwork, ball marks bounced against walls. I must say, it was always a pleasure to come home, as if the house itself had enjoyed a vacation.

But now, I was disgruntled by the monotony of our "museum white" walls, always the same dead color. I had found out at the paint store that they didn't add brown or yellow or red to the can of interior latex, but a jolt of black.

"What difference does it make," Jack wanted to know, "if you can't see it, if you can't tell?"

I was working on a new mirror, which Barbara Bell had ordered as a Christmas present for her mother — an underwater scene with pearly strings of lustrous algae, flowing grasses, a turtle on the rise, and several slender fish. She had given me *carte blanche*, saying that she trusted my instincts, but I always felt apprehensive about working this way, on commission. The buyer usually had some vague idea in mind, and the finished piece rarely reflected that unconveyed image.

For a previous commission, I had sketched out the entire four-part design, just to avoid this problem, and Roberta Bricker had given her enthusiastic OK. But on my presentation of the finished work, I could see her surprise — it was not disappointment exactly, just a moment of mental adjustment, but still, it was a little awkward for me when she didn't say anything and just stood there. It wasn't how she had pictured it.

Of course she had taken the four Tree Altars, paid for them in full, and learned to live with them, just as she had taken Bill, and learned to live with him, I suppose. I'm sure he wasn't exactly what she'd imagined either.

I knew my life was charmed, that I had a wonderful family and all the creature comforts, but at the bottom of it all, I felt alone. I think I felt this most keenly when my daughter, Jen, came home from school. Colleges have the longest god-awful vacations, and though Jen and I were never close, there was always this attempt on both parts to establish a mother-daughter relationship. In many ways I feared her.

"You and Dad don't really look like a couple, do you," she began. "He's more of a city person. Maybe it's because you grew up in the country, or because you don't have a job. I'm going to get an apartment in New York when I graduate." Jen wore black as a rule, and it made her look even thinner. She was wearing tight stretch pants, and a short chenille sweater. Even her running shoes and socks were black.

"I'd worry about you in New York," I responded, "but I guess you'll have to go where you can find a job." This idea had not occurred to her. She believed that there were plenty of opportunities, and I was glad that she could be optimistic, that she could see the calendar of her future life stretching out like one long, athletic vacation, moving from season to season, sport to sport.

When she had first announced that she was majoring in PE, I had made the mistake of saying, "What kind of a major is that?" Somehow it seemed a poor excuse for a twenty-eight-thousand-dollar-a-year education, running around a gym with a whistle, doing stunts on a mat. But Jen's response was, *If your body isn't fit, what good are you.* She had me there. And I had to admire her flexible spine, how she could put the palms of her hands flat on the floor, or hold a difficult yoga position. She ran up and down the front stairs when the weather was too grizzly to go out. Her greatest fear was slipping on ice, those damned askew bricks in the Beacon Hill sidewalks.

As a child she didn't even like chocolate, and now she admonished me for popping Tic-Tacs. She knew the fat content of all sorts of food, eternally on vigilant calorie patrol, shocked when I mashed up an avocado for a pre-dinner guacamole, pointing out the surprising percentage of fat in my beloved smoked tofu. Like most children her age, she was passionate about her new-found beliefs, and wanted to convert everyone to a more mindful state of awareness, but I felt, after forty, I should give myself permission not to feel any remorse for spreading butter on the occasional piece of warm bread. I would have a second glass of wine if I wanted.

"What if you hadn't married Dad, how would you have made any money?"

She had me there. I didn't make much of an hourly wage selling my hand-carved mirrors. "As you must know," I said wearily, "I don't have to work in the *real world.* Your father has always been a good provider."

"That sounds so archaic. What if he divorced you and married someone else? Who do you think would hire you?"

"Maybe I'd sell my body on the street, Jen, at a discount rate — like Filene's basement."

I could tell from the minute retraction of her face that I hadn't amused her, that we were back to issue number one — Who would want me?

"Will you help me chop?" I asked, peeling the skin of a purple onion. I was making a winter lima bean soup in her honor, vegetarian, though I could swear these recipes took twice as much time. Nutritional yeast... now where did I put that?

"I don't see you ever asking Jovey to help. I was just going out for a run."

I shook my head — *Run along, run along.* Soon I'd only have Buster to cook for anyway, and he looked like he was about to burst. The pug had actually been Jackson's choice. He insisted that more designers owned pugs than any other breed, because they were decorative — i.e., useless, but they lent a certain quality to a room. Never mind that one never saw pictures of dogs in commercial spaces, which were always photographed empty.

"Why don't you take The Sausage out for a walk once in a while. Exercise might do him good."

I wanted to say — *Jen*, can't we just get along? Can't we drop this endless sparring? But instead I muttered, "What we really need is a second dog, then they could exercise each other."

I turned to rinse my hands, but Jennifer stopped me. "Is that why you had two children?"

"No, Jen," I answered — but thank God I did. Thank God for Jovey. She knew that was how I felt. She knew it in her bones, and she hated me for it.

"What if Dad had refused to marry you, just because you were pregnant with me. Would you have even had me?"

"Of course," I said.

"I'm never going to have kids. Women only do it by accident, or out of some sort of reflex. Who'd want to put themselves through all that — it's grotesque."

I looked at her mean, little, perfect body that held not an ounce of compassion for anything, and wondered if she were a changeling. Her breasts were ample, bigger than mine, despite the fact that she was so thin, but pregnancy would surely weigh those perfect breasts down. I imagined white, rippled striations all over her flawless, global parts.

Selfishness was surely the disease of the decade — but I had to blame myself in a way, for what had I offered these children? I had rarely taken them to church, or offered them any alternative. They knew not to steal or murder or lie, but where was reverence, where was grace? Did either of them think about how they could give, give back to the world, to others, life?

"If I got pregnant right now, I wouldn't keep it," she told me, and I knew in her mind, she was turning it around — if she were the mother, back then, she would have gotten rid of me.

MY DISCUSSION WITH JEN disturbed me. It made me wonder if I would have married Jack if I hadn't gotten pregnant. I had been so young, and Jack had been my first lover. It wasn't as if we were being careless, for Jack always carried prophylactics in his wallet, and as far as either of us knew, the rubber hadn't broken. Jennifer had just wanted to be born, I guess. And Jack was so supportive. All of my girlfriends thought Jackson Hawkins was an excellent catch.

In retrospect it does seem strange that we sought out my mother's grave on our honeymoon, but I suppose it's the same impulse that leads a couple to make love in the broom closet during a wake, trying to raise Lazarus, pouring water on the dried porcine mushrooms. My mother was buried on the Isle of Capri. Before she left on that supposed vacation, she had said that she needed a swan song. I was eight, and didn't know that swans only sang when they were about to die. Jimmy and I didn't go to the funeral because it cost too much to get there.

I remember the day when Jackson and I first came to Capri, how the weather was brilliant yet mild. Gazing up at the wild outcroppings of stone, far above the village, I sang my Italian in broken phrases. The owner of the little *trattoria* where we settled for lunch seemed to enjoy my efforts, crouching, hands out, as if to catch a ball thrown wildly by a baby — *Magnifico* — insisting that we disregard the *menu turistico* and eat only the *specialita della casa*, beginning with an extraordinary puffed-up, homemade ravioli, filled with three kinds of cheese, floating in a fresh tomato sauce. Jackson liked nothing better than to sit in the sun and eat good food. I was famished one moment, wretched the next, consuming enormous quantities of breadsticks instead of the second course — a freshly caught whitefish, doused with lemon and oil. We had a carafe of red wine from the old man's private reserve — "Too young," Jackson thought, for it had a bit of a bite to it. He didn't want me drinking too much wine or lifting heavy suitcases. He tried to help me keep track of my weight.

When I wasn't feeling sick, I thought I was happy, sitting by the sun-drenched wall writing postcards, dazzled by the looks of my tall, handsome husband, with his wiry blond hair and blue-green eyes, *il colore del mare.* I felt I could get lost in that color — I could float out to sea on those eyes.

But during this first phase of our pregnant honeymoon, I was mostly thinking about my mother — excited that I was finally this close to her. It was as if *she* were the lover I was finally coming home to — *she* was the one who made my heart beat faster. After lunch, we found *il cimitero,* surrounded by a tell-tale border of cypress. I was thrilled, a little dazed by the sun and glass of red wine, feeling the child-like joyfulness of anticipation.

I could smell the jasmine even before we entered the gates of the cemetery, but I had never seen anything like this. The entire small graveyard was covered with flowers, arrangements on every tomb, not just one bouquet, but masses of flowers — the giddy sweet scent of spatter-striped lilies, sweating with fragrance, ten blooms to a stalk, gladiolas galore, chartreuse starburst mums mixed in with vibrant purple, voluminous roses — I wanted to bury my face in them. Flickering candles in votive cups stood beneath photographs of the various deceased, and I wondered if I'd recognize my mother.

There is some primitive element in the Catholic Church that connects material things — candles, flowers, fetishes, candy— with the souls of the dead. The air was so thick with that sultry perfume it seemed to be coaxing spirits back to recall a physical past life with all its sensate pleasures. When I asked the caretaker why the cemetery was filled with *tanti fiori,* he insisted that it was always this way.

"We're looking for the grave of Edith Weston," I explained, writing her name out. He looked at the card, and then up at me kindly, suggesting that perhaps we should look in the Protestant cemetery down on the lower part of Capri. I was surprised that there would be two cemeteries on such a small island, surprised that they would segregate Protestants from Catholics.

When we found the other cemetery and my mother's grave, what a travesty it was — a dark and dismal dumpsite of a place, unkempt, uncared for — broken bits of bottle lay between the headstones. The earth of the hillside was collapsing into the yard. A few two-by-fours were propped there, but the wall was caving in, and the random graves looked abandoned, as if they housed discarded souls. It must have been the only gloomy place on the island. I grieved for my mother, left in such a place. I wanted to move her, to have her moved, but Jack thought that was impossible.

Through an opening further on, Jack saw that locals had dumped their garbage — old broken relics, cracked vases— but there were also masses of wild nasturtium, bright peppery orange and yellow, and he began gathering a handful from the refuse. Together we lay them on my mother's grave, and with his arm around my shoulder, I think I felt truly married at that moment.

Sometimes I wondered why my father had insisted that my mother convert from Catholicism when she had married him. He never went to church anyway. Funny what women were willing to give up when they got married. Jack had asked for no such thing from me.

Later that day, we climbed to the ruins of Jovis, far above the cluster of villas and hotels and walled-in gardens that made up the charming maze of Capri. The air seemed to open as we made our way up to the tumble-down stones of the ancient fortress. As we sat there watching the sun set into the waters of the bay, a blush of light spread over the crest of Vesuvius. How close the world seemed, as if our hands hovered over it, as a hand over a map, pointing here and there. We decided that evening, if we ever had a son, we would name him Jovis and call him "Jovey." So that day not only encompassed the past death of my mother, but the future birth of our son. I remember trumpet vines in profusion.

I WAS ALWAYS PROUD TO WALK into a party on Jackson's arm — glad that he was my husband. Big parties were not my forte, but Jack always made me feel somewhat safe. Unlike his guarded, private self at home, in public, he brought me in, arm around waist, opening doors, taking my coat, introducing me to everyone.

The Brickers' house was decorated to the hilt. You could smell the orange-clove *potpourri* on entering. Evergreen boughs had been stapled around the entrance, with twinkling lights and golden bulbs. Unwisely, Wally had not been restrained — he must have gotten a whiff of Buster, for when the Lhasa apso rushed to greet us, one of the lower bulbs crashed and fell into glistening splinters. Then off he ran to jump up on various guests, ripping one woman's pantyhose.

Whatever they were serving from the punch bowl must have been stiff, for there was a great deal of jostling beneath the ball of mistletoe, and even the Beacon Hill dowagers and men in business suits were on their merry way to getting plastered. Roberta had invited several black basketball players, who didn't look terribly comfortable, but I admired the way that Jack walked right over and started up a conversation, before Bobbi Comstock cornered him. There was a party photographer — probably from Roberta's professional life — with a heavy protruding camera, and several fashion models who were far from pregnant, making Roberta look (I had to forgive my daughter at that moment) somewhat grotesque.

Roberta planted a kiss on Jackson's lips, "Welcome, welcome. Isn't this jolly?" Gripping her belly, "*Ho ho ho.*" He took the assault good-naturedly. Only I could tell that he was put off. Jackson was like some glorious knight in polished armor. No one perceived the darkness lurking within, for he was the perfect partygoer, naturally charming. With his hand sweeping out across the room, he regaled Roberta on her *largesse*, but she got the pun and shook her finger at him, taking a swig of bubbly water from a silver flask, resting the trophy on her enormous bump. She was only in her seventh month, but she looked like she was ready to deliver at any moment. "We've got loads of turkey sandwiches, so help yourself!" And then leaning forward, she whispered to Jack, "At nine we're going to have mummers."

I paused by the console table in the front hall and looked into the Oriental bowl — it displayed a wealth of Christmas cards. I guessed that ours was buried in there somewhere, the four of us sitting on the side of some catboat we'd rented to sail to Block Island last summer, the photograph of our suntanned faces framed by a red and green holly-bedecked frame.

Pushing on, I found Bill muttering in the kitchen. He was wearing a festive green satin bow tie, but he looked disgruntled, preoccupied with how slowly the caterers were replenishing trays. "They should always look full," he told one frazzled server. Seeing me, he grimaced at his own frustration and then managed a party mood. "Allow me." He lifted the bottle ceremoniously. "Let me brighten your wit with champagne."

*Yes, and my eyes with tears*, I thought, trying to look ravishing and nonchalant, like Greta Garbo in *Camille*. Bill had been hoarding the champagne behind the counter, though he was drinking Scotch himself.

"Do you know any of these people? They're our neighbors, you know. Cows and chickens would make better friends. I swear this is the last time we do this. Christmas always makes me depressed." But Bill didn't seem depressed. He seemed manic. "Ever since I retired, I feel driven to seek pleasure, constantly, wherever I go. It's the only cure for what ails me."

"And what ails you?" I asked, enjoying his banter.

"Boredom, of course. I fear boredom more than I fear my own conscience."

"I'm never bored," I said blankly, and wondered if that made me a boring person. Did I bore Bill? Did I bore Jack? I sipped at my champagne, which made me sad, sadder still. I was worried about Jovey going away, and told Bill so. "At least he can come home on the weekends."

"Oh, once they get there, they never want to leave," Bill said matter-of-factly. "But you'll get used to it."

That was almost the worst part, that you could get used to damn near anything.

"Do you think anyone's having a decent time? Maybe I should strengthen the eggnog, but the sight of that stuff almost makes me gag. Loved your Tree Altars by the way — we just got them hung. They're upstairs in the hall if you want to take a look. I like that dress, very nice, very *tempting*. You should always wear red." He walked quickly toward the living room, carrying a bowl of cashews. I followed, and saw Jackson talking to Lark Mendel, the other most handsome man in the room. "Your husband is certainly an asset at these things, so good-natured. Such good taste!" Bill winked, as if including me in Jack's sense of selection.

"We try to keep the Yule log burning," I added, without much conviction, but it seemed the metaphorical thing to say.

"Pretty good turn out considering the rain. Has anyone prayed for snow?" he asked the hallway in general, and the hallway replied in the affirmative, as if it were some drunken congregation. "Sally!" Bill turned, passing his one free hand over her bony ass. "My God, you look twenty-eight years old tonight."

"Did you hear that?" Sally shrieked with hilarity. "Twenty-eight years old! I guess I *will* have to celebrate."

Hearing the commotion, Roberta came over, and was informed by Sally of her new age status. "Oh, Bill," Roberta laughed, waving it away, "he can't even read the numbers in the elevator."

Sally frowned, and decided she'd act twenty-eight anyway. She wanted to dance. She needed a partner. "If I'm going to enjoy this party, I've got to take off these tight shoes!"

Bill was a *schmooser*, a talker, a tease, a harmless flirt — if there was such a thing. His flirtations were simply the flip side of good Wasp restraint, for he certainly had no real intentions. Women my age seemed so eager, too ready — I could feel the same impulse rising in myself, the bubbling over of some wild brew. I imagined once the collective party was high enough on the rum-laced *schlag* and sugar cookies, we'd dim the lights and sing Christmas carols at the top of our lungs. Bill knew all the verses, despite his supposed aversion to the season.

"Do you mind if I check out the Tree Altars?" I asked Roberta, but Bill eagerly led the way up the stairs, nearly tripping on the thick, white carpet. I wondered what the twins would do to that. At the far end of the upstairs corridor, I could see the small gilded mirrors all lined up, votive candles flickering beneath each one, illuminating the panels that depicted the seasons — a willow tree for spring. I had carved a little fish as an emblem above it. The apple tree stood for summer, with a five-pointed star shape within a circle, the alder for autumn, and then a cedar. There were rays of light on the left side of each mirror, droplets of rain on the right. Together, the altars looked pagan and holy, and I was pleased with how they were hung.

"You are superb," Bill said. "Come here, come here." He acted as if he had something he wanted to show me, but he simply pulled me off into the Chinese guest room, murmuring, *"Mmmm,"* as he closed the door. A paper lantern barely lit the bedroom, and a set of ivory chopsticks lay crossed on the lacquered bedside table, as if some geisha had just pulled them from her hair. I felt flattered, but not prepared to realize the minor crush I'd been carrying for Bill all along. He touched the shoulder of my velvet dress and told me, again, how lovely it was, and then without further ado, he leaned down and kissed me. I let him, though it felt rather strange to be kissing anyone other than Jack.

I found myself thinking about toothpaste — did Bill hand squeeze his or use a paste pump? He probably thought of himself as the old-fashioned squeeze kind of person, though I suspected Roberta was switching him over to the pump. Putting my hands on his blackwatch vest to hold him off, made him even more amorous, and he insisted on giving me a boozy hug, pressing himself against me. It reminded me of those dances in high school, when guys just wanted a little friction. "Now look what you've done," he accentuated the modest bulge in his dark grey flannels. "You're just too pretty. And I love that dress. Do you want to see? Here," he offered, and before I knew it, he had pulled himself out, displaying himself like a little boy holding an astonishing bullfrog.

"It's very nice," I said, patting his arm, "but you better put it away now, or you'll spoil the party." He was far more drunk than I'd realized.

"I'll never use this thing again, I'll tell you that." At least he managed to zip himself up. "This is the last big shindig before we're blasted away by quintuplets or whatever else it happens to be. No one tells you the truth about babies. Oh so cute and *blah blah blah*, but they ruin your goddamn lives!"

I could hear the arrival of the mummers downstairs. They had entered with cymbals, the booming announcement of one big drum, displaying their well-stuffed jingle-bell hats — now the party was really rolling.

"Roberta doesn't care about this, you know." He meant our little encounter.

I didn't believe that for one minute, but it made me wonder if Jackson would mind if I had another interest. He would probably be too busy to notice. He wasn't the jealous type.

THE PRESBYTERIAN CHURCH WAS CRAMMED with familiar people I didn't really know, but at least our family was together, and I knew this was a treat for Granny Hawkins. I wondered why such a mild-mannered old lady held such power over Jack. Would I have the same effect on Jovey?

The kids were on their best behavior, which wasn't very good, whispering and poking and tickling each other — "This is so phony," and "God, what bull-shit." I was tempted to get up and sit between them, but then they finally settled down.

Granny Hawkins fell asleep almost immediately, which was lucky for her, because the minister went on dissecting the lyrics to *Away in the Manger*, ripping it to shreds. He kept saying how the manger was a feeding trough, as if that should wake us up to some harsher reality, and how baby Jesus was not peacefully sleeping, but probably howling, hungry, in pain. How would he know? Swaddling clothes were not soft and warm, but ripped strips of rough cloth. And the cows weren't lowing. Why not? I expected that next he would say that the star wasn't shining, but no, it was shining all right — he just wanted us to realize that it probably took years for the three wise men to get there. So much for the drama of the crèche.

The only saving moment in the entire service was the lighting of the hand-held candles with their little cardboard skirts for catching wax. After the lights were dimmed, two older men at the front of the church tipped their unlit candles into a flame, and then offered the light to their neighbors. Soon the entire church was filled with candlelight, very beautiful. The child could have slept. The cows could have lowed in such an atmosphere as this.

As we walked down the aisle, Granny Hawkins kept saying,

"Wasn't that lovely? I'm so glad we came," but before we were out the door, Jen turned to Jovey and said loud enough for all to hear, "Didn't that give you the creeps?"

I kept yearning for some image of serenity — a family huddled in a barn, the breath of big warm animals, the shining star in the darkness. Outside, it was misting, and Granny Hawkins continued the theme of the sermon she'd just slept through — "Oh well," she said cheerfully, "it probably never snowed in Bethlehem either."

I wished that I had passed on more to my children, found a way for them to accept the unseen element in their lives. I wished that I had passed on more than a tradition of desires and demands that almost always led to disappointment.

Jovey and Jackson each took an arm and walked Gran up the slippery walk to her apartment. I felt a moment of panic, left with Jen in the car. "I hope you're satisfied," she said. "That was about as boring as it gets."

Jen was ready to go out and party and Jovey wanted to join her, but he was coming down with a cold. I listened to the subtle rasping of his asthma, and insisted that he stay in. He needed a good night's rest.

Once home, Jack went directly to the answering machine and then fled upstairs to his study. What could he possibly have to work on now, Christmas Eve? Didn't he want to help fill the stockings? Or was that my job as well? Suddenly I felt achy, dull, lack luster, and wondered if I was coming down with something.

I was thinking of bowing out on Donna Marie, but when I waffled on the phone, she pleaded — "I can't go by myself — you promised! I'll pick you up and everything. *Please?*"

I didn't bother to remind her that she had this amazing habit of going to church alone and leaving accompanied. I wondered what it was exactly — how she attracted such a variety of men? Was it some natural perfume, some pheromone? She was like a butterfly bush, not exactly gorgeous but exceedingly attractive on some level.

Donna knew just how to toss her lustrous hair, glancing back in a guy's direction, as if welcoming him to follow her glitter of bracelets, her billowing scarves. She appeared shy and yet encouraging, never too available, but not overly protected. She gave the impression of having no needs, though men always liked to treat her, which was fortunate, for she rarely had money. She was as experienced as I was not.

Jack didn't like Donna Marie. He thought she was scary. She did have a hard, Sicilian side to her — I could imagine her shooting a guy in the kneecaps — but she had a soft and loving quality too, just like her eyes, obsidian spheres with compassionate centers.

Her father had been in the Mafia. She could barely remember him. Her only recollection was of moisture forming on his upper lip. This memory had endeared her to me. At the age of fifteen, Donna had run away from home, and had ended up in Boston, where she met an older man who put her through secretarial school. Donna was a faithful friend, but I wouldn't want to cross her.

As we parked she told me about Steve, the guy she'd just broken up with. "Did I tell you he called up asking for Nancy Smith? I said *who*, and he just hung up. So I called all the Nancy Smiths in the phone book — he was seeing her the whole damn time. She wasn't too pleased to hear about it either, believe me. Fucking lawyers always think they're above the law."

The chapel was filled with a variety of people who all looked like they came here regularly. I thought of the austere plainness of the Presbyterian church compared to this odd and friendly place, with its bright blue ceiling, decorated with angels peeping out over the dark, carved wood. I thought it curious that the Virgin was featured, a lamb nuzzling her outstretched hand, a little nick in his neck. There was something about this chapel that made me feel like an infant, reaching out for some gaudy necklace dangled just out of reach, wanting to put the whole world in my mouth.

The chapel was filled by the time the midnight bell began to ring. The processional started with an all-male choir, followed by a hierarchy of priests in their beautiful golden robes, made from a heavy, embroidered material. I liked the presence of Father Gregory, who was leading the service. He was older, and his voice reflected great warmth. I asked Donna about him, and she insisted that the priests had a special quality because they were celibate. "They put all that energy into their spiritual life. You know how good love is before it is consummated — well, it's something like that. I should try it sometime."

I liked the idea of cultivating patience, withholding. My children hardly understood the concept of waiting, with everything handed out so readily. If something was broken or lost, it was immediately replaced. Jen had asked me for a portable CD player for Christmas, and I told her that I already had her presents, hoping to make the CD player a surprise, but then two days before Christmas, she announced that she was going to go out and get one with her own money. She couldn't wait. I had to stop her and tell her, ruining the surprise for us both.

Donna Marie looked beautiful that Christmas Eve. She was wearing a loosely woven, pale blue scarf over her lustrous hair. Her skin was poreless, smooth as stone. It reminded me of solid olive oil, chilled, then smoothed back with a warm hand. Even if she didn't have money for meat, she always had a jar of olive oil to warm up her vegetables, to fry chopped onions until they sweetened, freeing red peppers from their indigestible skins. Even the simplest *fagiolini* tossed with sage and chopped *pancetta*, or roasted eggplant with its innards all creamy, sprinkled with parmesan, had a drizzle of oil to make the elements combine.

When the priest said, "Let us pray," she went up on her knees with such good posture, it seemed to confirm the candor of her faith. When I knelt, I slouched back on the edge of my pew, thinking about earthly things — Were the kids getting too old for Christmas stockings? What time should I start the twenty-pound bird? Would anyone help me clean up this year? Should we invite the Brickers over during the holidays, or would that be two-faced. I thought about kissing Bill, how I hadn't really liked it.

As we rested back together, I leaned over and whispered, "I think I might fall asleep." I was so exhausted. The whole Christmas week now wanted to be reckoned with, the entire year, my life — it all seemed to have ground to a halt, but I didn't want a struggle. I wanted to sink into the sound of the choir as they sang in harmony together. I felt happy and comfortable, not fighting the tiredness, going in and out of consciousness. I remembered my mother being very sick and asking for something — she was pleading with my father to see a priest. But he said no, "That's nonsense."

After she died, I created an altar in my bedroom. For some reason my father tolerated this setup, with its lace cloth and candles. I bound two sticks into a homemade cross and stuck it down into a jar of stones. Perhaps he thought I was only playing, but I was serious, collecting flowers for the vases set on either side. I kept a special collection of things beneath the apron of the altar — a china palomino with her frisky little foal, a rabbit's foot key chain, a collection of handkerchiefs, a baby bottle filled with disappearing milk that always reappeared again. These semi-sacred objects were kept beneath the altar with my mother's costume jewelry, secure in her pink leather jewelry box.

Donna always insisted that I had to meet her family and taste the homemade pasta of Sicily. Her mother, who now lived in the Bronx, still hand-rolled macaroni around long threads of iron, pulling them out, cutting it and cooking it *al dente*, tossing the noodles with a mash of anchovies, breadcrumbs, garlic, and parsley. Donna was the one who had told me that you had to dissolve your anchovies over steam, or they would become bitter. She wondered why Americans were so put off by garlic. Were they afraid to use their noses, or afraid that other people would?

Donna Marie's hometown of Erice was supposedly the birthplace of Venus. They made fabulous marzipan there, in every shape imaginable: split-open figs, bananas, peas in the pod, little pigs, Easter bonnets, bleeding lambs no doubt. The green bitter almonds were gathered from the hillsides. They contained a touch of arsenic, illegal in this country. Whenever she talked about Sicily, history and food both came together, and here in this chapel, I felt as if we could be in Syracusa or Palermo. Oddly, I felt at home.

The service was not a social event, the way it was on Beacon Hill — here it felt like necessity. I liked seeing the older people, along with the middle-aged working class, mixed in with a scattering of teenagers, who were particularly alert to each other, while I kept dozing, drifting off. I closed my eyes, and was back before the family fire, my head in my mother's lap. I could smell the pan of acorn squash mixed with butter and syrup, onions caramelizing to a savory sweetness — jerked back with a physical tug to the present, my head whipping up to attention.

Father Gregory's homily was about a man who felt he couldn't accompany his wife and children to church on Christmas Eve, because he couldn't reconcile the fact that God could be a human being. He felt bad letting his family go off without him, but at least, he thought, he was not a hypocrite. But as he sat at home alone that evening before the fire, reading his newspaper and waiting for their return, he thought he heard a soft thud against the picture window. The curtains had not been drawn, so that the outside world could witness their tree with its colorful lights. When the man got up to investigate, he saw a flock of sparrows fluttering about, three birds lying stunned in the snow. At that moment he realized how cold and blustery it was. The temperature was close to zero. He ran to open the garage door. The light inside came on automatically. He hoped the birds would fly in and get warm. But the birds refused to enter.

He thought maybe he could coax them into the warmth with bits of bread, so he hurried to the kitchen to get the bag of breadcrumbs his wife had set out for the Christmas turkey. Surely, this was more important. The birds dashed down and took the crumbs but then flew away, not understanding his impulse to save them. *If only I could be a bird*, he thought, *maybe then they would follow me*, and just as he thought this, the church bells from Midnight Mass began ringing. *If only I could be like one of them, then perhaps I could lead them to My Warmth and My Love.*

I closed my eyes and let myself drift — as if I could hear the wind whistling on the clapboards of our old white house, feel the rough wool quilt with its diamonds of red and green and brown, keeping me warm and cozy, the cracks of light through the floorboards, hearing my parents rustling around downstairs — such sweet security, their secretive hush.

The first Christmas after my mother was gone, the fire went out in the hearth of the family, and the feeling was cinder, frightening, cold. Our Christmas stockings were disappointing — a tube of toothpaste, a red potato, plain yellow pencils for school. We all tried to cheer up Dad, but he was glum. Even his sister, Aunt Carla, wasn't much of a help, though she was a good fire builder. She got a roaring fire to go in the living room. We had to draw back from the burning intensity. It seemed that nothing would ever be right again, either too hot or too cold. Our mother had taken some comforting quality away with her, that perfect, lulling temperature that had always calmed my soul.

The service went into the second hour, and when the parishioners began to take communion, filing out row after row, Donna excused herself and went forward. I felt out of place sitting there, all alone in the pew, slightly resentful that I couldn't join in because I was only a Protestant. Donna seemed dependent on confession and communion, for she repeatedly slept with married men. I didn't know how she'd ever meet the right man if she slept with everyone she dated.

As we left the chapel, I felt woozy from the lateness of the hour. Pushing through the double doors out to the street, we saw that the misting rain had changed to snow. It had covered the city with a lacy brightness. The big, thick flakes landed on Donna's face, on her blue head covering, dampening it with little stars. We walked arm in arm to the parking lot down toward the harbor, and I felt that this would be the best part of my Christmas, and that seemed a shame, not to share it with my children, or to be with Jack. I felt as if our family was all dispersed, shaken like a cupful of dice, thrown out to scatter all over the board, making no sense, tilted.

Standing there under the streetlamp, Donna went into the depths of her purse and pulled out a package, plain white tissue without any ribbon. My present for her was at home. The pavement in the parking lot was glistening, the air refreshed. The night had a buoyant quality, and I felt transformed — like a visionary baby with golden lines of insight traveling out to some far horizon, a tiny bonfire of happiness burning in my brain.

"Open it," she said. I could feel her eagerness, that she wanted to share in my delight. Falling out of the tissue were a string of lovely amethyst-colored beads with an ancient-looking cross. I stood there staring at it — a treasure — something too precious to own, but she insisted that she wanted me to have it. Then like an ignorant, well-meaning Protestant, I put the rosary over my head.

DONNA'S APARTMENT WAS FILLED with objects that drew my eye, a collection of starfish and plastic figurines, stone fetishes lined up on the windowsill. The one I liked best was a smooth black mole with a turquoise arrow embedded in its back. According to Donna, the mole connected women to their secret life, to the deep underearth, to healing.

I had promised her one of my mirrors for Christmas, a little one she had always admired. I had carved apples and oak leaves all around the frame. The apples represented the feminine aspect, while the oak leaves stood for the masculine part. Of all the people I knew, Donna Marie seemed to bring these forces together.

Pounding in a nail, she hung the mirror between a ceramic Black Madonna placed on top of her bookshelf and a Selena poster. The placement seemed perfect. Various necklaces and scarves were draped over pegs. A faux leopard-skin material covered her only armchair. Whenever I came over to Donna's place, there was always something new to see. That day, I was struck by a tin heart with wings, stuck above the doorway with a red push-pin.

"Look what I just got in the mail." She went over to her dresser and pulled out a rather discreet white box. Opening it, she displayed two luscious breasts, covered with a saran-like material. "*Curves*," she said. "Don't they feel real?"

I jiggled the gelatinous pink flesh with a finger, but then she reached in fearlessly and scooped one up, as if it were an oyster, a very large oyster with a nipple. You could see how the breasts fit into their box on top of two molded forms. Donna stripped her shirt off in order to exhibit their believability. "The only thing I hate is you have to wear a bra to keep these things in place."

She fastened the underwire in front, and then tucked the Curves in, so that she packed the cups. I'd never thought of her as lacking in that department, but she considered it a form of make-up. Romance was all about make-believe anyway. She felt the fullness of her newfound flesh, part her, part Jell-O, and began to jog. The Curves bounced. "I don't think I'd want to be this big all the time, but isn't it amazing? No surgery, nothing. I'm not trying to sell you. You're fine the way you are."

I'm glad she thought so, and yet I had to admit, I was losing interest in sex. Donna thought that this was the physical equivalent of being depressed. But unlike her, who wanted every guy on the street to do a full 360, I preferred to remain invisible. Perhaps I wasn't much of a sexual being. Perhaps there was more to life than coupling all the time. I had other sensual interests — cooking, gardening, mothering my son. I would rather carve a curve in one of my mirrors than display my own to the world. I liked the way a sharpened gauge cut into hardwood, making a curve so smooth I'd want to rub it with my fingers.

"You know, last night," I told Donna, "Jack really hit the ceiling. I was eating a banana upstairs, and I left the peel on a windowsill and he just freaked."

"That guy has so many rules. Do you know how great you'd be with someone who really loved you? I don't think you know how unhappy you are."

"Jack loves me," I protested, thinking Donna didn't understand long-term relationships, how love could not be judged by some initial attraction that was over as soon as the tension was resolved. I thought briefly of my feelings for Bill Bricker, the closest I'd come to a flirtation of late, but how I hadn't even liked kissing him.

"You might consider one of these," she handed me a catalogue. "You wouldn't believe the difference when you come with one of these things inside. Men have a hard time competing."

Paging through the catalogue, my mouth dropped open — Did people really use these things? She pointed to one called "The Lone

Ranger." It was a nice rubbery cock, *Ladies' Favorite,* described in pleasing terms — flexible, firm, sculpted realistically, from the shapely head to the prominent veins— it had everything but a set of balls. In place of them, there was a flat base, so that you could display it on your bedside table, I suppose. It was available in white, black or hi-ho-silver, if you wanted to stick to the western motif. But what if Jovey found it.

Donna was losing patience with my good-girl squeamishness. "Don't worry, I'll order you one."

I WAS ONLY ABOUT FOUR YEARS OLD when I locked myself into the bathroom. I thought it had been barred from the outside, that Jimmy had done it, and I started to scream. There weren't any windows, and I couldn't reach the light. I heard my mother explaining that the latch had fallen down, but I couldn't see where. I could only hear her calling from the crack beneath the door. She said that she couldn't open it, but that someone was coming. She said very calmly that I'd be OK. "Joanna," she said, "take hold of my hand." I lay down on the floor and found her finger while she said the Lord's Prayer. I didn't really understand it, but the words were impressed on my memory, like a seal on hot red wax.

Our Father who art in Heaven, Hallowed be Thy Name — halo, holy, the etched initials of INRI on that crumbling cross, found where the two trails met, the cross within the crossing. Sam scraped the dirt, while I looked on, wanting to kiss him — he wanted it too. Fear and desire, desire and fear — for he could have lost his job. Thy Kingdom Come, Thy Will be Done, On Earth as it is in Heaven — the welcomed rain quenching the thirst of the desert — the sky was clear, the earth smelled fresh, when Sam put his arm around my shoulder. I thought — if life could be this good, all hearts would rise to the brim. Give us this day our daily bread — the voluminous, silky mass of it rising, the airy punch, kneading three good loaves lifted out of the oven. Forgive us our trespasses, as we forgive those who trespass against us — stealing into my brother's room, ripping Mars from his homemade mobile, throwing it onto the highest shelf. Lead us not into temptation but deliver us from Evil — the chocolate egg wrapped in golden tinsel, solid, hard, bittersweet chocolate, little mouse marks gnawing away, until I succumbed to my eagerness — All! For Thine *is the Kingdom, and the Power and the Glory* — one peach shade dove, one rose, fluttering light all around them — gold, while they curved their wings still moving — in light's smashed eyes of awe — *Forever and ever and ever. Amen* — How they could swing so space-less.

And then the firemen came, inserted a screwdriver — "Get away from the door." I scooted back on the cold blue tile, thinking it would all crash in on me. There was a *bang* and the latch was ripped from the frame and light poured into the room. My mother was there on her hands and knees, as I crawled out of the darkness. She grabbed me and rocked me, back and forth, as if *she* were the one who was frightened.

Four years later she was gone, and there was no one there to protect me. That's when I found those sticks from the tree we called the Mother Apple and tied them together with yellow yarn. I was glad my father ignored me. I thought he might take my cross and throw it in the trash. I could hear Aunt Carla, who had stayed, it seemed, only to grind fresh coffee — the dark brown smell of it always brewing. They drank it night and day. Day and night I said my prayer like a long silver river floating slowly after her, into some peaceful place where I thought I might also belong, downriver, with an ease of splashing over many stones. I imagined heaven as all spring-lit, yellow leaves and the sound of water, her goodnight kiss on my cheek. I put myself to bed now. And found myself in the sheets. Father didn't remind me to brush my teeth. He didn't like to say goodnight. "See you in the morning," was the best he could do.

Once I got over the initial embarrassment, I found the Lone Ranger not only a useful implement but a reliable companion as well, never tiring, always willing and ready to ride. The only problem was the more I used it, the more awakened my sexuality became.

I tucked the Lone Ranger away when we weren't out riding, but sometimes I fell asleep with it still inside me, or I'd wake up to feel it there in the bed, like a minuscule partner, who wouldn't complain if I touched him by accident.

When I had my period, dark blood would cling to its molded form, and no one was repulsed. I only had to wash it off with soap and water, pat it dry. There was something endearing about it. I think I finally understood something about being male, as if this thing, this shapely piece of flexible rubber were my own little male homunculus. Gripping it in my hand, I felt complete, and yet on some other unacknowledged level, it underscored my loneliness.

I DIDN'T SEE HOW ONE COULD prepare for this, anymore than one could prepare for the death of a child. I kept pushing the inevitable away from me, all the while dragging this useless anchor that thudded along on the bottom of my stomach — Jovey was going away.

We tried to get ready by being overly cheerful, going on various shopping sprees. Recklessly sad, I bought him whatever he wanted — big black boots with tire-tread soles that came unglued after a single test-drive, cotton khakis, the bigger the better, a few nice button-down shirts. One soft to the touch houndstooth check complimented his dark brown hair. I wanted to wet my thumb and trace the line of his perfect eyebrows. I wanted to hold this moment to myself, but it kept racing away. I bought him a pair of sunglasses, though it was the darkest time of the year. Style had always meant a lot to him, a trait he didn't inherit from me. It was uncanny, the way he could put any old outfit together, that casual style so difficult to achieve. He did need a couple of sports coats, and these we bought secondhand. The students had to dress for class, and practice good table manners one night a week, in preparation for some other life, I guess.

Jack always made our dinner hour a bit of a strain, and now with Jen away at college, the focus was all on Jovey, whose behavior only became worse as a result. Every night, without fail, we would sit in silence, not in preparation for a blessing either, but waiting for Jovey to remove his grimy, turned-around baseball cap.

"Nobody else has a dinner ordeal like we do," he complained.

"If you want to go buy yourself a piece of pizza with your own allowance and eat out on the curb, that's fine, but if you're going to sit with us, you can keep your elbows off the table."

"Talk to the hand, Dad, talk to the hand."

"Jovey, don't be rude," I put in, for I didn't like it when he was disrespectful, though it must have seemed like we were ganging up on him, for he became silent then, sullen. Personally, I could see the logic of the once-a-week-manners approach, as long as they learned to tell the difference.

The next day we went out to buy a new desk lamp, a black one, with an adjustable arm and radon lightbulb. Jen insisted those bulbs gave you cancer, but I thought it might help Jovey read. He had a hard time focusing on the page. We got a carrying case for his CDs, and I had him write his name in indelible ink on each disc, because Lord knows, kids are always borrowing things. I wrote JWH on the inside labels of his new acquisitions. Why was so much attention paid to boxer shorts? Jovey did keep me current, and I was afraid that I'd now slip into a world of thoughtless routine — dismal dinners with Jackson and me facing-off over quickly cooling lasagna.

The night before I was to drive Jovey to school, we were sitting on the windowseat in the kitchen looking out at the winter garden — boxwood hedges laden with snow — and Jovey was toying with my hair, twisting it, as he often did. I liked the ticklish feel of it, until he plucked out a strand and said, "Hey, look at this," holding up a stiff grey hair to inspect.

We kept up some pretty jovial banter on the car ride north to Vermont, alternating tapes, his Metallica, my Pavarotti, his Jimi Hendrix, my Chopin nocturnes, his Smashing Pumpkins, our Bob Dylan. We reminisced about the Dylan concert I'd taken him to last spring, how Jovey had walked right up to the front. I had told him on the car ride home that he should try to find his own sound. "The most important thing," I repeated what Aunt Carla had always said, "is to live your own life, not somebody else's."

Underledge Academy had a good music department, and he would have guitar lessons. That had been a big plus. The administration had asked us not to arrive until late afternoon, and as we came across the wintry countryside, the sun was setting, and it made the sky glorious, the tree shapes vivid, but it didn't take away the chill of the New England landscape, mid-winter, nightfall. I saw the white church steeple of the school in the distance, and my stomach became queasy. I admitted to being nervous, and asked if he was.

"*Nah*," he answered, putting on the wrap-around sunglasses, pushing back his hair with both hands.

"Do you think you should maybe brush?" His hair did look a little ratty. But no, he didn't think he would.

Most of the other students wouldn't be returning until after dinner, though there were two very quiet Japanese boys in the dorm. Perhaps they hadn't gone home for the holidays. At least this school was only an hour and forty-five minutes from Boston, not impossible for weekend commutes, though with school in session six days a week, it would hardly be worth coming home.

They had told me that Jovey would have his own single, which appealed to my motherly sense of "his own room," but on arrival, lugging his duffels up three flights of stairs, we were shown a room that had obviously been occupied, much in the way one country occupies another. Grunge and litter were all over the floor — clothes lay in random piles, one flimsy chair for two Formica desks. One of the desks was laden with books and papers and raggedy notebooks, while the other was functioning as the music center — I could imagine the battle of the boom boxes. Federico Hidalgo was from Chile, and he liked Hard Rock, as in Cafe, one poster testified. Federico had gone home to Santiago for Christmas, and he was due to arrive later that evening.

The bottom bunk had already been claimed, and the top bunk displayed a broken mattress cover. Because Federico had used the room alone during the first semester, he had pushed the bed over to the side of the room where the ceiling dipped down two feet above the top bunk. If Jovey were to wake up with asthma or a bad dream, he could knock himself unconscious. The room seemed hot, at least seventy-five degrees. Coming from South America, Federico probably liked that. The carpet was stained. No one had come in to vacuum.

But what was most appalling was the lack of storage space. There were only two deep drawers for the two of them to share, and one half-closet with a couple of bins. How could they maintain any order and keep their thinking straight? All of this made me feel panicky.

I knew Jovey would have to deal, I could no longer come behind him, straightening, collecting his dirty clothes, offering him grapefruit in bed Sunday mornings, giving him late-night backrubs with citrus-scented oil. How I loved the feel of that boy's good shoulders, his long, smooth back, his muscular buttocks.

I knew I was being emotional, because it was the first day of my period, and it was a particularly heavy flow, but when I opened the miniature closet, and sports equipment tumbled out, I had to turn to the corner of that little, ugly room and bite my lip, pinching the bridge of my nose.

Jovey was up on the end of the upper bunk, trying to make the new sheet stretch over the flimsy mattress, and then suddenly he was down, hand bleeding — he had cut himself on a mirror embedded in the plaster. The glass was sharp and the blood was streaming. At least the bathroom was just across the hall.

He wrapped toilet paper around and around, while I felt the warm wetness of my own blood gushing through the Tampax. We were on a similar mission here, plasma control. When I pulled out the saturated tampon, a huge clot of blood dropped into the basin. I stared as it blossomed like a red camellia in the round white bowl. *L'Amour, la mort*, I thought.

Back in the dorm room, Jovey was flinging, single-handedly, his queen-sized comforter up onto the top bunk.

"Do you think I should buy you a dresser? Don't you want to unpack?"

"I'll wait til Federico gets here, then we'll decide," he responded, so thoughtful that I was ashamed of my take-over attitude. I had to hold myself back from straightening the room, throwing away candy wrappers, crushed Pepsi cans. What would Federico's mother think? How could she send her son so far away? Were they estranged?

Was he difficult?

Jovey's dorm parent arrived like a third party showing up at an important moment on a big date. I didn't want him taking my place, helping my son get settled. He was only in his mid-twenties, a relaxed-looking preppy professor with a ponytail. I could tell he thought I was in the way.

I looked at my watch — how anxious it made me. My life was marked by the metronome of its all too steady ticking. Why was I doing this? Turning my son over to an institution. I would be alone in the universe — bleak, grey, wintry Boston. Slippery ice, *Oh, Heaven help me.* I didn't want to leave. I didn't want to die. I felt like I was losing my baby forever. He would never be carried in my backpack again. I would never watch him winning a Little League game, or ride with him up a chair lift, or sit with him in some funky cafe, ordering a double *latte.* Yes, our love was cozy, and while I knew that I indulged him, he was not spoiled because of it. I admired his look-at-me antics, believing that true narcissists never had real mother love. His cut would not stop bleeding, and I could feel my own blood leaking through.

Excusing myself, I tried stuffing two Tampax up, one after the other (to be born in blood within the hour no doubt), and thought about the Brickers' imminent twins — how they would make Roberta insanely happy, but how a mother knows so little at the moment of birth. See what she had to look forward to!

The admissions lady who had encouraged Jovey to come mid-semester began telling him about dinner — the dining hall was across the quad, though who on earth could eat? He was holding up his bloody hand wrapped lamely in toilet paper, but she didn't seem to notice, until I asked for directions to the school infirmary. I had to drop off his medical records, an extra Ventalin inhaler, echinacea drops. Jovey didn't get asthma all the time, but when he got a cold, it was difficult for him to breathe. I wondered if Federico would mind switching bunks, if it came to a life or death situation.

I remembered when Jovey was six months old, and we took the

kids to Maine. On the first night there, he developed croup, and the rental cabin didn't have a humidifier. I got up with him every twenty minutes or so to turn on the shower. I was young then, but easily frightened, afraid my baby with the fish-bone bark would die in my arms. Things happened.

Was I over-reacting now too? Or was this a normal response for an average mother at the end of her mothering road? The nurse in the infirmary seemed cordial, though she'd never heard of echinacea drops before. She admitted that they did not have a hot steam humidifier, but she assured me that there were at least thirty other students with asthma here at Underledge. Why so many? Not enough vacuuming?

She handed Jovey a Band-Aid, and he tried to apply it while the blood trickled down. "I think I'm feeling faint," he smiled.

"I can see this one's going to be trouble," she laughed, and he laughed too, soft-hearted kid, no longer a boy but a young man now. Or was he an idiot infant, walking around campus without his jacket, though it was only sixteen degrees out — *Hello.*

I was sick of being a mother all of a sudden, all this anxiety we had to haul around, trying to keep others alive. But when I no longer had anyone to take care of, what would I do? A new hobby? I might have been aging, but I was too young for this. Most forty-two-year-old mothers wouldn't have to deal with abandonment for another half a decade. I had had my children too early. What was I thinking of way back then?

I thought of returning to Boston and shuddered. In many ways it was really Jackson's house. I simply went along with his choices. I was like a rather funky lamp, placed out of the way. I had my own room, "my rat's nest" and that's where I lived, along with my tell-the-truth mirrors, the dead finch embalmed in my closet.

I had never lived alone, truly on my own, and that was something to think about, that I'd moved from my father's ramshackle colonial into a supervised dorm, then on to an early, hasty marriage with immediate kids. There was something liberating, not at all lonely about the idea of living by myself, in some one-room cottage with a fire going. I would make plenty of fires and scatter the ashes, make my roses grow.

I realized that I was almost terrified about driving back to our empty house on Beacon Hill, each floor so isolate, a different world, no easy coming together. Jackson liked it, because he could shut out the rest of the world. Privacy was high on his list. There was a hearth in every room, but they were all swept and empty, like miniature, waiting mausoleums. Maybe I should cremate my bird. Why was I being so morbid? Why was my husband too clean for this world, too orderly for co-habitation? No grubby logs to carry in, no fly-away ashes to carry out. His idea of fun on a Sunday morning was to polish everyone's shoes. I wanted him to come sit beside me, to relax and read the Sunday paper. Love was cozy, hearth-warmed. My mother made a fire every night in the winter. We were drawn to it, drawn together. I remembered getting under my mother's wing, while she read to me and my brother, saying "ding" when it was time to turn the page. A *ding* went off in my brain.

I looked over at Jovey and thought — You'll do fine, my dear sweet boy, almost as tall as your mother. "Taller!" he'd claim. Well, he would be soon, by the end of the semester.

But what about Ping-Pong and one-egg omelets, cuddling up to watch *The King and I*, taking the T to the Isabella Gardner Museum for an afternoon concert, what about walking through the North End and listening to the old Italians, what about a million and one or two things? What was I ever thinking? That I could bear this? That I could behave like a grown-up person? That I could rationalize and say — *A gardener often takes a cutting off the mother plant, and places it in a fresh glass of water, so it can make its own roots, and eventually take hold in separate soil.* But Jovey was not a coleus. At home he had a dresser with eight workable drawers. He had his own phone. I could call him from the kitchen on the other line. Here there was only one pay phone for three floors of boys. Were their mothers all trying to reach them? Or had they given up.

Everyone had always loved Jovey, and he would make good friends. But now I was thirsty, for wine, for water, strong caffeine. I was cramping and knew it was time to go. Soon the other students would be returning, and he would want to face that on his own.

When we walked to the door, and he opened his arms for one last hug, he might as well have punched me in the stomach. My eyes widened, and I bent slightly forward as if gasping for breath before turning to run out into a seizure of cold. Good God, get me out of here — *Terrible, terrible, loving somebody, and having to leave him.* Oh my God, where is the car? I was already sobbing before I could get my body inside and put my head on the steering wheel. Nobody heard. Now it was over. He was certainly gone. It would never, ever be the same. I had done my job. I had gotten him here. I had set him sailing. His new life was beginning. Mine would only come in bits and pieces now, never the same whole deal.

At home, Buster was there to greet me as I walked in. He cocked his head, and witnessed my grief with knowing eyes. I bent down and patted his head, and told him, "Jovey's gone." Though I knew I was being maudlin, I didn't care — Buster and I were on the same wavelength. He was my familiar. Jackson was in Providence, doing a new law office — but I doubted if he would have been any comfort, saying something practical, like, *You can drive up and see him next weekend,* or — *You know it's for the best.*

I walked slowly up the flight of stairs to Jovey's level, and circled his room — the sight of his things gave me physical pain. Empty CD containers were scattered on the floor. Jovey's comforter was gone, so I spread out my old quilt, which he'd used since childhood — diamonds of green and red and brown. Placing his little yellow bear on the pillow, I felt like he was dead. I couldn't get over it, how bad I felt, but I wanted to get to the bottom of this. I wanted to touch my own damaged depths. It had something to do with my mother, losing her and feeling brokenhearted, that nothing in my life would ever be complete — that nothing ever came together.

JOVEY HAD BEEN AT UNDERLEDGE for several weeks when I called and could sense a change in his voice. I knew entering at midterm had not been easy, and he hated wearing a coat and tie. "What's wrong?" I asked.

"My advisor," he growled. "Mr. Folkedahl." I could hear other kids in the background, horsing around. It was difficult to have any privacy with only one pay phone for the entire dorm.

"Did you have an argument? Did you flunk something?" I thought from the pause that he might be fighting back tears. It was not beneath this boy to cry.

"He tried to comb my hair," Jovey said in a low voice, adding — "Cut it out! I'm talking to my mother, OK?"

"What do you mean? *Tried* to comb your hair."

He said, "Come see me after class, and when he finally showed up, he said — Your hair looks like shit! And then he took out his comb and started *shredding* my hair."

I could hardly believe this.

"He was yanking it out, and I said — Don't, you can't do that! And he said — I can do anything I damn well please. He said — Would your mother let you look like this? And I said — My mother doesn't judge me by my hair," which was true, but I was speechless. I wasn't keen on Jovey's dreadlocks, either, but I would never dream of taking a comb to his hair.

"He took a handful and threw it on the floor, and then told me I had to sit there until I got it all combed out."

I knew that hair, that ratty look. It would take a good soaking with heavy conditioner, hours of patience and pain to get it combed through. Far simpler just to cut it off. "I'd like to call your advisor," I told him.

"I hate him. I *hate* this place. Nobody likes me. I don't have any friends. They were going to put me on varsity — I'm better than most of those guys, and now I'm only JV. Don't call. What good would it do?"

I didn't call the school, but wondered if I should call Jack. I decided not to, waited a few more hours, and called Jovey back again, just to check his story. It wasn't easy reaching him on the pay phone. Often kids just left it dangling and went off hollering, or they'd pick up the receiver and slam it back down. But I figured this was a good time to call, the thirty-minute period between study hall and lights out.

I asked him to repeat what had happened, and he gave me the exact same lines — "Your hair looks like *shit!* I can do anything I want."

I told Jovey that maybe he should try to comb his hair, but he said, no, he wouldn't. "There are plenty of black kids here with dreadlocks. Nobody bothers them."

"Well, you're not black."

"I might as well be."

Jackson and I had always joked that Jovey wanted to be black. Even as a baby, he liked jazz and southern blues. Granny Hawkins had insisted that Jovis sounded like a *black* name. James or Jonathan would have been preferable. But most of his teenage heroes were black. Jovey walked like he wished he'd been born in the inner core, not the best neighborhood in Boston.

"Is there a code about hair?"

"You're supposed to look neat. *I* think it's neat." He was trying to goof for several other boys who were in line around the pay phone, and he was distracted. They seemed to be punching and wrestling each other like energetic little animals.

"I'd really like to talk to your advisor," I repeated. "I think what he did was wrong. Would you mind if I called?"

"I'm going to sue the dick-head."

"Don't say *sue*."

"I'm gonna," he insisted, good-naturedly.

"Why don't you write a song about it?"

"Yeah," he laughed, and I could feel him turning to perform for his friends — "*My hair might look like SHIT, but at least I'm not a pinhead...*" There was more shouting, rough-housing in the background.

"What did your friend say?"

Jovey said, "No!" but then laughed at somebody's antics.

"*Jove*," I tried to hold his attention.

"We're not allowed to swear in school."

"Oh," I said, wondering if that applied to the teachers as well, or could they do anything they damn well pleased?

I left a message on Mr. Folkedahl's answering machine, but my call was not returned. So on the following morning, I called the Dean of Students — Jan Baxter reported that she'd spoken to Mr. Folkedahl, who had apparently had enough time to run to her office, but had not returned my call. I told her exactly what Jovey had said, including the *shit* part, and could feel her flinch. "I know Terry Folkedahl," she responded, "and I don't believe he'd say anything like that."

I pressed on, using the words abusive, humiliating, inappropriate. I thought the teacher had stepped over a line. But Miss Baxter came back with a list of Jovis' problems, his inattention in class, in study hall. He had missed basketball practice and had said that he couldn't play because of an ingrown toenail, but then he was seen hiking in the woods. "He told Terry that wasn't a lie, just a story. But we feel at his age, he should know the difference." I agreed. "In the future," she sighed, breaking up her sentence into breathless pauses, "I think it would be best — if you told Jovey — to come directly to me with his problems."

I now saw that I was clearly off-base. This was an in-school issue, and I was trying to solve Jovey's problems for him. No matter what I did, it would not help. "I don't think you can always assume that the adult in any given situation is the one telling the truth," I added.

"We're just trying to get Jovis to own up to the things he does, to take responsibility for his actions."

"Fine," I said.

"Jovis is not a bad boy, not one of the worst."

Worst! I thought. I didn't like dreadlocks either, but if there was a code, couldn't the prescribed punishment address the given problem? Fairness, with children, counted above all things. I remembered my father taking the hard side of a hairbrush and beating both Jimmy and me for no reason. He was mad because we hadn't thanked Mrs. Helminiak for giving us both a ride home. He was frustrated and lonely without mother, not liking to depend on people.

"Jovey was probably just exaggerating, trying to get a response," Miss Baxter assured me. "We see it all the time. Children are lonely, and they want their parents' sympathy."

But Jovey already had my sympathy. He knew that. I almost expected her to say — *Maybe this isn't the right place for Jovis.* And maybe she would have been right.

EVERY YEAR ON FEBRUARY FOURTEENTH, we played up the fact that Jovey's birth was Cupid's most welcomed gift. Birth and love both bathed in red — we made homemade Valentine birthday cards with cut-out tissue and pastel candies — *Oh Boy, Don't Quit, Luv You.* This was the first year for as long as I could remember that I didn't get out the glitter and red hots, the first time we didn't have a bouquet of red helium balloons.

It was a Wednesday, which meant half-day at Underledge. Sports were scheduled for the afternoon. Jovey was playing first string JV basketball, and I was going to drive up and watch. Then afterward, I was hoping to take him and some friends out for pizza. I would spend the night in a local motel, and drive back to Boston in the morning. But halfway there it started to snow, coming down in big thick flakes, which made the drive a bit nerve-wracking. I made it to school in time to find out that the basketball game had been canceled. Jovey seemed happy to see me, but he was embarrassed by the heart-shaped chocolate cake. "What are you trying to do, ruin me?" He insisted on straightening the edges in the car. He at least liked the tape recorder I'd brought him so that he could keep track of his songs, but he seemed distracted, almost bored by my presence.

"You don't know how horrible it is here," he grumbled. "Nobody's well-rounded," which struck me as an odd complaint. I knew it had been hard coming in at the middle of the year, but there was something else. Jovey was in a sullen mood, which was unusual. The other boys we met seemed nice, polite and very friendly, but he claimed he had no friends. It worried me when he admitted that he didn't have anyone in particular that he wanted to invite out for dinner. He thought maybe it would be best if we just had lunch. He had so much homework anyway, and he had to be in study hall by seven. Apparently, he was off-standing, not to be confused with outstanding. What had he done? "Nothing," he claimed, just late to three or four classes. I began to feel like I was one more obstacle he had to navigate. He didn't know what to do with me.

If I left after lunch, he suggested, I could get home before the storm dumped its fourteen inches — he had heard the prediction on the radio.

It was true, I didn't want to get stuck in the storm, and then suddenly, I thought, I might surprise Jackson. He had always said how it wasn't his day — how only women were partial to heart shapes — lockets, stickers, quilted pillows. Jovey had always been my Valentine, anyway. Perhaps now I could make it up to Jackson.

After a rather hazardous return drive, I was relieved to find parking on Beacon Hill. Dashing into the liquor store, I bought a bottle of Merlot, purchased for the charming stag on the label. I selected a heart-shaped anthurium, which looked like it might last forever. Then walking up Pinckney, I snuck in through the garden, and heard Brazilian music coming from the library upstairs. That seemed odd, but I slipped off my boots and crept up the stairs, padded down the hallway. I swung open the door for a big — "*Surprise!*" And there was the father of my children, in bed with another man, both of them bare-chested, reading — reading like a married couple.

I remember their mutual expression of shock, and yet I also recall a giddy, whirling sensation, as if someone had taken me and spun me around — I was standing still but the walls were not. I dropped the bottle on the carpet, a harmless *thunk*, and began to back out. Turning, I sprang down the hall in slow motion — slammed my door shut and started digging through the drawers, digging insanely for something. Where was it? Jack appeared in the doorway, asking what had happened at Underledge, and I threw the Lone Ranger right at him. He caught it in his hand. "What's this?" he asked, as if he didn't know.

I could hear Jack's visitor scuttling down the stairs. "Sven!"

Jack called from the top of the banister, watching him descend the circular flights like a turd going down a toilet.

Rushing into my studio, I picked up a mirror and smashed it on the floor. Shards flew in every direction. I was surprised at how quickly it all fit together. The pieces of this intricate, obvious lie, my part in it, my necessary part. I shoved another mirror off the table and kicked over the birdcage — the poor finch began batting its wings against the bars. I could see that I didn't belong here. But where would I go.

Jack tried to stop me — this was all a mistake. He could explain. Nothing had happened. They weren't doing anything. They'd just been over at the gym, and they were relaxing. But I didn't believe it, and neither did he.

In a daze I went over to Donna's, taking Jovey's sleeping bag with me. Donna was always dependable when it came to an emergency — she made my cause her cause. But when I told her what had happened, she flipped out in Italian — "*Il cazzo, la minchia, i coglioni.* That bastard, do you realize what he's exposed you to?"

"He's been lying to me for who knows how long."

"*Yeah*, lying in your own fucking *bed*!"

Even Donna didn't know that we slept in separate rooms. Only the kids were aware of that, and they found it odd but acceptable. I had come to think that it was normal — don't confuse sleep with sex, right? But maybe I'd been confused for such a long time, I didn't even know my own husband.

Donna was on a rampage now, exhibiting all the anger I couldn't begin to feel. "He's been doing a *Gaslight* number on you! As if you weren't good enough, or sexy — *shit*! At least it now makes sense." She went over to the kitchen and got down a half bottle of Chianti, uncorking it with her teeth, pouring me a jelly glass full. I glugged it down, still in shock, not quite inside my own body, though I knew I was sitting on the floor, leaning back against her leopard-skin armchair. I realized then, that Jack and I were only still together because of his mother, because he was afraid she'd find out.

I felt like marching back over to the house with a hatchet,

smashing up her stupid mahogany furniture, filling those spotless mausoleum fireplaces with priceless kindling, making a fire in every room. But Donna discouraged me. "Don't do anything, yet. That junk might be part of the settlement." She poured me another glass of red wine, and said I could use her bed that night. "I'm probably going over to Steve's," she added, a bit sheepishly, for Steve had talked his way out of the Nancy Smith episode, and though the mention of her leaving made me slightly anxious, I didn't give her a hard time.

"So what should we have for dinner, baked beans, and weenies?"

This made us laugh, and reminded me of how I had thrown the Lone Ranger at him, how he'd caught it in his hand. *What's this?* As if he'd never seen one. We both began to giggle, and then slowly slid into uncontrollable hysterics. But then I stopped, oh no. "What if Buster finds it?"

"He'll probably just think it's a bone," she burst into wine-spitting guffaws, falling down on the day bed. Both of us were crying with laughter now.

"Maybe Jack'll set it in the hallway niche, make a little, you know — shrine!" But in the midst of our hilarity, I wished I'd never let her order that thing. It was like a pet alligator, bought on vacation, quickly turning into a monster, lost somewhere in the house. But now I didn't have a husband, or a lover, and I didn't even have my rubber *kemo sabe*. Perhaps my riding days were over.

Donna emptied the last of the Chianti into my glass. I was beginning to feel drunk, but I didn't care. I wanted to drink until I passed out. I wanted to be blind, like the black mole fetish, burrowing deep, deep, deep into the dark, silent earth.

A week later, just before Jack left on his bi-annual trip to Milano, I returned to the Beacon Hill house. I had agreed to stay there, to look after Buster while he was gone. It would give me a chance to box things up. Jack was still hoping for a reconciliation. I don't think he believed that I had the guts to move out. He didn't realize that the vase was broken, that it would never hold water again.

Standing in the hallway, ready to go, he looked fabulous as always. Even his grey-green raincoat looked immaculate, while I was disheveled. My hair wasn't clean. I could tell he felt regret, but mainly because his precious facade had crumbled, and he could see how shaky his whole life was — the stage set of his illicit desires. He wanted to put things back in order. He wanted me to acknowledge the difficulty of his position. He felt bad about not sharing his secret, but it was more than a secret — it was his life, the only thing that held any interest.

We hadn't really spoken much that week, and when we had, it had all been details, dates. I could see that he was alarmed, trying to remain calm and in control, which was our normal scenario. "I always thought we had a good marriage," he said, another lie, unless his idea of a good marriage was living together for eighteen years and not even knowing each other.

"Don't talk to me about marriage, Jack." I was surprised to hear the tone of my voice, for I rarely got mad. "You *used me*, as a front!" Buster was cowering down the hall, as if he were afraid of witnessing a scene. "I feel like such an idiot, just a piece of— crap."

"I thought you would hate me," Jack responded with lowered eyes.

I had to fight myself not to give in to this. "I wouldn't have hated you for telling me the truth. I would have understood, or tried to." *But I hate you now, with all my heart,* I didn't add, because I didn't want to give him the tiniest memento of melodrama that he could smile about later with somebody else. "You almost feel justified, don't you, as if you had no other choice. Well, I don't believe that. We could have shared our children in a decent, honest way. You shouldn't excuse yourself."

"I don't excuse myself," he answered, using that irritating mirror technique. "Don't be so angry."

This *made* me angry. For once I felt empowered. I was no longer the sleeper, the half-asleep mate, who turned her head and went to bed early without claiming a crumb for herself. Did he really think I could believe him? That he hadn't known exactly what he was doing, which he always knew at all other times? "Jesus, when did all of this happen?"

"When?" he repeated, as if he were in a stupor, as if I'd clubbed him with a hammer, instead of the other way around. I expected him to say a couple of months ago, but what he admitted floored me. "I guess it was right after Jovey was born. You were in the hospital, after the Caesarian." So what was he trying to preserve here? "I knew Jovey was the most important person in your life, not me."

"Oh give it up —" the displaced penis award. "Am I supposed to feel *sorry* for you? I wonder how you'll break the news to him, because you know what? I'm not going to do it."

"I *need* you," he responded.

That I could believe. But honestly, I was sick and tired of being needed in that way — like a mother needed to change the diapers, heat up the milk to the perfect wrist temperature — I was needed only to provide basic comforts. "And what about me, my needs?" As I recall, it hadn't been much of a Valentine's Day. I didn't even get a card, not to mention long-stem roses. I knew if I asked for anything, right then, he would have given it to me, but that wasn't the point. I wondered how Jovey would take this. Jen would probably blame me.

Jack was ready to go, and he wanted to leave on a good note, so that he could have an effective trip. "I'll call," he said, like he always said.

"Don't bother," I replied.

"But I'll want to talk to you." He looked at me as if he were trying to recognize me — I resembled someone he knew. But then he looked down at the black and white diamonds of the hallway tile. "This almost feels like a death."

It was, only worse, because we were still living. I didn't tell him that I'd miss him too — husband, partner, father, lover — yes, we were undeniably attached, through the many layers of common details — meals and trips and phone calls, upsets, parties, births and deaths, chores and laughs and choices. I was bound to him as a matter of habit, as a matter of fact, but now we were being ripped from each other, torn and chucked like reject plants. We had been wed in our own strange way, but to us it had felt familiar, and I'm sure that would also be true for the kids — they would feel the disruption of all they'd ever known, all that we took for granted.

A FEW DAYS LATER A PHONE CALL woke me up. It was 11:15 on a Sunday evening and I was sound asleep, certain that it was Jack with another apology. But no, it was the dorm master from Underledge wondering where Jovey was — Perhaps he was sick, and I'd forgotten to call?

I had just gotten back that evening from Skidmore, where I'd been watching Jennifer play volleyball. I tried to keep my visits somewhat even, because Jen kept track, and held any sign of inequality against me. I was disoriented by the dorm master's question, as if I were supposed to translate my recent experience of seeing one child into a bad dream of misplacing the other, and I wondered for a moment if Jovey was supposed to come meet us. "What?" I asked, feeling the first spurts of adrenaline shooting into my blood stream. I put my feet on the carpet, and hardly recognized the nubbly texture. At that moment I felt what Jack must have felt, what it meant to risk losing everything.

The dorm master informed me that Jovey was missing, and a strange sensation came over me — like a dream state — a hampered rush — I wanted to jump into my clothes, but could not reach them — dash off in the car, which would not go. That impulse was met by an inward feeling of falling, the slow, deliberate descent one must feel before hitting the bottom. I knew I could figure this out. There must be an explanation. What had Jen said? That she knew about Dad and me, but didn't want to talk about it?

The dorm master went on to explain that Jovey had signed out Saturday after class with Cookson Palmer and his parents — he'd gotten a ride with them to New York. "He was supposed to meet your husband at the St. Moritz."

But Jackson would never stay there. All the while my mind was racing — how could I reach him in Milano, or was this some new scheme to get the kids on his side? If Jovey had been dropped off in the city, where would he be staying now? I thought to call friends in the village, Jack's cousin on Park, but what could they do at this hour?

When I couldn't reach Jack, I woke up Jen, who admitted to calling her brother. "I don't know, last week sometime."

"What did you say?" I demanded.

"I said, you were leaving Dad, that's all. What else is there to say. What is this, a mid-life crisis? Jovey took it all in stride. Don't worry about it. I don't see you worrying about *me*."

"Well, *you* haven't disappeared," I reminded her.

"Would you like me to? It can be arranged."

"Stop it!" I wanted to yell at her — *You don't even know what's going on!*

"Maybe you should have told us together, you know? That might have been nicer." That stopped me, for she was probably right. It would have been better for both of them. Why hadn't I thought of that? Because I feared that together they'd gang up on me, that the truth would slip out? Why did I feel this need to protect everyone?

"I need your help," I said to Jennifer. "Where do you think he is?"

"How should I know?" She was cranky. I'd disturbed her sleep, and she had a chemistry test the following day. "You could try calling those places for homeless people, though he probably wouldn't use his real name. I don't know why you sent him to Underledge anyway. An all-boys school? That place was way too straight."

After hanging up, I made fifteen more phone calls to official departments of disinterest, then got out the Underledge Parent Directory and called the Palmers. They were both still awake, chagrined that they'd had any part in this upset. And yet I could hear an underlying layer of relief in Mrs. Palmer's voice, grateful that it wasn't Cookson who was missing. She implied that Jovey had been quite convincing. "He said he was going to the Whitney and then out to dinner for Cuban food. I did wonder why he had his guitar and a suit-case just for an overnight."

She paused to inform her husband what had happened, and then he got on — his tone more sympathetic. "If there's anything we can do, anything at all. I know of several agencies, but it's difficult at this age. There are so many younger ones out there. I thought Jovey had a real head on his shoulders, if that's any consolation. We had quite a discussion coming down. He'll probably turn up tomorrow or the next day, but I know how distressing this must be."

"Yes," I whispered.

"If there's anything we can do."

I thanked him, absurdly, for giving Jovey a ride. I really wanted to thank him for the sound of his voice, for his deep, even tone of concern, which almost reassured me that everything would work out, even if it wasn't what I had planned. It was the reassurance that fate often had it's own reasoning, and it spoke to me on some other level.

Jack was relieved to hear from me long-distance. Apparently, I still needed him. He seemed grateful that another emergency had replaced the one he'd left. We had to stick together. He urged me to call every precinct in New York, but Donna thought I'd be wasting my time. "Keep the phone lines open. He'll call. He's going to run out of money."

That first morning I sat by the phone until I thought I'd go crazy. I couldn't work. I couldn't read. I could only drink Coke and eat Tic-Tacs. I imagined the worst — he was so attractive and not very street smart — too spaced out, too innocent, trusting. He'd be a mark, just hanging around, trying to act cool. I made myself frantic, thinking of every possible scenario, and then a phone call came. It was only Donna, checking up on me, but I didn't dare talk. What if he was trying to call? I wondered if I should change the message on the machine — tell Jovey that we only wanted to know that he was all right — but I was afraid of other people hearing it, that it would set up a snowball effect of phone calls, and that it might even scare him away.

That evening as I sat there waiting to hear some word, I felt that I was connected to every mother in the world who had ever lost a child. I knew what it was like to hear that sickening silence in utero, what it would be like to stand helpless before some inexplicable fever — where did it come from, who sent it, why? The VW loaded with teenagers — skidding on ice, the milk-carton children, each face a radiant beam in the darkness. My nerves had become like talons. The clock kept making its progressive chimes, until I began to believe, with a superstition people have, that if I went out for a little while, I would return to find an answer.

I decided to take a chance and ran down the street — I needed bread, milk, and more Tic-Tacs. They were out of white, so I bought green. When I came home the red light was pulsing. The machine had registered two calls. The first was from Monica, Jack's assistant, and then — *"Hi Mom, it's me. Sorry if you've been worried. I'm OK. I just couldn't take that place anymore. Guess what, I shaved my head. It feels really weird. I met some people at a concert, and I'm staying with them for now. But I want to come back to Boston, get a job and a place — I really want to work on my music."* I thought about what I had always said — as long as you live your own life. *"Jen told me about you and Dad breaking up."* His voice sounded slightly worried at this point. *"Don't try to find me, OK?"* And then finally, after another long pause, he added, *"Love you."* He was then gone, dropped back into the masses of Manhattan, lost to me, out of reach, but at least I had his voice. I played the tape over and over.

I called Jack in Milano to tell him the news. He acted as if he had known it would all turn out, that everything would be OK. He said he wanted to return home early, but I didn't think that was necessary. There was a silence, which felt extremely long for international long-distance. Within that thirty-second pause, I think we both realized that we would always be connected, even if apart, but that we would never get back together.

SEVEN DAYS LATER I RECEIVED a postcard from Jovey, saying that he'd landed a job in the school cafeteria at the Berklee School of Music. He was sharing an apartment with a drummer friend, and he'd already joined a band.

I tried calling him at work, and when he came to the phone, I said, "Don't hang up." His silence seemed slightly paranoid. I wasn't even sure if he were still there. "Jovey?" I asked. "I just want to see you."

"I told you where I was." He sounded wary, trying to figure out if this were a trap. Did I mean to shove him into the back of my Audi and lock all the doors with the jab of an elbow, keep him nice and cozy under lock and key? Would I make him see a shrink?

I just wanted to hug him, kiss him, assure myself — "Are you really all right?"

"Sure, I told you. Don't worry so much.""

"You're probably upset about me and Dad. I just want to talk."

"I'm not upset."

"That's good. Great." I waited, but he didn't respond. This wasn't going too well. We used to talk so easily. It was as if we'd broken up, and were awkward now over the least bit of intimacy. I told him that I'd decided to move out. "Maybe I have to grow up too, you know — get a job, pay the rent."

"Starve," he added.

"Money doesn't go too far, does it. How's that going for you?"

"I wouldn't do this forever, but the music is *dope*."

"Do you think I could come to a performance? Don't forget, I'm your number-one fan."

"I *know*, Mom."

There was another moment of silence, and I felt as if I had lost my best friend. I wanted to make it OK again. We could still continue on his terms. And then for some reason, he began to warm up.

"Do you know how many guitar players there are over here? Maybe a thousand, and this band wanted me. They even want to play my songs." He went on about all the opportunities, how they were cutting a CD, how there were always talent scouts around, but then he asked about Buster. "I was just thinking about that ingrown toenail he got, you know the one the kennel lady discovered?" Yes, I remembered my negligence. One of Buster's toenails had grown in a complete circle, and had come back to pierce the pad of his foot. "I thought maybe I was getting an ingrown toenail too, but I got all the gunk out."

"Just cut straight across, that's the main thing."

"*Right*," he responded, not in the old way, which was loving, warm, but now with a cynical edge that hurt my feelings.

"Would you like to see the Jellies Exhibit?" I asked, as if trying to get the old days back, when he was a small boy and liked to go to the aquarium. "We could go to the Oyster House afterward." The food wasn't great there, but it was his favorite, *the oldest restaurant in continuous operation in the United States*. I did like the dark, timbered rooms, the yellowing plaster — it felt nice and protected, a good place to talk.

"Sure, fine."

"Tomorrow's a Thursday. The aquarium shouldn't be too crowded. How about one o'clock?"

"Just don't be shocked. My hair's real short. And Mom..."

"Yes, sweetheart?"

"Will you control yourself? No crying scenes or cops or anything."

"I miss you," I said.

"I miss you, too. Don't worry so much. I'll be there."

I waited for Jovey for half an hour at the entrance to the aquarium. I could not believe he wasn't going to show up. I had bought two tickets, and now I took his back to the woman in the booth and told her that if a sixteen-year-old boy with a shaved head came to the window and answered to the name of Jovey Hawkins, it was his ticket — I'd be inside.

"Sure," she said, looking at me as if I were some poor, silly creature, stood up.

I hadn't eaten anything that morning, and felt mildly dizzy with anticipation, but as soon as I turned my eyes to the first tank of Moon Jellies, something inside me began to unwind. They were pancake-sized creatures, pulsating, white-grey, ghostly diaphragms with silky skirts, a blossom of ovals etched on top of each one.

I walked into the darkened corridor that held the main show and stood for a long while before the Lion's Manes with their long, stringy tentacles — globular, trailing, like edible seaweed, half-cooked yolks. Across the way there were small orange parachutes, their delicate tentacles streaming behind. Their brilliant color was vibrant against the artificial blue of the background, but the intensity of it was strangely peaceful. I stood there transfixed by their orgasmic undulations. Did nobody see this but me? Such quiet, rhythmical, pulsating contractions. There was a certain release in just giving myself over to watching them there — no brain, no heart, no bones. Nothing to break, no memory. The celestial music was soothingly piped in as if it had been composed to assure me that the universe had its own rhythm and that I could just let myself float.

*Now I lay me down to sleep, my health and love and joy to keep. Grant me strength and wisdom too, to do the things I have to do.* But then one night we went upstairs, and just didn't say it anymore. We stopped singing grace before dinner, like you stop going out for pony rides, or no longer think to plant pole beans, making a teepee of leaves.

Walking on, I stood and stared into the black tank with the smaller Moon Jellies and felt as if I were in some space craft that was carrying me further and further out into another realm of serenity.

How diaphanous they were, encircled by tiny dots of light. I read —
*Light passes through them in nearly the same way that it passes
through water. Transparency helps to avoid being eaten.*

And then the thimble-sized Umbrella Jellies — a microcosm of
the night skies, a smear of constellations. It reminded me of those
summer evenings when my brother and I stole out from our sleeping-
porch beds, each dragging a flannel blanket, and how I liked to roll up
in mine like a white cocoon because the grass blades were damp —
scanning the bowl of the sky. I imagined our mother was up there,
watching over us. And when I was a little older, my eyes drifted to
Venus. I wondered if Venus brought couples together, what star-
crossed lovers meant.

Did Jackson and I marry only to produce our two beautiful children — was that our only purpose? Perhaps our stars were not perfectly aligned, not balanced like Orion's belt. I had always wanted to
have a third child, and now I felt like I'd driven away the two I had.

Turning, I slowly walked back through the darkened exhibit,
wishing that it went on and on, not wanting to face the cold streets
of Boston. I had always thought that having children would fill up my
heart, but now I couldn't believe the emptiness.

I had wanted to take Jovey out for clam chowder. I had wanted
to watch him opening the plastic-covered crackers with his good
teeth, how he'd sprinkle those tiny sea biscuits and then pick each
one off with his spoon. I had wanted to feast on his features, the dark
strokes of his eyebrows, the outline of his mouth. I had wanted to rub
the soft flat bristle of his new-grown hair, perhaps an eighth of an inch
by now. Would it seem a different color? Darker? I wanted to take his
hand across the table, tell him how great it was to see him. Why had
he run away? It wasn't just school. Why hadn't he come? Had he
missed the train, overslept, forgotten? Perhaps I had too many tentacles.

I imagined those jellies drifting out into the dark, entrapping
small creatures in their stinging arms. Perhaps Jovey was afraid of my
enveloping him again. Was I simply trying to hold onto him, to fill an

emptiness that wasn't being met? Did I just want to keep him within the motherly flesh of my too-great concern, keeping him, in that sense, a child? Could I give him up in order to let him grow? Could I give myself over to this floating motion?

A little girl peered into a tank and said, "*Ahhh,*" as one would beneath a starburst of fireworks, or before any newborn creature. I felt all of that week's exhaustion, as if molten lead had solidified in every limb, adrenaline empty, too tired to feel much of anything, really. I was shipwrecked, a useless vessel, but gratefully becalmed. *No heart, no brain, no bones.*

MY FATHER, UNFORTUNATELY, no antidote to despair, delivered the typical third blow — Aunt Carla was dying of cancer. I could hardly believe it, for she'd always seemed invincible to me. He thought he should go out to Arizona and get her, bring her back east where she'd have top care. Apparently, she didn't want to leave the ranch, but like most older brothers, he thought he could make up her mind for her, and wondered if I would take care of the cat and the chickens while he was gone. It would only be for several days.

I said, sure — it would get me out of Boston, but it was odd being back home, odd sleeping in my drafty, childhood room. I still had cartoons and memorabilia taped to the inside of my closet door, and there was the scrapbook I'd made in sixth grade — *Everything You'll Ever Need to Know About Horses*. For the first time I sensed what it would be like to live by myself. I wasn't lonely, exactly — there was just too much time.

I wandered around poking my nose into everything, snooping through every drawer. I sat on the couch and went through old photo albums with their brittle black paper, snapshots slipping from their corner tabs. There was one with a tooled leather cover that featured Aunt Carla on the ranch, back in the early days, stacking adobe, doctoring cows. One shot might have even been Sam, but I wasn't sure, because it was taken from behind. I wondered what he was up to now. Did he have five kids? Or was he still a loner? I remembered the postcard Sam had written after our first summer of teenage love — how he had found my hairbrush, but wasn't going to return it, because it smelled like me. My father intercepted the postcard, and tore it up. I was not to write to Samuel again.

I thought I should take the album to Aunt Carla in the hospital, but distracted by the towering stacks of *National Geographics* and all the attic storage, I forgot to set it aside. Rummaging through old clothes, toys, and treasures, I felt I was stealing magic from my own past, sifting through my mother's costume jewelry, seeing once-sacred objects as common trinkets. I began to feel as if I were house-sitting some past life, a displaced person in charge of pets and plants.

I walked the boundary of our five-acre property — it seemed so much smaller now. I even sat under the Mother Apple, with her low hanging limbs where I used to hang dishcloths, and gazed out at the pasture where we once kept Rosie, the half-draft albino that Jimmy and I rode.

During those few days I spent a lot of time day-dreaming, lying on the sofa with blankets heaped over me, thinking constantly about Sam. It seemed weird to be fixated on him still, but it made me happy, so I succumbed. When I thought of Arizona, I could almost feel the sun pouring over me — I could feel his sinewy arms, how hard he used to hold me, and yet how gently he could kiss — it was almost like eating pudding.

I laughed at the thought until I remembered that time in the tack room when I was sixteen. I was lying on a saddle blanket, and Sam was on top of me, when Pedro came in. Aunt Carla was furious, for she was supposed to be keeping an eye out. She told Pedro to handle the situation — he could either whip the boy or let him go. Pedro told Sam he couldn't thrash him, so he would have to do it himself. Even Aunt Carla was satisfied with the results, for Sam gave himself a bloody back of nasty, raised welts. A week later I was sent home.

Aunt Carla had always wanted to be a cowboy. And though she was told — That's impossible — after finishing high school, she bought a one-way bus ticket and headed out west, ending up in Magdalena, New Mexico. She met her first boss, Mr. Watson, in a local bar. He needed a hard-working, young woman, for his wife had recently passed away and he had six kids. He owned the Lazy K Ranch — their brand was a K, lying down — he drew the letter with his finger on the bar top. "The K is for Kids," he laughed, but Carla didn't get it. "Well, they aren't *all* kids. My twins are older than you are, and one of them's already married. But Lundy's wife, she's sullen, no good in the kitchen."

Ross and Lundy were the epitome of good-looking Western boys — tough, strong, bright-eyed, tan. Ross was blond, dark blond, and Lundy, the married son, was dark as a Mexican, but he had bright blue, flashing eyes. He was the perfect incarnation of all Aunt Carla had ever dreamed of, right down to his well-worn spurs and greasy chaps, his rolled-up work shirt, same color as his eyes. She found herself staring at his forearms. Sometimes he'd take his shirt off, coil up his rope, make a loop, and practice catching a turned-over bucket — the muscles in his arms did a corresponding dance to the twisting movement of the lasso.

Lundy's wife hardly paid him any attention. She was a pretty girl, but she'd lost her zip, her sense of humor and feeling for life, while Lundy was bursting with the raw commodity, brimming over, as if he could barely stay put — joking, tumbling his little brothers and sisters, howling at his own silly jokes, singing old tunes at the top of his lungs, taking off his hat and filling it with fresh-pumped water, splashing it all over himself. He and his brother were always wrestling in the dust, ending up bloody but laughing, falling down.

Even the girls were tough in the Watson clan. Rosalie was a bull rider, one of the best. Unfairly, as nature can sometimes be, she was as plain as her brothers were handsome. She was heavy for a fifteen-year-old girl, heavy-handed in the kitchen, banging the frying pans down with a vengeance. That's when they'd sought out Aunt Carla. Rosalie took on the role of bossing the little ones who ran barefoot around the yard, whooping it up like Indians. It took the crack of a bullwhip to make them line up.

Carla tried to keep her eyes off Lundy, but the harder she tried the more irresistible he became, as if the hand-carved leather of his belt was some sort of delicious jerky. He had a creative bent, and she liked that about him, that he could sit back and tool a little basketweave. "It's relaxing," he'd declare, "but I don't mind *you* as a bit of a distraction." He'd wink, and she'd feel a rush of blood lacing through her veins.

When he came in from work, the dust was often caked on his neck above the well-worn kerchief. That grey-green bit of cloth was as soft as a pail full of ashes — it had been washed so many times. She smelled piñon smoke on his hands one time when he put his calloused palm to her cheek, and said she was too pretty for ranch work. She threw his hand off, denying that, tough as any of the Watsons. She could prove it too, and she did, riding out with him, doing the same jobs as any of the men, cutting out heifers, driving bulls into their pasture, branding, calving.

After a month on the job, Mr. Watson gave her a quarter horse that would spin on command and cut like butter. He was small and sturdy and she named him Ease. All the rest of that life on the Lazy K Ranch was good hard work, nothing easy about it.

Ross and Lundy were twenty-two, still quite impressionable, though they thought they were all grown up. They had seen a film star named "Pancho" who had a gold tooth, and they were both set on getting one like it. Their father told them, absolutely not, that they weren't going to finance that kind of foolishness. But the boys were bound and determined. Using an old pair of pliers, they took turns yanking a front tooth out of each other's mouth. They came into the kitchen crying with laughter, bloody and spitting. Aunt Carla had rescued Lundy's stained handkerchief, soaked it in ice water. She then ironed it into a triangle, and slept with it under her pillow where she could stroke its worn softness like a skin.

The boys saved up their nickels and dimes and finally had enough for a trip to the dentist. Lundy seemed especially proud, his front tooth gaudy and doubly sinister, like deliberate sin, and something about it made Aunt Carla turn away as if she couldn't handle the radiance.

Lundy never laid a finger on Carla, though his eyes were like hands all over her body. She could feel him watching her washing the dishes, a chore she didn't particularly like. Once he came and stood behind her, offering to wipe, but they were always sparring, and she told him to go sit down — it was more sanitary to just let them air dry.

Aunt Carla had been a good-looking woman, big-breasted, with a dark brown braid hanging down her back. Any cattleman knowing the over-all impact of an animal would have appreciated her proportions, just as he might run a hand over a horse's rump, or feel the strong, straight back of a steer.

She imagined Lundy's rough, firm handling, ashamed of such thoughts, creeping up inside her — still, she stirred them around and around, as if her insides were all a smooth sweet batter and she was only borrowing his spoon.

Everyone but Lundy's wife seemed to notice. Ross even laughed and said, "You're in some trouble now!" The way Carla lit up, setting his milk down before all the others, hopping up, mid-meal, to refill it, sitting across from him, listening to him intently when he talked about feeding his little doggie from a bottle.

Watching the light on that tooth, it was a temptation to imagine the metal sweetness of his mouth. She'd have to get out the cards as a kind of distraction, and they'd play Slapjack, Hearts or Casino. He'd chase her around the room if she ever dared beat him. Lord, he was unbelievably handsome, big and brown and hard as nails. They were some family, those Watsons.

But then one night at a carnival on the outskirts of Albuquerque, the twins got drunk, and they were talking pretty wild. "My brother is after you," Rosalie whispered. It was then Carla knew it had gone too far, that she had to get away. She didn't ever give an explanation, but at the first opportunity, she took her savings, packed up, and went. She'd always had mixed feelings about it.

Aunt Carla knew that she had missed out on something, but maybe she had kept something special too. Maybe she had known pure desire, untainted by any actual experience. She must have recognized some resemblance and feared it when I fell in love with Sam Mendoza.

But Aunt Carla's denial had stopped up the potential for anything like that ever happening to her again. She was doubly secure from any invasion of masculine plundering, as she became more masculine herself, gaining weight around the middle, letting her looks go, hefting up her sleeve and showing her muscle. She could throw a bale as high as any man, and she liked to put her boots up and smoke with the cowboys, one puff of Salem, one puff of Old Golds. She seemed to live on coffee, *quesadillas*, and Coke. She drank tequila with the worm in the bottle. She seemed like neither man nor woman to me, but I adored her just the same. She taught me that it really didn't matter what anybody thought, as long as you lived your own life.

When Aunt Carla first came to the San Rafael Valley, she heard about a piece of land for sale. There was nothing on it but the ruins of an old adobe schoolhouse, and she was determined to rebuild. She even set out to make her own bricks. But one day, when she was just beginning, she saw four dark Mexicans sneaking up the valley. They were just sort of creeping along, and she was all by herself, with only her chow dog who wouldn't hurt anybody. It worried her that the chow didn't seem to bother the men. Two of them slipped off into the oak trees, and another headed straight for her truck. She saw he had a burlap bag tied around his waist, and he was putting his hand down into it. She was sure he had a knife, that he would finish her off before she'd even begun. She didn't know if she could make it to her truck, get the doors locked and the windows rolled up in time, so she held her ground, and pointed to the dog — "*Malo, malo*," but the Mexican kept coming, and then reaching into his burlap sack — she always paused here for effect — "He pulled out a trowel!"

We were all relieved to hear that. "They only wanted work," she said, "and yes, I told them they could help me rebuild the place." She took one of the men into town for supplies, and that man turned out to be Pedro. It took several months of steady labor to put the place back together, but after that, she never hired anyone but Mexicans.

94

Aunt Carla loved birds and animals the way other women nurtured their kids. Her place was alive with stock and poultry. She had a special fondness for a certain French goose, which she held in her arms like a baby. She also had a pet javelina, named Gentry. That wild pig just loved her, and nobody else could do anything with him. He just about fit in her hand when she found him. He followed her everywhere, because she always kept a handful of acorns in her pocket. She even let him up on the bed sometimes. He was really quite endearing, nudging and snorting, rutting around, though if any of us tried to hold him, he'd squirm and squeal and make ugly, violent noises.

I can remember the first time my father drove me down the county road to the fork that led to La Querencia — I was only sixteen, there for a summer of work. Jimmy had gone off to be a counselor at a camp in Maine, and Aunt Carla said she'd take me. As we drove down the dusty road, I remembered seeing the rustic outbuildings clustered together, bunkhouse, corrals, the main adobe set across the yard with its ocotillo fence, all of it rather ramshackle. Frightening black and tan dogs charged the car, and then almost the first thing I noticed was a mountain lion's paw hung up on a bent coat hanger, dangling there in the shed. "What's that?" I asked, before I would kiss her. I wasn't sure at that point if I wanted to stay.

"Don't go feeling sorry for that ole thing! He was picking off my heifers, one by one. That paw's for the fish and game warden, in case he wants to know. We're making a rug out of that big ole fella."

Life on the ranch seemed brutal, dazzling, bright. Peacocks wandered about the yard, and guinea hens pecked amongst the roosters and cats. There was one white peahen in the flock of brilliant blue-green birds. Aunt Carla said it had arrived out of nowhere. "It just lit in and liked the vittles I guess. Pedro calls it our angel in residence. That's why we're so darn affluent around here!" The horses looked scruffy, old Pay Day the bay and one tired palomino, two paints, and a burro. I wondered which one I'd get to ride. I had always wanted an all-black horse.

When I came into the kitchen, Aunt Carla was still talking about predators. They'd found the body of a deer with two newborns, the bones of the babies picked clean. "Probably just born when they got eaten." The lion dogs looked like huge beagles with some Walker hound in them. They were kind, good dogs once you got to know them. Aunt Carla also had a corgi, which seemed out of place.

I was a bit shocked by my Aunt Carla's kitchen. There were things all over the counters. It looked like no one had ever scrubbed down the yellow painted clapboard that ran tongue and groove up the walls and over the ceiling. It didn't even look like she'd done the breakfast dishes, but there was fresh, hot coffee, and she poured me a cup. It was my first taste of coffee, very bitter. She laughed when she saw my expression, and pushed the milk and sugar over in my direction, though she always drank hers black.

The rest of her house was more civilized. It wasn't fussy, but you had a sense that she had traveled. She had a deep feather sofa in the living room, covered with a faded, pale green material. You could sink back into it, even if you were wearing blue jeans. She didn't care. There was a big stone fireplace with an Oriental screen, Navaho pillows. She had an English secretary where she did her book work, wrote her letters, and paid her bills, a grandmother clock that she had shipped from Massachusetts along with her four-poster bed — that lent the house some elegance.

I can still remember when she invited Pedro and the men inside to have a bowl of chili, how uncomfortable my father was, especially when Sam Mendoza came in, telling Pedro in Spanish how he'd just fixed the calf-puller. Then Gentry the pet javelina came squealing through, disturbed by the unfamiliar company. I thought it the funniest thing I'd ever seen, though Samuel Harrigan Sixkiller Mendoza refused to even look at me. He was about my age, but seemed older somehow, tall and thin, with long black hair pulled back with a piece of rawhide. I'd never seen anything like him. Aunt Carla told us he was part Apache, and that was enough to alarm my dad. He told me to stay away from him. Apaches were known to be so untrustworthy, they couldn't even trust each other.

But I was mesmerized. After I had settled in, Sam taught me how to cinch a Western saddle, how to neck rein a horse. I had always ridden bareback in the woods back home — Rosie was bomb-proof, but out here, Sam rode fast, and after chores were done, we'd chase each other over the bare, baked earth. Once he made me a bracelet out of our horses' manes, pulling white and brown and black, braiding them together.

Another time we went hiking in the foothills, and sat for over an hour on a lookout rock. He pointed out things I barely saw, antelope in the distance, circling hawks. On the way back down he found an old, metal cross half-buried in the dirt. He scraped it off, saying, "I'm going to keep this," but then he just stood there, blocking the path. I stepped forward, into his arms.

DETERMINED TO SEE JOVEY face to face, I decided I would go and find him. I knew he was working at the school cafeteria at the Berklee School of Music, and if I didn't locate him there, I would speak to the person in charge and get his address. In my gut I knew this was the wrong thing to do, that this would only make things worse, but I felt I had no alternative.

Taking the T over to the Mass. Ave. exit, I jogged up the stairs to the street, walked past Urban Outfitters, where just a few months before I'd bought him clothes for school.

It was late for lunch, but there were still a good twelve students sitting around, and I was about to ask a black girl with *real* dreadlocks if she knew Jovey Hawkins, but then I spotted him myself. My heart was pounding. He looked like a convict, pale and self-absorbed, clearing tables in a big white apron that made him look like a large child. I walked in his direction, and could tell that he saw me, for he stopped for an instant, before making a retreat back toward the kitchen.

"Hey," I shouted, waving my hand. "Where you going?"

He turned on me then. "Can't you *see* that I'm working?"

"I can see that you're being very rude."

I hadn't laid eyes on him since his birthday, February fourteenth, and now without a hug or a kiss after all this time, he added, "Why don't you just give it a break, Mom."

I didn't know what to say to this, but blurted out, "Don't you ever think about anything other than yourself?" He looked embarrassed, ashamed of this outbreak, but I went on. "Did you know your Aunt Carla has cancer? She's right here in town, at Mass General."

"So what am I supposed to do about it?" He looked at me with such hatred, his eyes became smaller, as if my presence were weighing

98

him down, compressing some part of his brain. And then without speaking, he turned to go.

"You can't do this to me!" I yelled.

"Do *what*, live my own fucking life? Do you want to get me fucking fired?"

"Don't *speak* to me," I growled, "*like that.*" I took hold of his apron, and he jerked himself free — the cups and plates he was carrying on a plastic tray clattered to the floor. We both stepped back.

"Now look what you've done. I'll have to *pay* for that. *Shit*," he muttered. "Why don't you *do* something with your own *friggin'* life, Mom, instead of feeding off of me!"

He stormed away and I was left standing there. I could feel the few students staring at me, and I avoided their gaze, bending down to pick a few shards from the floor, remarking on how sharp they were, careful not to cut myself as I lay them on a table.

I waited until I was up on Newberry Street, standing in front of a mural, before I started to cry. I pretended I was examining the artwork closely, intrigued by the geeky creatures climbing around, but all I could see was a world of beaked bodies with striped parts, trying to fly. Jovey didn't need me. He wanted to be off on his own. That was natural. He was trying to make his own way. That was good. I had turned it all around into an impossible situation. Of course he had to hate me.

There was nothing left to do but get out of town. He was right — I had to "give it a break." But I was the one who felt broken. It seemed as final and horrible as the death of my mother, but I had survived that, hadn't I?

MASS GENERAL WAS ONLY A SHORT WALK from our house on Beacon Hill, and I went to see Aunt Carla almost every day. She was just as I had remembered, only more so. She wanted me to sneak her in cigarettes — preferably Old Golds. She would smoke them, she promised, standing on the toilet seat blowing up into the ceiling fan. "You can't expect me to quit at this age!" She claimed she didn't like the hospital atmosphere, which also made me feel a peculiar form of panic, as if my own life were balanced on the rim, teetering one way, then the other.

"I know your father means well, but he's such a big bully. He always thinks he knows the only way. I was too weak to fight him. Let him win for a change. I never should have told him anything. Pedro's always doctored me before." I poured her some water, and urged her to drink, but she mainly wanted to talk about the ranch.

When she had first come to the San Rafael Valley, it had clearly been a man's world, and the other local ranchers weren't too keen on her ideas about diversification — she thought maybe they should raise some sheep, as well as cattle, in part because she loved eating lamb. "But sheep are so dumb," she admitted to me now. "You can mark a pig, put an X on its forehead, and *bam,* one shot, it's dead. But you shoot a sheep, it just looks at you. Shoot it again, and it shakes its head. It gave me the willies. Turner Treat drove his truck right off the road, when he came over the hill and saw those sheep. I guess it was worth it just to see his expression."

I took her hand, but her grip was weak, a side of her I'd never known before. It made me think of a tender pole plant, needing a stake for support.

"I've got one request," she told me. "If I don't make it, will you take my ashes out to Ben's Spring? I doubt your father would honor that. He has it in his mind that both of us should end up in that cold little cemetery with the rest of the family, but it just about makes my bones shake to think of that cemetery under snow. It would give me some peace to think of being on the ranch."

I promised, and told her not to worry — "You should think about other things."

"I think about things!" she responded. "I was just now thinking about Gentry. Remember him? Not so little when that idiot trapped him. Boy that made me mad, madder than anything. Remember how he used to come snuffling around? Wasn't he the cutest little creature? And I tell you, after flying, I miss those trains. I always liked the way they jiggled you."

I got the feeling that her sense of time was a great big jumble, that the years were something like spools of thread, all tangled up, and she was trying to put her basket in order.

"You know, at shipping time, it used to be so damn exciting, having that train pull into town — big black coal smoke pouring from the engine. Seeing a truck pull out is not the same." She shook her head, and reached for a cigarette, then frowned at me because she didn't have one.

"You know, I always had this crazy notion, that menthol would somehow clean the regular tobacco up — sort of like a mountain breeze." She laughed, laughing until she went into a coughing fit. Her face turned red, and she had to lean forward to get her breath. I rubbed her back in circles, and then eased her onto the pillows.

"Now, don't go giving me your sad expression. I've lived my whole life just the way I wanted. That's the trouble with you — you've been living everybody else's. When's the last time you did something for yourself? When's the last time you were even happy?"

The first thing that came to mind was riding alongside Sam — out across the valley floor. It didn't seem like such a long time ago. "I was happy," I told her, "I was always happy in the sunshine."

She glanced toward the window — Boston was at its worst in

March. She thought I should get out of town, not to worry about her. "Take what's left of your life and just go." Then a nurse came in to take her temperature, and Aunt Carla almost knocked the thermometer out of her hand. "What do you want to do that for? Get the darn hell out!" The nurse retreated, to Aunt Carla's delight. "Scare 'em a bit, and they shape right up. I learned that rule with young horses. Remember when they used to stick those things up your bum? That really gave me the willies. So, what do you hear from that brother of yours?"

"Not much," I said, not telling her how Jimmy only called when he needed money. He gambled, and seemed to blame the world for his losses. He also had the sorry habit of getting into debt on his credit card, and Pop had bailed him out three times. Our father couldn't stand to see him paying such high interest, but I didn't think Pop was doing Jim a favor.

"Never did care for that boy," she admitted. "Isn't that awful?" I had to laugh, because I felt the same way. "You got to go out and party," she said to me then. "Don't throw away your chances. You're still good and young. Go buy yourself a six-pack, drink a couple of beers. Go eat a piece of pizza for me!"

Donna claimed she had entered a new celibate phase. She was going to wait now and see what happened. Steve was truly out of her life. She wanted to meet new people, nice men. In fact, she wanted to take me off to a party after dinner, somewhere in the Back Bay. I wasn't so sure about that.

"But I have something for you," Donna announced, as if it were a bribe. We were sharing a big bowl of *pasta putenesca*. Fishing a package from the depths of her bag, she dangled it before me. "This is to celebrate your new life, free from misery, free from tyranny." She wanted me to open it there on the spot. Donna was like that, and I was a child when it came to presents, though this one seemed a little odd — a glass hen egg-holder with an egg-shaped candle, charming with a touch of hokiness about it, which was identifiably Donna's. So

I lit the candle and watched it burn, until a yellow waxy yolk appeared. I was fascinated by the simple magic of the molten egg, especially when a pearly white bead appeared in its melting center. I captured my treasure, but it wasn't a pearl — it was a strange silver capsule, shaped like a bullet, tightly sealed. "You have to unscrew it," Donna said. Inside the bullet was a scroll of paper — *One heartfelt joy dispels all woes. Your love waits some place special.* Donna thought that was fortuitous. Maybe it meant that someone was waiting for me at the party she wanted to drag me to. I didn't think so, but the red wine had made me almost amenable, and finally I agreed to go along.

The living room was filled with people who were all drinking and talking intensely. I didn't know a soul, but Donna pulled me in and introduced me around to a few acquaintances, and then with her expert eye, she nodded toward the windows that faced the street — there stood a particularly attractive man, in a loose white shirt and blue jeans. He had long, dark hair pulled back in a ponytail — he immediately reminded me of Sam. The mere sight of him, standing there, with his back to the room, shot a visceral response right through me. Donna gave me a little nudge of encouragement, and I went and stood at a neighboring window, hoping that he might notice my presence. He was smoking a Krakatoa cigarette that snapped with clove as he inhaled, but he didn't look my way. He was so good-looking, he was almost pretty, about six feet tall, but with a rather fleshy, sensual quality. When he finally turned to face the room, he rested back against the wall and casually offered me a cigarette, which I refused. He then walked closer, offering me something to drink, which I didn't refuse. I said I wanted a beer, which seemed mundane, but they had quite an array from all the local micro-breweries. I handled several, examining their labels, before selecting a *Dos Equis*. He smiled, and asked me if I was hungry. I explained that I'd just had a big bowl of *pasta putenesca*.

"Do you know what that means?" he asked.

I knew it meant that I was very full. I stood next to him at the bar, with an unusual feeling of possessiveness, even though he made small talk with an anorexic brunette who looked like she was about to slip out of her dress, the material was that flimsy. She kept saying his name as if she were pleading, *Tonio* this and *Tonio* that, but then he took my arm and led me away, giving me a casual, sleepy look that I knew would be my downfall. I didn't care — I had already given myself over to the idea. I wouldn't even bother with birth control if it came to that. How could I be thinking this way! His shirt was unbuttoned one notch more than necessary, but his dark, smooth skin looked tempting. I sensed that he could read my response as he led me over to a low red couch with numerous pillows. The couch was deep — we had to crawl back onto it. He pulled me under his arm. "I like you," he said, "American woman," accepting a joint that was being passed, taking a drag, handing it on to me. Why not, I thought, though I hadn't smoked in years.

I took a drag, and the room instantly came into focus. All the people seemed socially fierce, but they were also at a great emotional distance. I felt amused by his voice, soothing and toying, and thought he was marvelous. I felt as if we were brother and sister, wed in some world between life and death. We knew without knowing — we understood each other. We talked about nothing in particular, though it all seemed full of import — where we were from — how this meeting was inevitable — he had arrived that week from Tunis to visit his cousin — he was staying in the guest room — did I want to see? I stared at the concupiscent outline of his lips. Everything he said seemed loaded, a prelude to a forgone conclusion.

A tray of strawberries was brought around, and I began to giggle as he rolled one in powdered sugar that made me sneeze. I blew some onto his chest, and he took my hand and rubbed it in, then drew me over to the opening of his shirt as if he meant for me to lick it. He said something suggestive in some other language, that sounded as if he wanted to pull the covers up over us. "Maybe better alone," he added, and I worried that he was going to leave me then, but instead, he took my bottle and placed it on the floor, and pulled me up, pulled me along with him. I was astonished by the invitation, but thought he was so considerate, such a nice young man. I was angry at Jack, though I thought he was forgotten. I would do what I would not normally have done because of my forgotten husband.

Tonio pulled me up close to him as if he wanted to breathe the essence of my hair. Donna nodded from across the room, lifting her eyebrows. Tonio was so sure of himself, and in no big hurry. His mother was Venetian, he explained, his father a Tunisian. "That makes me a Venutian," he smiled.

When he opened the door to the guest room, I was appalled by the eggplant color, the pink satin spread, and ornate chandelier. What was this, a brothel? But soon he eased me back onto the slippery looking bedspread and began to undress me, button by button, taking his time. I was alarmed, and tried to stop his hand, but he took my fingers and kissed them. "I'm not going to let you sleep tonight, anyway. You have such a beautiful body. Did your husband always tell you?" I was amazed that this was so easy, giving myself over to some unknown man, amazed that he found me attractive.

"You're just like a delicious plate of polenta," he added. "Such perfect breasts." Tonio had probably seduced many women and would tire of my plain old dish of polenta after an hour or two, but I didn't care. I was ready to offer myself, overly ready. He had to calm me down, smoothing my skin with the palm of his hand, and then he began to breathe on my neck, his mouth hovering over my body.

We slept together without really sleeping, making love again and again. All he had to do was run his hand down my spine, and I would roll over and present myself. We smoked more grass, and drank straight from a tall clear bottle of grappa. Everything he said, no matter how practiced, everything he did, made me more responsive than I had ever been. I knew that I didn't love him, but for those few hours, I pretended I did. My body certainly responded as if it loved him, until everything began to feel raw.

I wondered what it would be like to be in love and to feel this physical passion, to know your partner felt it too, but this experience alone was some kind of carpet ride. I wondered if it kept on going, where it would take us, where it would leave me, but the next morning the room smelled of liquor and ashes. Tonio rolled over, and looked at me with tired eyes — *Baby, the party's over.*

I was longing for one more session in the big pink bed, for the seduction to go on, for I had done things with him I'd never done with anyone. He had dropped into my life like an angel, a dark, seductive angel with a quota to fill.

He got up and pulled on his blue jeans, "We can see each other tomorrow, yes?"

I agreed. I would like that. I even believed him, and was anxious when he didn't call. I couldn't get him out of my mind, and pestered Donna with details.

Finally my period came, which helped relieve the tension. I was grateful that my carelessness hadn't gotten me pregnant. I wasn't heartbroken. I had had an affair.

"At *last*," Donna said, "you've lost your virginity. It's much better like this, for the first time, with someone you don't really care about."

"I care about him."

"I know, I know, you care about everyone. "

But soon I *would* forget about him, because of my Aunt Carla. I felt terrible that I had forgotten that tooled-leather album — how she would have loved paging through that.

She had been forced to leave the place she loved most in the world, only to spend her last days in Mass General. When they opened her up, they decided not to operate — she was too far gone with cancer. My brother Jimmy was furious, because she'd left La Querencia to me.

# Part Two

# PATAGONIA

I KEPT THINKING ABOUT my Aunt Carla, how she used to pick up her big grey goose and hold it in her arms, so naturally, how it lay its long, goose neck down along her shoulder, and what a sculptural vision that was, the long goose neck all stretched out. I thought of how I'd like to carve that image — the feminine lines encircling the bird, its head nestled against her heart.

I had decided to go back to my maiden name, Weston, which had been my Aunt Carla's name too. "Hawkins" now made me think of a bird's sharp beak — Jack always on the lookout for some infringement of his rules — *Don't slam the door. Don't walk so loud.* I wondered if I would even recognize myself, without someone finding fault with me. Well, good-bye to all that. Let him take a good long look at himself for a change.

How hard it would have been to imagine such freedom just three short months ago, but here was this new life spread out before me — dry, bright, a dazzling kind of energy that made me feel like a teenager.

Taking a right on Route 83, I soon began to recognize familiar landmarks — the buckaroo shape of the Mustang Mountains, and then the majestic Huachucas up ahead, the ripple of the Canelo Hills enclosing the valley on just the other side. I passed the Empire-Cienaga, Gardener Canyon, where the Trappistine nuns sang so beautifully. There on the roadside, off to the right, stood a white wooden cross with the words: *We Love Our Son*, written in script, a pile of stones holding the cross in place. Some teenager had crashed his car. It was always a marker for a boy, and I could imagine his mother mourning — how mothers everywhere were grieving for their sons, lost in battle, lost in bars, lost to other women.

Right before I'd left Boston, Jovey had called to apologize for our fight, for not meeting me at the aquarium, saying how he'd overslept that day, a reasonable excuse, but I didn't believe him and told him so. Then he admitted that his band had to practice that morning. So why didn't he just tell me the truth in the first place? I didn't mind a change of plan, as long as he cared about how I felt, and could empathize with anyone put in that position.

"Put in what position," he had to ask.

I told him that I was also upset that he'd never gone to see his Aunt Carla. And then as if clearing the board, he announced that he had made up that story about his advisor — Terry Folkedahl had never touched him.

At that moment I realized I didn't even know my own son. He had simply been working on me, hugging me at appropriate moments, feigning love in order to obtain certain goods, getting a rise when it suited his purposes. A promise meant nothing if it didn't work out for him at that particular moment. Everything decided by impulse. To steal or not to steal. To lie or "tell a story," fudge on the truth so that he might look good. Appearances were all.

"I've got to go play now," he told me, and briefly, I imagined him going outside to sit on his small, metal tractor, moving it forward with his two feet. I saw him in his overalls with a make-believe stick, but then realized, he meant — play music.

I asked if his band had a name and he said, "Excarnation," like incarnation, but going out. That seemed appropriate for this generation, snuffing the candles, one by one, so that we could all sleep in the dark, in silence.

Driving into Patagonia, I felt the nervous churning of excitement mounting. There was the high school on the right, with its baseball field and tennis courts, and then the big boulevard with the yellow train depot across from the Stage Stop Inn.

Going up Harshaw Creek Road, the terrain looked familiar with its giant sycamores and cottonwoods, the steep red wall with the chartreuse lichen, even more brilliant now at this time of day, the shape of

Saddle Rock as I climbed to the rim, and then the roller coaster feeling in my stomach as I topped up onto the edge overlooking the valley. I had to stop the car and kill the ignition. It was so silent, just the subtle hum of wind breezing over the cattle guard, and there across the valley, the rosy Huachucas sprang up from the grassland floor, catching the glow of the sunset. The expanse of it opened inside of me, and made me understand why Aunt Carla had called her place La Querencia — the special haunt where one feels good, the home place one comes back to.

Driving out over the valley, the road dust billowed, marking the air behind me for a good two miles. Soon the summer rains would come, raindrops big as acorn nuts, hitting the dirt road, sending up small explosions of powder. I remembered the power of falling rain, the Santa Cruz rising, arroyos full. By August, the grass would be brushing my stirrups.

As I pulled into the driveway, which took a downward slant away from the county road, back to where the large cottonwoods made a shady place of protection, I saw Pedro sitting in his rocking chair out beneath the ramada. When he saw me coming, he got up and went inside. His catahoula dog came out barking. It had a blue-grey cataract over one eye. Everything seemed a bit shoddy, run down. The old water tank by the windmill had been so abused by woodpecker holes that it had partially collapsed, but there was a motorized water tank now.

Pedro reappeared wearing his good dress hat, and walking calmly up to the car, he shook my hand very gently. Then he stood there nodding, as if acknowledging that this was a big change for him too, and it would take time like everything else. He picked up my suitcases, and led me into the house. I could smell *carne asada* simmering on the stove, and it made me pause, but Pedro walked on toward the living room, explaining that Rosa had been out to clean, but that she didn't know what to throw away. "She changed the sheets on the big bed, and did the bathroom real good, but otherwise she pretty much left things."

I wouldn't have minded her clearing a path. Rosa was the Mexican maid from across the line. Aunt Carla used to go and fetch her by the back roads. I noticed a familiar clay pot by the fireplace, with geese flying around the rim. I thought — that's where I'll put her ashes. We will bury her ashes in that beautiful pot, with the geese in flight, encircling her.

A calico cat jumped onto the back of the sofa, and Pedro whisked her away. "That cat, she thinks she runs this place. My dog got no use for that Hairball. But out here," he added, good-naturedly, "even enemies got to get along."

I sat down for a moment on the old feather sofa — it was so comfortable, real goose down, though the slipcover still smelled of cigarettes. I put my new suede boots up on the rough-hewn table. They were giving me blisters. I felt overwhelmed, and was grateful for the beer Pedro offered.

He had cubed a couple of small zucchini and fried them up, tossing them with crumbled Saltine crackers — oddly delicious, but one taste of the meat dish and my eyes dilated — a glow formed on my forehead.

Pedro chuckled and blew at his bowl, in imitation. "I guess we're going to have to break those boots in one teaspoon at a time." And then like most cowboys who were comfortable with themselves, he sank into silence, savoring each bite.

"She was a pretty good boss, you know. If she knew you took an interest, she'd give you a chance. She'd trust you. And when somebody trust you, you do the best you can." Pedro got up to clear the dishes, stacking them in the sink. Every move he made seemed meditative, slower than normal, and I wasn't used to anybody serving me. "You never say *no* to the Boss," he continued. "If she say one ice cube in a glass of Scotch, you didn't give her two."

Normally, I would have said no to dessert, but this was a special evening — he had knocked himself out, so I ate the vanilla custard he'd prepared from scratch, ladled with a little Tia Maria, a comforting, creamy combination. Then, sitting back in my chair, I knew I was home. It was a sobering moment.

I HAD NEVER SLEPT BETTER IN MY ENTIRE LIFE, and I was so hungry. Such heavenly air! It was the most luminous day. Pedro had made *pan dulce*, but had then gone out to do some chores. I took my breakfast outside to a little wicker chair that sat in the corner of the yard. Sitting down under the shade of the poplar, I watched a violet-crowned hummingbird whirring about its red plastic feeder, threading back and forth, glistening with its metallic blue-green body. The yard had gone to seed, but I could imagine planting delphinium and hollyhocks up against the adobe wall. I wanted strong, cheerful colors surrounding me — sunflowers, zinnias, nicotiana, phlox. I would bring this desert soil to life, work it with compost and horse manure. I wasn't fully aware of the severity of the drought, but surely there would be enough water for a garden.

When Pedro suggested we take our first ride, I was ready to go, only a little reluctant, for I hadn't ridden in so long. But he assured me that riding was like anything — "Once you know, you never forget it." And he had a special horse for me, an eight-year-old, "Name of Banner." She was all black, with a definite quality, easy to pick out amongst the other sleepy-looking horses. She came right over as if expecting a treat, though I had nothing to give her. She remained expectant, rubbing her forehead against my hand.

Pedro slipped her halter on, and led her out of the corral, talking to her steadily with a calm, sing-song voice. He moved so slowly, I began to sense the pace of this work — gradual, easy, getting the job done step by step. Pedro generally rode *Dos* or Target, though there was also a palomino called Omelet, which Pedro referred to as *Huevos* because he was stud proud. Then there was the rest of the motley crew — Rivet, Ransom, Old Mike, Chink, but Banner was by far the prettiest.

Aunt Carla's saddle was there in the tack room. On the back of the leather seat were two etched oak leaves with a cluster of nuts. Pedro threw the thick pad and saddle up on Banner's back. She didn't like it when he cinched the girth, but once it was set, I took the reins, turned a stirrup, and swung up into the saddle. It was a comfortable fit.

Walking Banner around the dusty yard, I leaned forward to stroke her neck. The sun was quickly becoming a factor — I felt dazed, a bit jet-lagged. Possibly it was the altitude, over five thousand feet. The intense sun flattened out my perception. I wished I'd brought a canteen or at least my Tic-Tacs. Pedro wanted to go up to Ben's Spring, see if there was still enough water up there for the cattle in that section.

I followed along, thinking — How absurd, here I am, a rancher, and I know next to nothing about cattle, plus I'm afraid of bulls. I feared one might charge me and gore my horse. I would certainly fall and get trampled. But Pedro assured me, as we rode by a couple of Hereford bulls, that this breed was tame, though their balls hung down like massive bags of gunpowder ready to be ignited. I was glad when we passed on out of their pasture. Pedro hopped off to shut the gate behind us — it was only kept together by a wire loop squeezed over two mesquite posts.

As we headed up into the foothills, a pack of bristle-backed javelina went scuttling by, and I couldn't help but think they might be related to Gentry. Within half an hour we had climbed to where we could look out over the valley. A small herd of white-tail deer could be seen bounding away in the distance, cattle placed here and there — it was like a great big game preserve, our last frontier, what my father had once called "that inhospitable land," but why should it want any visitors, when its charm was its desolate vastness, its unpopulated space.

I could tell Pedro was used to mirroring this quietness as he rode, but I felt I had so much to learn, I kept asking him questions —

Wasn't it dry? The grass appeared worthless, and I wondered if the cattle were getting anything out of it. Pedro admitted that even he would have to call this a dry spell. "But you got to be patient. Things come around."

Luckily, Ben's Spring was still providing water for the cows up here, making a verdant little groove against the rubble of the earth. It was obvious that the cattle came here often— the mud had been freshly worked by their hooves, and I could imagine the cool relief of it, scrubbing their hides against the curved earthen wall. There in the bushes lay a newborn calf, catching a little piece of shade. It was so beautiful, small and soft-looking. I thought — This is where I'll bury her ashes.

Pedro pointed out a big red longhorn he called "Lasagna." Her horns came in handy protecting the calves from predators. Packs of coyote had become a problem. Another old cow he called "Shoog," short for sugar, because she was so sour, and so on. "Down in Mexico, when I was a kid," Pedro told me, "in those days you didn't hardly have to learn this heifer or that calf — they were just ole cows, you know. If you were driving and one calf got tired, and she lay down, you'd just go on and let her lay. The owner didn't pay much attention."

Aunt Carla kept about three-hundred and fifty head, and the ranch used nine-thousand acres of land, but only one hundred and sixty were deeded; the rest was leased from the government. You needed about eighteen acres per cow in this part of the country, and if you were lucky, and got ninety percent of the herd to drop calves, you could just about make it.

As we rode back toward the ranch, I knew I had the rhythm of riding stored in my body. I guess I hadn't forgotten. My muscles certainly remembered, and reminded me the next morning. But the only cure for that was another ride, and another ride after that.

LATER THAT MONTH AN UNSEASONABLE wind started up and continued for several days. It made the horses uneasy. I felt the same way,
and stayed inside, trying to distract myself with household projects,
boxing up Aunt Carla's old clothes, taking in the smell of her — alco-
hol potions and baby powder — tossing the stiff, store-bought, poly-
ester curtains and yanking up the green shag carpet.

Maybe it was the work of the living to go on remembering, hon-
oring the dead, but there was so much to do here, so much stuff —
piles of magazines, newspapers, letters opened, but probably not
answered, a stack of bills, her "cattlelog" — that it began to feel like
a burden. I just wanted a simple, cleaned-out life. Begin with the
obvious, I said to myself — exit the Budweiser beer sign and the horse
yoke mirror. The lion skin rug that had always lain by the side of Aunt
Carla's bed must have given her some satisfaction as she stepped on
his hide every morning, but I had no desire to prolong that grudge. I
painted the bedroom floor a pale blue-green, and covered the bed
with a white cotton comforter and big white pillows. I took the dusty
piñata down from the corner of the bedroom and pried the elk horn
handle off the door. I couldn't help but think that Jackson would
approve of the changes I was making, how his aesthetics had somehow merged with my own.

As the wind continued, I tried to drown it out with local
Mexican music, interspersed with the street-hawker exuberance of
noisy sell-something announcers. We were only a twenty-minute
drive from the border, but even with the radio turned up high, the
wind was still rasping, and by the third day, it started to get to me.

Late that night the wind seemed to carry this haunting tune
that came and went, very creepy. I wondered if Pedro was playing his

radio in the bunkhouse, but no, it sounded more like the cry of some spirit circling the place, sensed one minute and lost the next. I couldn't flick on the outside lights since the generator had been turned off for the evening, and I felt too wary to step outside and start it up again. All I had was the high-powered flashlight by my bed.

Standing by the window, I shone the light around the yard, until suddenly my heart spooked — for there was this crazy-looking man just outside the fence. Now that I could see him, I could hear him too. He seemed to be talking in two different voices, waggling his fingers in the air. I could hear Pedro's dog barking in the darkness, not daring to come any closer. The man was leading a burro burdened with boxes and mining tools. He had a gruesome scar closing one eye, but the other eye peered right at me. He shouted at my light, as if it angered him. Maybe he had lost his way in the wind. Thank God Pedro appeared, and led the man away.

Shortly after Pedro knocked at the kitchen door and said he could use some coffee. Did I have any leftovers?

"Who was that?" I asked.

"Oh that," he responded, as if it were an answer.

"Good grief, Pedro. He scared me to death."

"I know, I know, but he's not harmful. That was only Manzanita Man," an old miner who lived in the mountains near Sunnyside, one of those ole hangers-on who had dreams of a pure vein of copper. "He comes by here once in a while, to gather nuts. He always talk crazy. Don't pay it much attention."

"What was he saying?" I persisted.

Pedro paused by the door with the cold coffee pot in hand. "Best to let him sleep and send him off in the morning."

"*Pedro*," I insisted.

"Oh, he say something about a sickle of blood over your door, but he probably only saw the moon. He say stuff like that all the time—angels of death and sky blotted out. It don't come to nothing. He'll be gone in the morning."

Pedro shook his head and went out into the darkness, but his words had a chilling effect on me. I bolted the kitchen door and then lay awake on my bed, tense as a fresh pine board before the saw blade. How did I ever think I could live out here, with only one old Mexican cowboy to protect me, wild men roaming the foothills, screaming for a midnight snack. I wanted Buster to cuddle up in bed with me — I almost wished I'd never left Boston.

AUNT CARLA NEVER HAD ANY USE for Maggie or Turner Treat though the Crown T was the closest neighboring ranch. Maggie was the president of the local Cowbelles, and she was always bullying people to come to her meetings, urging them to bring their latest beef recipes — *Sassy Beef on Tasty Taco,* or *Quick Fix Wagon Wheel Stew* — but Aunt Carla didn't like new-fangled combinations, preferring Pedro's savory simplicity. And she didn't really care for the noisy gatherings of gossipy women all trying to out-peck each other. Maggie Treat was a small, determined woman, the do-gooder type that would send over a tin of cookies on your birthday and expect a cake in return.

Turner, her husband, had a strange sense of humor, which bordered on right-wing lunacy. He had an arsenal of guns, which he supposedly used to protect his ranch. A sign at the foot of their property read: IS THERE LIFE AFTER DEATH? COME DOWN THIS ROAD AND FIND OUT. Turner liked to pull a cork, and he let his wife boss him, resorting to a sulky vindictiveness when he encountered other women. Aunt Carla fought back by not listening to him, and that made him even more angry. Turner didn't like the fact that she was a woman boss, hiring only Mexicans, didn't like the fact that she came from back east and was trying to change the nature of things.

"I'm not trying to change the nature of anything. Nature can stay just as it is."

Turner tried to make things difficult for her, opening gates and leaving them open, until Pedro suggested that they hire Treat's son. "He might be useless on a horse, but at least he can throw down a bull calf."

A couple of nights before the roundup Pedro told me, "I guess we'll be seeing Ken Treat pretty soon." He had also hired Eleazar, an older Mexican man, as well as some kids from town, but he wasn't sure of who was going to show up. I thought of how Ken used to swagger, challenging everyone to a game of "stretch" because he had the longest legs. Ken had always been a dandy, even back then, buying fancy boots, riding a Paso Fino Thoroughbred cross, having to have the best of everything.

I wondered what role I'd play on this roundup. I didn't know how to move a herd of cows, and I was afraid of being a hindrance. Pedro said not to worry, that the dogs did most of the hard work anyway. I could give injections. We'd be inoculating for black leg, which sounded to me like the plague.

That night around eight, I heard a truck pull in. Pedro got up and excused himself as I stood by the sink, finishing the dishes. I had reclaimed this chore, for it put me at ease. The next thing I knew, I was wiping my hands on the side of my pants when I saw someone standing outside the doorway. In the half-light I wasn't sure, but my heart started banging when I heard his voice, though he only said — "Remember me?"

It was Sam Mendoza. Yes, I remembered — as if I'd been remembering him all along. I felt dizzy, ebullient. It made me say the first silly thing that came into my head. "Hey, aren't you the guy who traded his cowboy boots for a bottle of beer in Nogales?"

He made a little bow as if to say — *I'm the one*, and took another step forward into the kitchen, putting a hand on the back of a chair to steady himself. He looked winded, nervous, gazing around the room, as if it were too much to stare at me directly. He was older, thinner, but still unbelievably handsome. His eyes and cheeks were more sunken, severe, his hair still long, drawn back in a ponytail.

"I can't believe this." I found myself grinning — "Are you going out with us tomorrow?

He nodded yes.

So, Pedro had known all along. How could he not tell me! Let me get prepared? I'd never get to sleep now, never, what with Samuel

Harrigan Sixkiller Mendoza out in the bunkhouse. How many times had I said his name, as if he were some hero come to protect me. I remembered how I'd felt that spinning sensation when I'd first found out about Jack, and now I felt like I'd been spun in the opposite direction, as if it were taking all the cord kinks out. When it stopped, I was back inside myself, ready for whatever might happen. "I bet you're still good with a rope," I smiled.

"Only about as good as the wind blows. Sometimes it does, and sometimes it doesn't." He looked back up at me and his dark eyes narrowed. "It's sure good to see you. You haven't changed, not much anyway."

"Not much can mean a *lot* where I come from."

"Well, out here it's mighty insignificant." He was trying not to smile, and it contorted his face in a subtle way.

I wanted to ask him to come on in, sit down, talk to me. What had he been doing with himself? For some reason I thought he was over in New Mexico. Did he have a wife, a family? I wanted to tell him about Jen and Jovey — he hadn't seen them since they were kids, but then someone else appeared at the kitchen door — a scruffy little guy peering through the screen. He put his hand on the mesh, and I could see he was missing an index finger.

Sam nodded for him to enter. "This here's my pardner, Cove."

I could feel myself bristle. Cove was one of the most unattractive men I'd ever met, with his buckteeth askew, big saucer-like eyes and scraggly dirt-blond hair. It looked like javelinas had been playing with his once-white hat. Even though he was short, he managed to slump in his grubby clothes. I couldn't imagine why Pedro had hired him, unless it was the only way to get Sam on the job.

"Cove?" I repeated, shaking his hand, worried about feeling the missing finger. "You must have been born by the sea."

"Actually," Cove drawled, "I was named after a bowling alley, up in Wyoming." A round tin of Skoal marked his worn shirt pocket, and he looked like he needed to spit. "I'm gonna hit the hay," he informed Sam. "You coming?"

Cove gave me a sideways glare before leaving, and Sam read my reaction. "Don't worry about him."

Why was everyone always saying that around here?

I took a step forward, wanting to give Sam a hug, but jammed my hands in my pockets instead, looking up into his dark, amused eyes, the kind of eyes that were so steady you weren't prepared for the inevitable jolt they gave. "Will you look out for me tomorrow?"

He considered this. Then nodded, yes. "That I will," he said.

That night I dreamt I was the mother of myself. I was telling my daughter to get ready, to go get her boots on, but she was ragged and dirty. Tossing her hair back, she announced to me, "I'm tired of being the Queen!" Then I became the daughter, galloping a horse over the swelling water of a dark night sea, misty smoke in the distance. A battleship with a red wood hull turned its bow in my direction.

I was awakened around 5:00 a.m. by the clip-clop sound of Pedro slapping flour tortillas back and forth in his cupped hands. The smell of fresh coffee reached me, and I climbed out of bed, put my chapstick and Tic-Tacs in either pocket, tied a pale blue bandanna around my neck, and tried to act casual sauntering into the kitchen. I was the first one there. Pedro was whipping up his typical roundup breakfast — baked *frijoles*, shredded beef, eggs with green chili and cheese on top, fried potatoes and *chorizo*.

I poured myself a cup of coffee as the others filed in — Cove, Sam, and an older Mexican man named Eleazar. Sam said "Mornin'," but then sat down and concentrated on his food, while Cove put his elbows on the table and scowled at me. He didn't like the fact that I was going to ride with Sam, while he had to ride with the *jefe*. Sam referred to Ken as the *jefe de pinacate*, boss of the stinkbugs.

Back when we were all teenagers, there had been quite a rivalry between Sam and Ken. They'd had an aversion for each other, even then. Sam didn't like Treat's easy money, and Ken was jealous of Sam's talent with horses. I mainly felt sorry for Ken, because he tried so hard, and because his mother was domineering. I felt bad that the cowboys made jokes behind his back, about his buckaroo outfits and sissy Paso Fino.

Sam was clean-shaven that morning, and he looked great in his blue work shirt, with his rough, dark features and deep-set eyes, but he also seemed distant, guarded. I had forgotten that he was by nature self-sufficient, and that he tended to hide strong feelings, even from himself.

Ken's truck finally pulled up outside. He was not about to miss one of Pedro's big breakfasts. He entered with a boisterous good morning for everyone; Pedro and Eleazar both said, "*Buenos dias,*" and I almost welcomed Ken's animation. He made a big point of shaking hands with me, holding on a bit too long, and I could tell that Sam didn't like it.

"Looks like the wind's finally settled down." Ken reported the obvious as Pedro loaded up a plate for him. Ken went on to tell us about some article he'd just read, how more and more people were ordering beef in restaurants now, especially in steak houses. "Five billion burgers last year. Who says this country's going vegetarian!" Ken looked around for approval, but Sam ignored him, almost wolfing his food. He wanted to get going. I thought he was being a bit rude, wadding his napkin and standing up abruptly.

Cove rose on cue, saying to me, "You ready to eat some dust?"

Once Sam and I were off alone, he rode by my side. I was already glowing from the heat, and yet Sam appeared cool. His skin was used to this kind of intensity. Skin parched as easily as the earth out here. Most of the horses seemed tougher too. They had to be tough in order to handle the terrain.

Sam's three-colored paint, Arivaca, was a true cow pony, almost an extension of Sam. He had found the colt over in the town of Arivaca, hence the name, and he'd raised and trained the pony himself, gentled him by riding him bareback with a hackamore. The horse was sturdy, compact, fast, but not terribly good-looking.

"You see this Roman nose," Sam said. "Some people think that's ugly, but a curve like this means a horse is bold. Those dish-faced horses are way too sensitive. You want a horse that will do anything for you, go anywhere you want."

"Even over a cliff?"

"Well," he paused, tilting his hat down, "there are times when going over a cliff is the only way out. It's not the horse's business to ask questions."

Banner felt overly eager that morning. Maybe she was aware of my nerves, my excitement, or perhaps it was from being around the new horse. And then a mile away from home, I discovered I had to pee. Why had I drunk so much coffee? I decided to hold it — but the further we went the more uncomfortable I felt, until I was almost in agony.

Sam suggested that he hold my horse. "I won't look," he promised. I ran down a little dip, where I was out of sight, but when I returned, Sam held up two crossed fingers, and smiled, though I don't think that he had seen anything. Before I could get back in the saddle, Banner stretched herself out and let loose a stream of her own. I was grateful that he didn't make a comment, though I enjoyed the warm uric scent of her soaking the crumbly soil.

"We'll go on down to the far end," he told me, "and work on up, get whatever we can. We don't want to chase them. They'll go right along. Look at Blue." He pointed to his dog. "See how she moves them, just back and forth. We don't want the cows to get hot, 'cause then they lose weight. Will you look at that little ole dog?"

We rode another mile or so to the far fence line, and Sam gave me a few quick words of advice. It looked like he had to get to work now. Apparently, I would have to ride off on my own. Banner swung her head up and down as if asking for more rein.

"The easier you ride around them and give them a chance, the better it is, better than trying to force them. Animals know if you treat them right. If you treat them right, they'll work along with you."

He was going to head on up the far ridge, while I could ride along this side. He reached out his hand, and I brushed mine against his — a sensation plunged through me. I wanted to say — *Sam,* but he had already turned and was loping out of view.

I wasn't afraid — in fact, I felt a strange calm. I think I felt the kindness of the cosmos at that moment. Way up above — a blue heron flew over, wafting through the air, on its way to the Sonoita Creek no doubt. It seemed as if everything were perfectly made, in this mysterious, tranquil harmony — even the scrub oaks beside me and the Cry Baby Hills, curving off into the distance.

The cows began to move without much urging from me. They seemed to know what was happening, bawling out to each other as they went. I rode on up to the top of the ridge, shooing them along, and they moved as they were supposed to move — like dusty, slow-moving cattle water. But then, looking down on the other side of the ridge, I saw Cove alone, crowding a steer. Apparently, it wouldn't budge. I didn't know why he was bothering with a steer, as we were only collecting cows and calves, but then I saw him rope the animal by the hind feet. He seemed to be taunting it, riding around, and then the animal dropped and he started to drag it. Cove kept trying to get it up, but it wouldn't move, so he dragged it some more. I wanted to yell — Hey! What are you doing? But I thought I had better get out of sight, and started winding my way back down. Banner moved instinctively to catch a couple of young heifers, which were trying to back paddle, and then I saw Sam riding my way.

"Good work," Sam said, as he rode up. "If a heifer runs out, do just as you did — go around her and turn her back. Give her a chance to make up her mind." Sam was pushing a small herd of about twenty head along, Arivaca swimming easily back and forth to keep them contained in their low river of dust.

When I told him what I had seen up above, he said it must have been Ken — they were both riding light bay horses. "We can't have that guy around if he treats cattle like that." I didn't want to argue but I knew what I'd seen — Cove's hat was white, dirty white granted, but Ken's was black with silver conchos.

When we got back to the ranch, the confusion in the corral became even more alive with all the dust and persistent bawling. Sam told me to go tie up. He and Cove would cut out the calves, pushing them into a smaller pen, where they cowered as far away as they could. There was a certain feeling of urgency, wanting to get the job done before it got too hot. Ken fired up the gas-stove for the branding irons. Pedro would do the branding. I was shown how to measure 5 cc's of medication, drawn into a thick syringe. Derrick and a couple of high school boys had arrived from town to help. Sometimes it took three men to hold a calf if it really struggled. It seemed brutal, stretching out the haunch that way, bracing the small exposed animal with a boot, kneeling with full force on its shoulder. Some of the calves were so puny.

As soon as they had one secure, I knelt in the dust, grabbed a handful of skin, and sank my needle, trying to avoid hitting bone. At the same time El sliced the end off the scrotum, pulling the balls out til the attaching threads looked like thin, white string — cutting there, tossing the grey-white "oysters" into a tin pan on the back of the pickup. The dogs sniffed around, hoping for a morsel.

The baby bulls didn't seem to mind the castrating so much. What really got them struggling was the branding iron. That sizzling piece of metal made them pitch and kick and thrash and holler, until it seared down to the orangey leather-like surface of burnt skin.

Sam picked out calf after calf — his movements were so liquid, you might have called it lazy-looking, but he almost always hit his mark, throwing his rope in a kind of slow motion, waiting til the calf made a little hop — then he jerked the rope toward him and caught both feet. He let it hop backward, before the boys tipped it over. Some of the little ones gave right in, but others were fighters. I knelt in the dust, over and over, sinking the needle into unfattened flesh. The irons were heated, red hot, and Pedro rocked the Q brand back and forth, nice and even and not too deep, making a stench of hair and hide. The left ear was notched and then the calf was released — off it went, hopping away as if nothing had happened. Coffee was passed

126

in Styrofoam cups. I noticed dark, dried blood on Eleazar's hand.

A little pile of scrotums lay there in the dust. I picked one up, and the caramel-colored fur was the softest thing I'd ever felt. "Eskimo nose warmers," Cove said, looking down from his horse. He had been watching me.

I wanted to say — I saw you do it, but then realized I was just feeling jealous. He was probably angry for the exact same reason. We both glanced in Sam's direction. But at that moment, Sam wasn't aware of either of us, and that made him all the more appealing. Concentrated, he coiled his rope, making a loop, swinging, tossing — hitting his mark. Arivaca knew just how to move, keeping the rope taut but not too tight, stretching the calf out.

Ken brought the red hot Q iron over and looked up at Cove. "I always wondered if this Q stood for Queer. It sure is one odd little out-fit."

Cove looked down from Cotton Eye Joe, screwed up his face, and spat in the dust. "Why don't you just do your job."

Ken went back to the blaring butane, but I could hear him muttering beneath his breath, "Screw that little screwworm."

I finished the bottle of medication, and Ken went and found me another. When I bent a needle, Ken inserted a new one. Sam looked suspicious when Ken stood next to me. Maybe he was jealous too. I hoped so. Calf after calf was released and went scampering back into the crowd for protection. When the job was done, Pedro opened the gate and it was a joyous reunion as the little calves searched out their anxious mothers. I couldn't believe how quickly they'd recovered from that morning's butchery, how little it seemed to bother them now, though one or two were limping, and one little fellow had blood dripping down his hind leg.

Leaning back against the rail, covered with dust and sweat, I watched Cove fooling around, standing up in the saddle, arms out for balance — Cowboy Cove, the center of attention. Sam lit a cigarette and tossed it up. Cove tried to catch it in his mouth, and the bay started to buck — Cove landed back down in the saddle, hooting.

Sam was laughing too, enjoying the moment — there was definitely a camaraderie that put me off. I headed back to the house to wash up.

Later that evening before dinner, the guys wanted to have a shooting contest. Derrick lined up a series of fresh tin cans and they took turns blasting them off an old stump. Part of the contest was the speed with which you could knock them all off. With his old .45, Sam got all six quicker than anybody. Ken protested and said that was only because he had gone first. The cans weren't full of holes.

"Start over with new ones," Cove suggested, but of course that didn't help Ken's aim.

Sam asked me if I'd like to have a go, and I agreed to give it a try. Standing behind me, he loaded the cartridge, slipping a couple of extra bullets into the tight front pocket of my blue jeans. As he adjusted his body to my body, his arms holding mine in position, I could feel his breath on the side of my face, his eye centering mine, and when I pulled the trigger, the jump kicked me back into closer contact with him.

"Nice," he smiled.

"Let'er try it alone once," Cove suggested.

"Go ahead," Sam said. "You can do it."

The gun seemed heavy in my hands, and when I pulled the trigger, I missed by a long shot. Oh well.

"We'll practice later." Sam winked at me, before spinning around to blast four empty bottles. "Loser sweeps up," he taunted Ken, but Ken wasn't about to pick up after Sam Mendoza.

After dinner, sitting around together, I asked Cove why he'd left Wyoming. I was just trying to make conversation, but he gave me a one word answer, "Snow." Funny how cowboys were either reticent, slow to speak up, lost in their natures, lost in the quietness of the space that surrounded them, or they switched into this other mode — where the words rolled out, steadily, easily, especially if there was an audience.

"Cove grew up on a ranch," Sam told me. But apparently as a teenager, Cove preferred the family snowmobile over his buckskin mare. One afternoon, he came blasting over a hill and saw a huge, eight-foot moose on the path. He was going so fast he couldn't stop and went right under her, crashing into a snow bank.

"She was so mad, she squatted down and started to pee," Cove said. "The hair on her back was standing straight up, and then she came at me and hammered me down. She just leapt up and pounded me into that snow bank — my nose an' ears all crammed with snow. Just like being buried alive. That was it for my Mama. She packed us up and moved us down to *Airyzona*."

"At least you learned how to cowboy," Sam put in. "And now you can make this terrific living. I guess you'd send them a paycheck every month if you didn't spend it trying to teach *someone* who's the best poker player around here."

And so it went, on into the evening. There was something congenial about a bunch of cowboys sitting around a table, drinking beer, telling jokes. It made me realize how little most people talked, as if it made them nervous — meals finished in a hurry, TVs left on, everyone rushing off to see the next movie. We had lost the art of storytelling, just sitting around, hashing over the day's events.

"Did you hear that one about the midget and the vet?" Derrick asked the group, a bottle of *Negro Modelo* propped on his big silver buckle. He was only nineteen, about Jennifer's age, but somehow he seemed much older.

A night owl warbled, and the full moon rose over the deepening blue of the Huachuca Mountains. Even Pedro got loosened up and told stories about the good old days, when cowboys rode out for a week at a time and ended up sitting around the campfire. "We had quite a remuda back then, seven horses a hand, and a big chuck wagon."

But Eleazar wanted to hear that story about ole Juan, when he fought Red Howell down by the fairgrounds. Pedro put his two hands on the table and rubbed them back and forth as if someone had sprinkled cornmeal there. "Oh yeah, ole Juan," Pedro began, rather slowly. "Ole Juan had a horse name-a Peppy. Seemed that little horse beat Red Howell's big Thoroughbred, not only once, but two, three times. And of course it wasn't enough just to race each other, because then they wanted to fight.

"By the time they was done, ole Juan was cut up and his eye was turning purple. On the way back home he said to me, 'What we gonna tell the Boss?'

"I don't know what you gonna tell her, but I'm gonna tell her the truth," I said.

"*Aw,* I'm gonna tell her my horse fell down on me."

"She won't believe that. You're better off tellin' her the truth."

Cove looked over at me, as if he could read my mind. I was already wondering how we could keep Sam on and get rid of his unsavory pardner. After the roundup we wouldn't need three hands.

Pedro went on, stroking his chin, leaning back in his chair, his eyes warm, unfocused. "So ole Juan, he told her his horse had fallen down. But later she asked me — 'Juan get in a fight?'

"I said, 'Yeah, I guess so. With that Red Howell.'

"'Did he win?' — she wanted to know." Pedro chuckled over that, but then continued. "'I'm glad you told me the truth,' she said to me. 'You always told me the truth.'

"So I stayed on, but Juan had to go. We never did see ole Juan after that."

IT SEEMED CASUAL ENOUGH going out for lunch at the Home Plate Restaurant. It was just that I so badly wanted to be alone with him, that it made me feel as if at last my fate was taking a certain swing and I'd have no more say about it.

Sam ordered an egg-salad sandwich, and I enjoyed watching him open his mouth to it, though I was too wound up to have anything more than a cup of soup. We sat in the corner as if seeking refuge, some peace and protection, which the ranch had not been able to provide. But even with his back to the few old cronies who would be happy to yak the day away — how this had once been a booming mine town, how cattle were driven right down the road and into waiting boxcars — even if we almost felt safe for a moment, it was a very small town, and people made assumptions. I could imagine them saying that Sam was a half-breed hired hand moving in on the new *gringa* rancher, though that had nothing to do with us.

I asked him if he thought about staying on, and he said he'd been thinking about it, though Cove had a couple of other ideas. He admitted that he'd been fired from his last job, and then waited to see my reaction. When I asked why, he explained that the boss had wanted to ride his horse. And nobody rode Arivaca.

"'You don't lend out your wife, so why loan your horse?' That's what I said to him. I always would have been in trouble over there, the way they worked those horses, never giving them grain. They never even took their bulls away from the cows. Pedro is the man to work for, not just some dude with a big wad of money."

After Sam and Cove were let go, they camped out in a line shack. When they finally got to town, they met up with Pedro. "That's when he told me about your Aunt Carla. He said he needed a man

*131*

pretty bad."

Taking a breath, taking a sip of hot soup, looking up into those bright, brown eyes of his, I knew I was beginning some great descent — down into the unfathomable reaches, that this journey could take me the rest of my life, and that it was both frightening and sacred.

I wanted to have the proper restraint, and yet I wanted to fling myself over some ledge. My heart felt buoyant. There was something about this borderland. Perhaps it was the *latino* culture, their love of color, music, good food, a quality of sun, but it made me feel like a flower. I had never before realized what a visceral response one long-held look could have, as if buckets of slow-pouring liquid were being spread between us — alchemical, two common people making this precious stuff.

I told him what had happened with Jack, how I'd discovered him in bed with a younger man. Sam could hardly believe it. He wondered if I was going to get a divorce. He even thought, in this particular instance, that the Church would be willing to annul the marriage. I knew he was only thinking about me, but *annul* was such a weighty word. What would that mean to our children? It put me off and I wanted to change the subject. I didn't want to think about Jack.

"Remember when we found that cross?" I said. He admitted that he still had it. I was amazed that he would have kept that old rusty cross for all these years. We had had our first kiss years ago at that spot. Maybe a man's early feelings of love ran deeper — women were forced to spread their love out over so much surface, over the busy details of life, while men went down, looking for water. My marriage to Jackson had all but dried up, a shallow well, but I realized now, like a dowser, that I was standing on a gusher. Twenty gallons a minute in the desert — that was Sam Mendoza.

We talked about the Christmas when I'd come with my kids, and he said how it had made him feel wild for a spell. He'd been so fired up, he'd gone and gotten a sixteen-year-old pregnant.

I asked him her name, and he said, "Manuelita," but he didn't go into great detail, only saying that he had intended to marry her, but then she had lost the baby. "It would have been a big mistake."

I told him how I'd been four months pregnant when Jack and I had casually gone off to the courthouse, not the best way to begin a marriage. Five months later I had Jennifer. Odd, how I didn't miss Beacon Hill, though I often thought about Buster snoring in his round wicker basket. I called the kids once or twice a week, but they rarely called me back, all wrapped up in their own lives. For once, I was also consumed by my own, and it felt good, something different.

Looking up at Sam, it was as if I were caught in a current, or whirlpool. I was responding with such velocity to the presence of this man. I was already taken by the quality of his skin, his blue work shirt, open at the neck. I wanted to see him lying on his bunk bed, both arms raised, to feel his sinewy shoulders, his hair in my hands — I wanted to comb back that long dark hair of his, to rub his shoulders and make him relax.

I wiped a little egg-salad off his chin, and then as I looked down at his bony hands, he moved one finger, ever so slightly, over to rub the tip of mine. I was amazed, delirious. If such a simple gesture could make me die and go to heaven, what on earth was still in store for us?

"I like your T-shirt," he nodded.

It was small on me, and well worn, but I could tell he was looking beneath the tactile cotton of the grey-black material. I laughed a little, imagining him pulling my T-shirt out, descending on me, pressing his long skinny legs between mine, pushing me back against his battered truck — there was something famished about him.

He certainly polished off his egg-salad sandwich, crunching his napkin into the closed wedge of the paper plate. "We better go and pick up a sack of lime," he said, standing up, as if we needed an excuse for our absence.

It was difficult leaving the table, our precious, newfound, separate world. We would now step back into the afternoon light of chores and time and pretense. I knew the glimpse I'd had that hour, I couldn't hold continuously. It was too dazzling, like some forbidden scene — the awesome gods ablaze with light, and we were only mortals.

I BEGAN TO NOTICE THE DIFFERENCE between what I called "real time," time alone with Sam, and everything else. In real time everything stopped. I was completely in the moment — the air itself felt heightened — jokes were funnier, food tasted great, sunsets were remarkable. But when he walked out of the picture, when he was sent into town, or had to go over to the Crown T for a two-day job, or took a drive up to Tucson with Pedro, then real time started to fade. Often, it lasted an hour, half a day, but then in its place came a kind of distraction. I was beside myself. I couldn't carry on an engaged conversation, as if I were waiting to hear his truck on the road. I became easily annoyed with all the mundane aspects of daily life. I became restless in the company of other people. If I couldn't be with Sam in real time, I wanted to be left alone, to brood.

I was either sky high or crashing, recovering — all of this tired me out, and I wondered if there was something wrong with me. Maybe I had chronic fatigue — I felt so exhausted, yet exhilarated at the same time. I was losing weight, just like you're supposed to when you fall in love, but I didn't like to feel so eager, so needy, needing his presence to hear my own voice, wanting to touch his dry, calloused hands — touchstone, bloodstone, mouth to mouth. I wanted to breathe the air he was breathing. I wanted to walk in the footprints he'd left, little wells of happiness watering the desert. This, I reasoned, was the nature of passion. I wanted to feast in isolation. I wanted Sam all to myself.

I THINK I REALIZED AS I BRUSHED Banner down, stroking her shiny sleekness and fussing over her mane and tail, how little Jen had let me mother her. She hadn't liked me to brush or braid her hair. She had preferred to dress herself. She didn't even like me coming into the bathroom when she was a child. It was as if she shrank from the touch of me, always running to her father.

Now, when I groomed Banner, it was like a meditation. I straightened her forelock and stroked her neck, and she leaned into my caresses, resting her head down on top of my shoulder. She was eager to please, and I gave her no reason not to trust me. I never whacked her with a rope or spurred her, for she was responsive to a gentle squeeze or cluck. When I sat back and said — whoa, she responded — I hardly had to rein her in. She could feel me shifting in the saddle, and she'd turn in that direction. Though Sam disapproved of feeding by hand, she'd lift her head when I called her, eager for the carrot she knew I had tucked away in the pocket of my blue-jean jacket. She liked the way I pulled her ears, and scratched beneath her chin. I took her muzzle in both hands and smooched her on the lips, pinched her lovingly along the mane. Sam taught me that horses often groomed each other this way as a sign of affection or acceptance, and that a horse responded better to this kind of attention than to a walloping slap against the neck.

I had come to like Banner's twitchy ways. She was definitely a female. Her squirting, winking behavior and her back-off attitude taught me something about myself and made me laugh at our common qualities. She did not like another horse coming up behind her. Sometimes Sam ran a hand over her rump as he rode by, and she'd lay her ears back, preferring to follow.

135

As we rode, Sam was always scanning the horizon. He could spot a coyote half a mile away, saying how he saw the flick of an ear. Further on, he looked down at the path and pointed out the track of a roadrunner, "Pretty smart bird. The footprint's an X so the Devil can't follow. The Devil can't tell which way he went."

We took a left, uphill, riding side by side, though the trail was only meant for one. Sam saw me looking at Arivaca's muzzle, a pale-orange, rubber-baby-doll color, not very pretty, and he said defensively, "Arivaca's a *mestizo,* like me, like some kind of crazy mixed-up drink — a good dose of tequila, a shot of Irish whiskey, and a bit of Apache black water."

"What do you think would happen if I drank some?"

"You'd probably get sick."

"Or drunk," I suggested. "Maybe I'm already a little bit tipsy."

"Too bad for you then." Sam ran his hands through Arivaca's mane. We bantered on like this for a while — teasing each other — flirting, I guess is what you'd call it. I hadn't flirted like this for decades, and I had to admit it was the most invigorating activity. I felt as if Sam were bringing me back to life, mostly through the pure, easy tonic of laughter, releasing a love that had gone to waste, that had been stored up and covered over, buried in dust, only to be brought out and shaken. And it was a wide-open atmosphere I was breathing — more expansive than any I'd ever taken into my lungs. I felt full of it — full of wind and high, loose laughter, flapping in the wind like cotton sheets, making that galloping sound as they fought the line. Our talk went a bit that way.

Though the roundup was over, Cove and Sam and Pedro and I still ate our meals together. I was beginning to wonder how things would evolve. We didn't really need two extra men. Often I found myself staring at Cove's stub finger, thinking how grotesque it was, until one night he lifted it up for me to inspect. "I won't charge you for looking or nothing."

I asked him how it had happened, and he glanced over at Sam

as if needing permission. Apparently, they'd been roping some bull.

"It was my fault," Sam interrupted.

"That was one mighty mean bull, too, wasn't it?" Apparently Cove had roped the big bull's head and was dallying the rope around his horn, without really thinking, when Sam threw his rope and the bull took off. "It just *snapped* my finger — sort a popped right off. It hardly bled or nothing."

That morning Pedro and Cove had gone for a load of alfalfa over in Tumacacori, and they'd loaded the shed without our help. Cove insinuated that we'd been out on a pleasure ride, though checking the fences was a regular part of the operation.

As Pedro scooped out the steaming chicken enchiladas that had all melted together into one steaming mass, I asked him what he thought of a Roman-nose horse, knowing that would turn the conversation.

"Well, a horse with a Roman nose is more apt to buck," Pedro responded, "but I don't know — I think some of those horses are pretty good horses."

Sam couldn't stand our talking about this particular subject without putting in his two cents — "When I broke Arivaca, and he went to buck, I got right after him. I turned him around, and then turned him the other way. He got the idea. If he tries to hang his head, I jerk him up a little and swing him around — that keeps his mind off of bucking."

"I don't like a horse with a little eye," Pedro added, teasing Sam, because Arivaca had a pale blue, appaloosa kind of eye, without any natural black liner to make it stand out. "I like a big round eye, a dark eye."

"They say a horse with a small eye probably lacks intelligence," Cove put in.

"Arivaca, he's smart. He knows what I'm thinking before I even know it myself."

"That horse, he's a mind reader," Pedro played along. "Can tell your future, an' everything. That horse he whisper in my ear the other day — *Sam maybe don't know it, but he gonna get thrown.*"

"Well, it won't be the first time, now will it," Cove said.

After hearing about Manuelita, I couldn't let it rest. I kept thinking about her, about their past. I could picture her coming around to the bunkhouse with a basket of homemade, buttermilk biscuits. I imagined they'd been pretty wild.

When I asked Pedro about it, he told me that Sam used to see this one girl from over at Lochiel — "She had real long hair, hung down to here. He liked her pretty good, but then he got her into trouble. Sam went sort a crazy 'round that time. Oh, maybe he gets into fights now and then, but he can work hard as five men put together. I guess we'll do OK, I said, if we get Sam Mendoza."

Then one afternoon Ken informed me that he knew where Manuelita was working now — the Red Cantina, in downtown Nogales. He tipped back on his heels and grinned as he told me, "She sure likes to take off her clothes. Some of those girls look all used up, but she's still got the fire in her. Real nice body, great legs too — that's unusual for a Mexican lady. Most of them are pretty overweight, but she's a little *saltimboca*."

As much as I wanted to picture her, I didn't want to hear all these details. But then he asked me if I'd like to go down and see her perform. I was surprised to hear myself answer, yes, if he could keep it a secret.

He insisted he would, because he couldn't let his mother know either. She was always scolding about the diseases you could catch across the border — saying those Mexicans didn't even speak Spanish, as if the language itself had been corrupted.

I wasn't interested in Ken, so I had no need to feel guilty on that score. Sam hadn't been with Manuelita for years, but still I knew he wouldn't like me going down there, especially with Ken as my escort.

I told Ken I'd meet him over at his place Thursday night when Sam and Cove and Pedro went into town for their weekly night of poker. We could take the back road through Washington Camp over to Kino Springs. He wanted to take me out to La Rocha for dinner, and since I hadn't seen much of Nogales, nor eaten out since I left home, I thought it would be nice for a change.

Walking up the steps to the restaurant, chattering away, mainly because we both felt nervous, we could hear the sound of *mariachi* music filtering down. Entering the dining hall was like walking into a huge white-washed cave — the walls were sculpted with a cavernous texture, and the wrought iron sconces lent a feeling of elegance.

Our waiter took the pose of formality, bending at the waist to light our candle, and I wanted to tell him — *This is not a date.* But at the same time, there was no reason not to make our outing festive. Only an hour from the ranch, and we were in another country — that alone made me feel both vulnerable and, in another sense, safe. I was relying on Ken to protect me, but his grin had the slightly lascivious quality that comes from too much success with the ladies, or too little. I couldn't tell which.

He ordered us both margaritas — they were quite strong, coarse salt on the rim. Thirsty as always, I gulped most of mine down, and he quickly ordered us another. I told him about leaving Boston, about the mirrors I used to make, my problems with Jennifer. He surprised me by saying that he guessed things might get better between me and my daughter now that I was getting a divorce, no more competition. It always amazed me when a man seemed to have any kind of insight. Then my plate of hot tortilla soup arrived and it was fiery — flecks of red chili floating on top along with bits of chopped cilantro. I had another margarita with my Guaymas shrimp fried in oil with lots of garlic, Mexican rice on the side, indulgent but delicious.

I thought maybe I should pick up the tab, so I wouldn't feel beholden, but Ken had already slipped his credit card to the waiter. He made it clear that he was not the kind of cowboy who would let a woman pay. I was feeling a little looped and he was acting a bit too friendly, saying I reminded him of a little coyote, but I let it pass. After all, I *was* sniffing around down here, checking things out on the sly.

Waving a five-dollar bill, he hailed a taxi, which wasn't difficult on a Thursday night, but Ken was all show, a slightly obnoxious brand of machismo that I might have found appealing in a *Chicano* guy. At least he knew enough Spanish to instruct the driver, who drove deeper and deeper into the heart of the city, away from the border atmosphere.

As we pulled up to the club, I began to have a change of heart. I didn't feel comfortable, but then Ken shocked me by saying, "Don't worry, Sam still comes down here himself sometimes."

Just the thought of Sam watching Manuelita made me prickle, but it also excited me — I could imagine him simmering, fighting his desires. I got out of the cab. Only men were out on the streets, and they looked our way, but Ken was so big and beefy and his swagger had such an imposing quality, I knew I would be all right. The bouncer outside the club pointed to a sign that said in English, *No cover, No minimum, No knifes.* Ken handed over a large silver switchblade, saying to me, "You can need these things down here."

Only male customers were inside the noisy, smoke-filled bar, disco music blaring. I was glad that I'd worn my blue jeans, a long-sleeved shirt, but no one paid me much attention. The girls were friendly, and a couple of them smiled my way.

"Which one's Manuelita?" I asked, but he didn't see her. He figured she'd come on stage in a while. Ken ordered us two Kahluas, sweet and syrupy, and I asked for a bottle of *agua minerale.* Something in the dinner had made me very thirsty. A girl named Cassandra was dancing on stage — an invisible announcer shouted her praises over the droning music. She had a good figure, and yet she seemed almost shameless, totally unphased by the baring of her body, top, bottom, all of it. Her lack of modesty seemed to lack sexual tension, but I found myself sitting closer to Ken, so I didn't have to yell, making comments.

The next girl wore a see-through negligee, and managed to

make a bit of a stir by dropping her garment. She untied the filmy scarf around her neck and began to buff it back and forth between her legs. At that moment, an overweight, bearded, professor-type came in. He turned his attention to a lap dancer who was grinding away right next to our table.

"Do you think it's her boyfriend?" I asked Ken. "It must be her boyfriend." She seemed to really like him, but I could only hear Ken's low guttural response, as she bent forward, lifting her dress to expose her flawless buttocks working in machine-like motion. Some of the other girls, drinking with customers, smiled at the aggressive way she rubbed herself against this guy, pulling his hands around to feel her breasts. Then turning to face him, she straddled his lap, wiggling and squirming while he just sat there. I could imagine Sam remaining that still, withholding, letting Manuelita do all the work.

The next girl wore a little sailor suit with a perky naval beret. She had the most fit body of all the dancers, and was very athletic as she worked the pole, jumping up onto it, sliding down slowly, doing various tricks with her legs, but she didn't have much of a sensual feeling — she was more like a kinky aerobics instructor.

Ken asked the waiter about Manuelita, and the man raised his eyebrows, and pointed upstairs. She was an upstairs girl now, where the show got raunchier. I let Ken pay the tab and followed him out. The bouncer nodded as we climbed the iron stairs, pushing through the beads that hung at the entrance.

A dancer named Marie had just come onto the stage; she had big bursting breasts that looked like they'd been inflated with helium. I asked Ken if he thought she'd had implants. "No way," he responded. "They can't afford cosmetics down here." She was not a good-looking woman, but she was very juicy, having fun, jumping down into the audience to slap her enormous titties in front of one dazzled customer, a small Mexican business man with a big grin on his face. The audience, which was denser and drunker, hooted at her antics.

Across from us, a young Indian girl, no more than fourteen or fifteen, was sitting on a customer's lap — he was trying to feed her

Fritos from a small blue bag, but she refused, turning her head, as if bored or disgusted. Ken ordered us both a shot of tequila, though I didn't want anything more.

Marie was taking off the businessman's glasses now and slipping them up into her private parts. After a couple of spins, she handed the glasses back, but he couldn't see through them and everybody laughed. Ken leaned forward and snickered, "Goose grease."

I began to feel rather slimy, degraded, as if a film of scum had settled over everything. When Ken put his hand on my thigh, I pushed it away, though I had to admit to feeling a zap of sexual energy. "Aw," he said, not terribly offended. "It's not the arrow, but the Indian, right?" I worried about the long drive home, and wondered whether he was sober enough to handle it, but then he surprised me, leaning over to whisper, "Hold onto your pommel — here she is."

A beautiful, delicate girl came onto the stage then. It was true, she did have exquisite legs. Her breasts filled the red lace cup bra she was wearing. She looked comfortable in her body, in no big hurry. Her hair was still long, pushed back from her face with a silver tiara. She moved in a slightly unconscious manner that made her even more appealing, almost innocent, as she looked around, over one glistening shoulder, then the other, enjoying the response she created. I felt a surge of maternal protectiveness — she didn't look much older than Jen, and she had carried Sam's baby. Her eyes still had a lively sparkle, and it was clear that she liked to provoke the men.

A waiter brought a tray of *Dos Equis* up to the stage where Manuelita danced. She bent to take one, and her bra popped open — perhaps by accident, perhaps not. She immediately turned, hiding herself with both hands, laughing, wiggling her short red fringe skirt. She was wearing high-heeled slippers, and I thought she could easily trip, especially when a Mexican man in a dinner jacket climbed onto the stage and she leapt past him. He stood there for a moment with his hands on his hips, before grabbing her mane of long dark hair, yanking her toward him.

She pretended to swoon, sliding down the length of his body

onto her knees, offering him a beer as if to placate him. He took the bottle but proceeded to feed it to her at groin level. She drank all of it down, with both hands on the neck of the brown beer bottle, some of it spilling out of her mouth. The audience clapped as a kind of encouragement, until she threw back her head and swallowed the last of it.

"Not exactly the Colonel's daughter just out of the convent," Ken grimaced. A lot of girls were sitting on customers' laps, and it seemed like anything could happen here. It was Mexico after all, and there were no rules, only commandments, and they had already been broken.

A tough-looking guy with crude backyard tattoos and slicked-back hair jumped onto the stage next. Manuelita was up now — spinning to the music. He picked her up, and lay her back on the table, stroking her gently, but then he put his hand on her crotch and yanked off her skirt, tossing it into the audience.

The more sordid the scene got, the more I worried about my own excitement. She struggled and screamed and her shoes fell off. The crowd was shouting, throwing coins on the stage. Ken, half-drunk, leaned over and leered — "I guess we're a long ways from Boston."

Manuelita then pushed this guy off the stage. Facing us, she leaned back, holding a bare breast in both hands, squeezing an arcing stream of breast milk out into the audience. It spurted a good four feet, and one man jumped up as if to catch it in his mouth. I was shocked, confused. Was she nursing a baby?

As she turned to exit, the overweight, bearded professor followed her out. Ken said, "Sixty-five dollars, and she's worth every *peso*." I wondered if he knew first hand, if his Spanish had also been corrupted.

I was ready to go, relieved when Ken suggested I drive. He passed out almost immediately, and remained asleep even when we drove through the Border Patrol station a few miles out of town. As the officer peered in, I remembered that Ken had forgotten his switchblade, but I wasn't about to go back.

The influence of the evening was working its way into me, but I was resolved not to talk about what I'd seen. I knew Ken was afraid of Sam's temper, and was sure to keep quiet. Ken had told me how Sam had gotten kicked out of high school for carrying a gun, how he had a reputation not only for starting fights, but for finishing them too, how recently he had made a scene at the Wagon Wheel Saloon on karaoke night because he didn't like the way some guy was mocking one of his favorite Patsy Cline songs. Sam had made the papers when he shot a rustler who'd been butchering a calf in the back of his Weekender. Sam had gotten off because the thief was armed and had a previous dope record. Sam was a local hero, but at the same time he was considered a *chollo* — not someone to mess around with. I was scared of Sam myself, but reasoned that that was a good sign, for it made me feel feminine. I had never been afraid of Jack.

After leaving Ken asleep in his truck, I drove myself home over the moonlit valley. It was such a beautiful night, I stopped my car and got out. There were no fences on this part of the valley. The earth in the moonlight looked graceful, not parched. The outline of the Huachucas was inky against the star-strewn sky. It was so peaceful that I was startled when a big jackrabbit came bounding past me. Another followed with spoon-like ears — its mate no doubt.

LATER THAT WEEK WHILE I WAS WORKING in the flowerbed, Sam came galloping into the corral. He leapt off his horse, slammed into the bunkhouse, and banged around inside. I was afraid that he'd found out about Ken and me going down to Nogales.

I followed him, asking, "What's the matter?"

But he turned on me — "None of your business!" Storming back outside, he pounded his hand against the side of the barn. "I just can't believe it. I thought I *knew* that guy."

"Who, Ken?"

"Cove, Goddamn it!" Sam took off Arivaca's saddle and threw it on a bale. "Good thing I surprised him, too. Breaking one cow's tail after another. For no good reason! How can you do that to a poor dumb animal? You were probably right about that dragging. Now it all fits together."

For the rest of the week Sam was sullen, depressed. I couldn't begin to jolly him out of it. Eleazar had moved on to another job, and so now with Cove gone, we had to rely on Ken Treat if we needed extra help.

Ken would come stand in the doorway and gab, about the latest weather prediction, about his mother's new litter of *tepizquincle* dogs — how they looked like little rats — about the nutty astronomer over at Kitt's Peak. Did I want to go visit? I told him I didn't have time, though I felt like I had to remain polite, nervous that Ken would say something.

Finally, one morning, desperate to get away from Ken's loitering presence, I suggested to Sam that we ride up the canyon to doctor some cows. As we climbed the crumbly terrain, the mood seemed to lift. Sam seemed eager to get back to work again, and began by roping one sickly-looking cow, swinging out of the saddle while Arivaca held her. He applied a little wipe of disinfectant to an open wound, released her, remounted and caught another cow, while I handed him whatever he needed — a jar of medicine, a rag, some spray.

After this part of the herd was all checked out, he suggested we ride down into the valley, tie up our horses, loosen their girths, and take a break. He had put a pack lunch together.

We tied up in the shade of some cottonwoods and then settled down in the warm sand of the riverbed. It felt good working my body down into the sand, munching on the turkey and iceberg lettuce sandwich slathered with mustard and mayonnaise. We shared an orange to cut our thirst. He had even packed a couple of ginger cookies, and he held mine just out of reach, so I had to lean toward him to get a nibble — licking the sugar off the tips of his fingers. I wanted to kiss him so badly, but instead of moving closer, he lay back in the mottled light and rolled a cigarette, scrunching down deeper in the sand for a rest. I lay down beside him, but hardly felt restful. There was way too much energy pulsing through my body, and I wondered if he felt it too. Perhaps he quelled his desire by smoking the cigarette, blowing the blue-grey smoke up into the mottled light. I almost asked for a drag, but resisted the urge. He tipped his hat forward over his eyes and seemed to fall asleep for a moment.

Looking down at the angles of his cheekbones, the shadow of a beard already appearing, I wanted to run my hand over the dark, rough surface. Seeing him lying so still, suddenly unconscious, my feelings became confused with a very deep sadness — I felt like crying, for all I'd ever lost, my mother, my children, my family, but I was also incredibly happy. I wanted to kiss Sam, as if he were an infant — I wanted access to every single part of him. But then he stirred, and vaguely brushed himself off. "Nothing like sleeping in a riverbed."

Everyone was hoping for rain, and trying not to talk about it. I could understand now why people prayed for rain, fell down on their knees when it finally arrived. I too wanted to feel that push of ozone that came before a storm, to smell the drenched earth at last easing itself, to hear the rain pelting the metal roof of the ranch house. I wanted to spot at least one bright-orange, vermilion flycatcher as it fluttered and bathed in it. I wanted to see the grasses revive and turn brilliant green. Everything was crackling with heat now, brittle. The bare earth looked like ancient tortoise hide. I preferred riding early in the morning, or late afternoon. The midday sun was relentless.

We rode further out onto the valley floor, where we had a nice view of the Patagonias, the Santa Rita peaks and Saddle Mountain. Sam stopped his horse so we could take it all in. "This must be the prettiest place on earth," he said, and I felt a rush of well-being — it seemed to flow through my body in waves, spilling over onto him. "Some people say this land's too big — it makes them feel uneasy, but it could never be too big for me." Sam leaned forward on his pommel, gazing out. There was no interference out here, no telephone poles, no *jingle jangle*, just the solid earth and this heavenly air.

I thought of how claustrophobic he'd feel walking the streets of Boston. What would it be like to go back there with him? Would he feel out of place, self-conscious? I wondered what the children would think of him now, what they'd think of the two of us together.

I tried to call Jen and Jovey at least once a week, but more often than not, I got an answering machine and left a rather perfunctory message. Sometimes I thought Jovey might be screening his calls, sitting there listening, because more than once, he'd pick up in the middle of my one-way conversation, saying, "Hi, I just walked in."

I no longer wanted to grill him. I just wanted to stay in touch. Both Jen and Jovey were so involved with their own lives, they rarely asked about mine. I once casually mentioned that Sam Mendoza was back on the ranch, and Jovey said simply, "Cool."

Jovey was sitting in on a jazz class, and he was "psyched," though money continued to be a problem. I sent him two-hundred dollars a month, and he was waiting tables at Davio's. "Dad's not giving me a dime," Jovey added, though I had to remind him that his father would pay for his education if he wanted to finish school, but he liked being out on his own. It was a tentative age, testing the ice of independence. I thought it was good that he had to work.

"We might get another roommate," he added, and I wondered if that meant a girl. Jen had told me that Jovey was dating a dancer, who had gotten her tongue pierced. When I asked him about it, fearing that he might do something like that himself, he answered, "No way. It makes your tongue swell up like a baked potato. But I'm thinking about getting a tattoo."

"Nothing visible, I hope."

"No, *invisible,* Mom."

STACKING A LOAD OF FRESH BALES in the back of the truck, I watched the hay dust sticking to Sam's forearms and wanted to take a cool, wet cloth to his skin. Without any rain, the grass was so poor, we had to supplement the feed now. Together we drove out to the upper pasture, where he turned the wheel over to me. I had to move the truck forward slowly in first gear, while he stood in the back, cutting the plastic cords that bound the big bales, tossing out flakes of hay as we went, littering them all over the pasture. Sam's dog Blue ran alongside the battered truck as we bounced over the terrain, and the cows began their chorus of bawling, running toward us to claim a bite.

When Sam worked, he worked hard, and I couldn't keep my eyes off the tension in his body, whether he was heaving a bale, or straining to pull a piece of barbed wire taut, cutting off the twisted ends. There was certainly a quicksilver charge between us. Sam seemed made of sparks, and yet there was something removed about him too, that refused to be captured for any common hearth.

If he was intense by day, at night he seemed to settle down. He liked a couple of beers with dinner, and afterward, he smoked, rolling out cigarettes. I had given up smoking when I was pregnant with Jovey, years ago, but now I actually liked the smell of it — a smell that seemed to mix in with sweat and leather, a combination of animal and manly smells that summed up this work life for me.

But later that night, when the dew settled on the thirsty grass and the scent of earth met the warm August air as it cooled to a comforting seventy-five degrees, the atmosphere was amniotic. I didn't feel like sleep. The lights in the bunkhouse were all extinguished, and I felt like a spirit wandering around in my moccasins — a couple of cows lowing in the distance. I kept thinking I wanted a cigarette, and imagined holding the wineskin leather of Sam's tobacco pouch. I hadn't had this craving for years.

It kicked off a lot of physical feelings in me that went way back to my childhood, waking up in the middle of the night, crying for my mother, who could no longer come, and when my father turned on the bedside table lamp, and sat there with his dour, sleep-disturbed expression, I knew I'd be alone for the rest of my life. At the bottom of everything, that was the truth, the only thing I could hold onto.

And yet now I was feeling a contradiction, the preliminary thaw of that early iceberg, as if my secret, frozen, lonely notion would now be proven wrong. Perhaps I had found the one man who could match me, make me whole. I simply knew it hurt in a familiar way. I felt the agony of it driven back into my stomach like the blade of love come down from heaven, twisting and cutting my insides up. I tried to relax, to float with the feeling — *Let the stars take over, let them work their course* — and then the pain was transformed into a sexy kind of pleasure, and I wanted to move closer to its source.

That night in the misted-out moonlight, the aroma of manure from the paddock was close. I was surprised to see Sam standing by the corral with one foot up on the four-bar pen. He was wearing a fresh white shirt, as if he'd just come from town. When he heard me, he turned, and I couldn't read his face, but I could feel the pull from his gut to mine, as if a rope had been thrown and we were cinched together — I gave way, I just succumbed — in fact I'd never in my life felt more like yielding to whatever it was he wanted. And when he bent to kiss me, tentative at first, it was as if some switch had been suddenly thrown — we kissed with an urgency that took us over — we kissed as if with a terrible thirst and with such a sweet, welcoming relief at having at last found water.

I thought I'd collapse right there in the dirt, but he maneuvered me back against the battered truck, and slowly pulled out my T-shirt. He bent to a breast, and I could tell he was liking the bright, firm feel of it — I watched him gathering me in. Everything happened so quickly. He couldn't seem to get to all parts fast enough, like a boy

*151*

gone crazy with sampling. But then he said something that drove the knife in — "We can't do this, you know." And so the blade twisted.

I didn't contradict, or even ask why. I only sensed that whatever was drawing us together had met some deep restriction, like the barbed wire fence that marked this range, and I was like some wide-eyed, torn-up creature, heart still beating, flung upon it.

The next day he was distant, cool, as if our taste of intimacy had made him pull back. Instead of seeing that we were all little shimmering dots in the landscape, spilling and connecting with all that we touched, he needed to make sure of his boundaries, where his limits began and ended.

Shoeing the horses, he said, "Go get a bucket," with such harshness, I felt slapped. I went and filled one of the black rubber buckets and splashed it down beside him. He took the shoe and plunged it from the heat of the furnace into the cold shrinking water, making it hiss.

I didn't understand his mood, though I felt it was some very basic, internal struggle, as if he didn't believe he were worthy, or felt he had nothing to give. I turned to go, and he called out — "Hey, why don't you stay and watch this?" So I came back and stood there, as he carved the frog of the hind foot clean — it came out looking as white as coconut meat. His little dog, Blue, grabbed a piece of the hoof and ran off chewing. Sam yelled, "You bum. That's going to make you sick now."

"I feel sick too," I told him, turning away. I could see that he was making a face in his effort to keep the hoof braced up on his oily chaps.

"Maybe it's something you ate."

"Something I tasted anyway."

"Maybe you should stay away from things that disgust you." He took the rasp, filed the hoof all around, a rough but accurate manicure. Then, placing four nails in his mouth, he grabbed the shoe and hammered it on.

"You don't disgust me, Sam."

Hearing that, he seemed to lighten up. Letting the foot drop, he stood up and wiped himself off, saying how he'd like to take me over to Elgin for a cup of coffee and a piece of pie.

"Or we could go to the Sonoita Winery," I suggested. He didn't care for wine, but he said, if I insisted, and it drew us closer, like an understood joke we were playing on each other. We collapsed from the seriousness of our little upset back into being whole. Yet how sad that we couldn't love each other simply. I felt that I wanted to live with this man, to share my life with him — he probably sensed that, and it scared him. He wasn't used to being this close to anyone.

I was crazy about Sam. Crazy about the way he looked. I loved his cool reserve. I loved the feel of his body and his passion for getting a job done. I believed he had never been so fully adored since his mother had wrapped him in flannel and chewed a bit of beans before feeding him with her fingers. I wanted to hold him, to stroke his hair, make him forget that to be alive was a painful thing, that we were all, without exception, born into pain, but that once in a great and fortunate while, love was offered, one to another, and that this was our time, our chance for it.

It's scary, I thought, how we go together. Scary, because if I lose this man, I don't think I'll ever find it again. I'll never come up to the mark.

I knew this dynamic of intimacy and retreat would have to repeat itself over again, until we both were secure the other wouldn't disappear. No matter what happened, I would never desert him. But even as I made that promise to myself, I imagined him gone, ephemeral, like smoke.

I went to the Catholic church in town, and prayed to let me love this man, to make it all right. I asked, and felt a sadness in return, that somehow it would never be fully given. At the heart of my prayer, my hope for him, I felt a heavy stone. It would be the one I'd carry. That I had come this close — to have had a taste, a visitation, but to have fallen, down, beneath the weight — that was my apprehension.

JEN WAS IN A PARTICULARLY GOOD MOOD when she called, but I was suspicious of her friendly tone, so unlike her. She quickly got around to telling me that she was seeing someone new, an older man. I didn't think that was such a bad idea. Someone had to get ahold of her, and shake some sense into that tough little head. Better that she be slightly intimidated. "What's his name?" I asked.

"Sven," she said. "Sven Saltet. He's Dutch."

I didn't answer right away, but then said, "Jennifer, doesn't he work in Dad's office?" Something stopped me. I couldn't go on. But I had to go on.

"Yeah, so what? What's the big problem now?"

"I've met Sven," I explained, proceeding cautiously. "I think he might be bi-sexual."

"Jesus, you're weird. I call up with this great news, and all you can do is your typical thing. Why do you always want to ruin everything? Why are you always so mean?"

"I'm not trying to be mean. I'm just trying to protect you."

"Oh, *right!*" she said. "Aren't you at least glad I'm happy?"

"Of course, I want you to be happy."

"I doubt it."

Obviously Jack had said nothing to either of the kids, and I didn't know how far to go. Though my AIDS tests had proven negative, I couldn't imagine Jackson wanting to expose his daughter to a potentially dangerous situation. "What does your father think about this? Does he know you're seeing Sven?"

"Why should he care, God. We've only had lunch a couple of times, and gone to the movies and stuff."

I had an instant replay of that afternoon when I had found Jack and Sven reading in our bed. Granted they weren't doing anything, and part of me still wanted to believe that it might have only been a platonic relationship. "I don't really feel comfortable getting into all this over the phone."

"So what am I supposed to do, fly out there?"

"You could," I realized, thinking — yes, I could offer her plane fare. Maybe out here, alone together, we'd have a chance for a dialogue without this constant bickering. I wanted to tell her how happy I was, how I wanted her to be happy, too, with a man who adored her in every way. "Or maybe you should talk to a counselor."

"Talk to a counselor about *what*? So now I need a shrink? *Christ.*"

"I thought all your friends had analysts." I paused, but she didn't answer. "I thought it might help, that's all. Do you mind not mentioning this to Jovey?"

"What does this have to do with *him*? Jesus, don't you ever think about how *I* might feel? Maybe all of this shit has been difficult for me too, you know."

"I'm sure you're right. I'm sorry."

"Oh, *sorry sorry* — you just don't care — you don't give a shit about me. Just your precious son."

"I love you both, Jennifer."

"That's a real crock, Mom. A total crock."

I could tell our conversation wouldn't get any better. "Can I call you back tomorrow?" I asked, extremely weary, but Jen wasn't done.

"You know what? I'm tired of being your daughter. As far as I'm concerned, I don't even *have* a mother anymore." She slammed down the phone, and I sat there in silence, wondering if I'd said the right thing. Was I really concerned about her, or just trying to get Jack to come out in the open, to own up to it with the children? We were all still living in a lie.

But in a way I could see that Jen was right. I didn't feel the proper love for her. I couldn't make myself, and she sensed it. Would things be better between us if I told her the flip side of her own fears

— that I was afraid of her, afraid she didn't like me, didn't need me, only her father, whom she had always twisted around her little finger. She got what she wanted out of him, and he had always been crazy about her, admiring her more as a feminine creature than he did me, his own wife. I had been jealous of my only daughter, and that *was* sick. I couldn't mother her as my mother would have mothered me. I had failed myself and my mother's memory. But then maybe I was angry too. Maybe I had a right to be angry. In fact, maybe my mother wasn't so perfect after all. Maybe she had wanted to escape us. Maybe it wouldn't have been all that easy for her, either, as we got older. I had built this impossible image, this altar to the Mother of all mothers, as if she were some ideal, up there with the Divine.

Or maybe it was just a chemical reaction between me and Jen, something neither of us could help. I thought back to the beginning, getting pregnant with her before we were even married, how she had made me violently nauseous. She had hurt me when she nursed — that had been such horrible, grimacing pain, and yet such a delight with Jovey. I hadn't really enjoyed mothering until I had my son. Then I always felt as if I had to protect him. She was so mean, hurting her baby brother when I wasn't looking, standing there with that little smile on her face. She would show no remorse, and that frightened me. I swore she was a changeling.

I USUALLY LOVED RIDING AROUND in Sam's beat-up truck, the hot air blowing in through the windows. Even when we didn't talk much, I felt like we shared an intimacy — sometimes I'd rest my hand on his leg, or give him a bit of a neck rub. But that particular day, I felt all wound up and wanted to talk. Funny, how talking can actually drive a wedge, rather than bringing you closer together.

I'd just had lunch with Maggie Treat, and though I was anxious to get home as soon as I got there, I found myself repeating the gossip I'd heard — how Miss Brightman of the Toro Grande Ranch had hired a jet to fly her and her poodle all the way out from Pittsburg. She said it was because she didn't want her pooch stuck in the baggage compartment, but Maggie insisted that it was only because Betty Brightman was an incurable chain-smoker and they won't let you smoke on commercial airplanes anymore.

"Was Ken there?" Sam inquired.

"I only saw him for a second, right before I left."

"Figures," Sam responded, sinking into a foul mood.

"Are you going to spend a beautiful day like this being jealous?"

"It's just that he's *always* there."

"But I'm always *here*," I assured him. Still, that did no good. We rode on in silence along the Harshaw Creek Road — someone's cassette tape had come unwound, and decorated the mesquite like modern-day tinsel. It glittered in the sun.

We stopped at the post office, the hardware, the cleaners — still no words — and by the time we pulled up to the Patagonia Market, I thought I'd go in and get the groceries myself.

Sam had parked next to a couple who seemed to be having even worse troubles than we were. Apparently, the husband had

157

locked the car keys into their gas-guzzling Olds, and his wife was saying how he was such an idiot, how he must be the most helpless man
on earth, on and on about the last time this happened, how he must
have Alzheimer's, how she was going to drive in the future. She kept
calling it "this godforsaken place" — "Now we're stuck in this godforsaken place. All I wanted was a diet Pepsi, for crying out loud."

As if to show me what a good person he was, Sam got out and
offered to help them. They looked a bit suspicious, but were willing to
let him take a coat hanger from one of my freshly laundered shirts. He
thought he could stick the wire down inside the window.

When I came back out, Sam looked aggravated. I thought I'd
better stay clear and sat inside the sweltering cab, beside my newly
laundered shirt, which was lying there in a heap, still wearing its torn
plastic cover. The woman kept bitching about the rubber around the
window, how it was going to get damaged by the metal hanger, and
how the lock was foolproof. You can guess who the fool was in this
case.

Sam finally said, "Well, I guess you're right. Maybe we better
call Frank Laguna," a local locksmith.

But just as Sam was heading for the pay phone, the woman
announced, "We should have just left the car right here. Sooner or
later, some Mexican would have come along and broken it open anyway."

Sam stopped and turned and said, "No kidding."

Right then little Wayne Lorta was walking by, heading for the
ball field with a couple of his buddies, and Sam said, "Hey, can I borrow that bat?"

*No*, I thought, but I stayed put. Sam took the metal bat and
walked over to the car, stood there for a moment, and then he hit a
homer, I tell you — that windshield flew all over their nice blue
upholstery. It just sort of crumbled.

Sam got back in the truck, and started the engine, leaving them
standing there with their mouths hanging open.

"Where do you think *you're* going?!" the woman yelled after us.

Sam stopped the truck, leaned out the window and looked at her. "You got a problem, maybe you should pay a visit to Sheriff Jimenez. His office is right over there." Sam only laughed as we rode out of town. "Guess someone's having an air-conditioned ride back up to Phoenix." He pulled me over close to him, oddly gleeful, like a hoodlum who'd gotten away with something, but I let him kiss me as we careened down the road. "Tourists like that should be shot."

I BEGAN TO REALIZE HOW IMPORTANT it was for Sam to always be right. When you were born with almost nothing, every gain was a big accomplishment. He was set on winning the barrel race at the local rodeo, practicing daily. If he won, he'd go on to Tucson, maybe even Kansas City. He thought there might be good money in it.

Arivaca was a natural racer, fast, responsive, athletic on the turns, but Sam had more than trained him, he had passed on something of his spirit, his will — he had made Arivaca want to win.

That Sunday morning we trailered out of the valley over the dusty gravel road through the Canelo Hills down to Sonoita and the racetrack. When we pulled into the parking lot, everyone we met had two things to talk about. One involved a well-aimed baseball bat, and the other was that Maggie Treat had just bought a fancy new cutting horse, which had been shipped all the way from California. Ken, apparently, was going to ride it that morning. I could see Sam's face set as he heard this news.

Just as Sam was about to tack up, the Treats' shiny black trailer pulled into the lot with its silver Crown sitting on its architectural T. Getting out of the cab, the Treats seemed all pumped up on themselves. Maggie, with her hair springing out around her head, announced to several other weathered-looking women, with cigarettes dangling, that this horse was the great-great grandson of Steeldust. But they were in no big hurry to unload the animal, maybe because he was pawing at the boards and giving a good kick every few minutes. The horse's high-pitched whinny was unnerving.

I wouldn't have wanted to be in Ken's position, opening the double back doors to the trailer, with his mother instructing every inch of the way — "You've got to take charge, Ken. Show him who's boss." Yeah, boss of the stinkbugs, I thought.

It was obvious that the animal was spirited, and hadn't had much time to settle in. When Ken lowered the ramp, the stallion jerked at its halter, stamping and screaming. I was nervous, afraid that the animal's crazy energy might work against Sam in the ring.

Surprisingly, when Ken entered the trailer from the front, the big chestnut backed out without any problem and stood relatively still for its saddle and blanket, but as soon as Ken lifted the bridle, it raised its head so high, Ken couldn't pull the leather over its ears. Maggie Treat looked like she was ready to box somebody. "Good grief," she yelled. "What's wrong with you? Can't you do anything?"

Sam shook his head, but he wasn't about to give any pointers. Clearly, he wanted to put some distance between himself and the Crown T crowd and was about to swing Arivaca around when he said to me — "Hey, can I borrow your kerchief?"

I untied my pale blue cotton scarf and handed it to him, hanging on for a moment, making him tug for it, wanting him to lean down and give me a kiss for good luck, not that he needed luck.

When Ken tried to mount, his horse spun in a circle, twirling away, until he lined him smack up against the big black trailer. Perhaps the poor animal heard the clink of Ken's spurs.

"What do you call him?" I asked.

"Mephisto," Ken answered, as Sam jogged away — angry that I'd spoken to Ken, but I reasoned that a little anger never hurt anyone when it came to a fight.

Climbing onto the bleachers, I looked around for Pedro. Two boys were dragging the track after the pole-bending event that had just taken place. Then three girls rolled out the barrels, tipped them over, and measured the exact distance between all three points.

I felt anxious for Sam, watching him on the outskirts of the ring, loping Arivaca in a tight circle, getting him to stop — right on the dime — making him back up, three steps, moving him forward, turning left, turning right, then loosening his reins and letting Arivaca stretch until his nose almost brushed the ground.

Sam had a good cheering section, a crowd of locals with their girlfriends, poker buddies, cowhands, a bunch of high school kids, all crowded together, munching on chips or gum or chewing tobacco. Pedro was sitting with George Lorta and his two sons. Pedro knew how to keep a low profile, but I was sure he felt just as I did — churning, excited, hopeful, worried. I worked my way over and sat down next to him. "So, what do you think?"

"I don't know," he responded. "I'm not doin' too much thinking, I guess. You saw that ole chestnut, didn't you?"

"Yeah, but I think it's kind of temperamental. They don't have much of a connection."

"A horse like that's professional though."

"Arivaca's got heart. He *wants* to win."

"He wants to, I know it. So maybe he will, and maybe he won't."

The ever-present sun had begun to cook, and I took a squirt of water from my plastic bottle, offered George and his kids a couple of Tic-Tacs before popping three into my mouth. Even at this distance I could see that Mephisto was getting lathered up. Arivaca was in such good shape, he rarely showed the heat.

"So I guess you're not placing any bets," I said to Pedro.

"I didn't say that," he looked straight ahead, teasing me a little. "I got ten dollar down on that ugly Roman-nose horse."

"And I got twenty," George said, glancing around. "Just don't tell Father Anthony."

When the announcer read off the name of the first contestant, the crowd seemed only half awake. The boy did well, but was not as fast as the second entry, Joey Hermosa, riding one of Hudson's geldings.

"Nice little quarter horse," Lorta said.

The third entry was a throwaway, an overweight dude on a pretty palomino. Pedro thought Arivaca could take them all easily. He wasn't worried until Ken Treat came into the ring.

Ken managed to make his horse stand behind the line — they

162

took off with the crack of the gun and headed for the first barrel on the right side, turning so close it looked like he meant to spin that barrel on its invisible axis — then on to the left, cutting hard there too. Ken had a black crop gripped in his teeth and an ugly expression on his face, willing to do anything to make that horse move. As he came around the far barrel, he took the crop in his hand and started whipping the animal, gashing into its sides with his oversized spurs, and that spitfire took off, racing across the finish line right up to the fence, where they jerked to a halt.

The announcer read out the time with a great deal of enthusiasm, and the crowd was alive now, liking a good show, wanting a winner. Ken spun his horse around once and whooped, as if it all were a done deal. He had beaten the other entries by a good three to four seconds, but there were bloody gashes on the horse's flanks, and the animal was heaving, lathered.

Sam and Ken had to ride by each other as Arivaca came into the ring, and Ken held up his hand as if he wanted acknowledgment, but Sam just rode past. For a moment I saw Sam as an Apache warrior, with a bone-sectioned breastplate, riding bareback with only a blanket to sit on — he rode straight, collected, as if he hadn't seen Ken. I thought of how he'd look with war paint on his cheekbones.

"Samuel Harrigan Sixkiller Mendoza, on Arivaca!" You could tell the announcer enjoyed reading out Sam's full name, and the fickle crowd was yelling for him now. Sam looked poised at the starting line, leaning slightly forward to whisper something to his horse — holding him back, centered, but as soon as the shot was fired, Arivaca exploded — it was a good start — maybe too much energy — but I was yelling for them, screaming *Go, Go!* As they leaned hard into the first turn, Arivaca cut at such a fierce angle I was afraid he might fall — but they were shaving off inches, milliseconds — his hooves seemed to want to devour the dirt as he scrambled for that third and final barrel. Coming around the turn Arivaca took off with a wild blast of speed — Sam was kicking hard too, but not gouging his sides out — flailing a piece of braided rawhide — they burst across the finish line and then danced to a stop, waiting for the pronouncement.

I collapsed back on the bench, and Pedro shook his head, "Gonna be a close one." I wondered if the judges could be bought in such a race, if that were a possibility. There was so much commotion I couldn't hear the announcer, but the judges were already coming out into the ring to hand out the ribbons. I didn't know who had actually won. They gave the yellow ribbon to Joey Hermosa, "and second place —" I held my breath — "goes to Kenny Treat." I heard myself bursting into a cheer that was really for the winner. Sam swooped down to collect his blue ribbon, and hooked it to the side of Arivaca's bridle. I knew Sam would say — *It was the horse who did it.* He rode out of the ring at a slow lope, scanning the crowd until he saw me, then he nodded, adjusting the pale blue scarf at his neck.

I kissed Pedro, hugged George, clapped hands with the kids, then ran down the rest of the bleachers to find Sam.

He didn't like any kind of public display, but he let me hug him without responding too much. "You were fabulous, *great!*" I patted Arivaca's side.

"Walk with me," Sam said. Arivaca's chest was still pumping, and we had to cool him down. Sam was accepting congratulations from all sides, while maintaining his composure. I knew he wanted to talk about every aspect of the race, how Ken had looked, how Arivaca had run. It would take a while before he unwound.

"Let's eat out tonight," Sam said, and I agreed, thinking how I'd like to get dressed up for a change, maybe go over to the Grasslands or Velvet Elvis. But once the trailer was loaded, and we pulled out of the lot, Sam stopped at the corner market. I thought he was just going in for a six-pack, and I stayed in the truck. But when he came back out, he had a sirloin steak and a can of baked beans. He wanted to eat out by the campfire.

Pedro had gone off with George Lorta and his family to have a picnic dinner down by the Sonoita Creek, and I was pleased that we would have the ranch to ourselves. What was the point of going out anyway, when I could make the best margaritas around? Measuring out the lime juice, tequila, and Triple Sec, I poured the potent concoction over ice cubes, then carried the pitcher out to the cottonwood where Aunt Carla had left a broken-down chuck wagon and a weathered picnic table.

Sam had a good fire going. There were stump seats around the ring of stones, though the flames were almost too hot now to sit there. Sam threw the meat on the grill, along with a few slices of onion and chili peppers. I had sliced up tomatoes and made some potato salad too, but best of all, there was a full moon rising over the inky Huachucas, so even our eyes would have their fill.

Sam was in an excellent mood, and the margaritas weren't hurting. He cut a bit of fat from his piece of steak and threw it over to Blue, who settled down in the dust with it. All the lights in the house were out now, and we might have been camped miles away from anywhere — we were that alone — though the presence of the sky was all around us, the fire creating its own warming hearth. It was as if we had the entire valley to ourselves, the foothills, the mountains, and yet I felt comfortable, almost cozy. Sam reached over to my side of the table and put a hand on top of mine. "I'm going to take care of you." And I felt those words catch, like a hook to the heart. No one had ever said that to me.

Sam pointed out Ursa Major and Minor, the bright star of Vega in Lyra above. I told him my favorite constellation was Orion. Though you couldn't see it this time of year. There was something so straight and true about those three stars, they made me think of my children, one balanced on either side.

But then Sam suggested we go for a ride. Everything was so pretty in the moonlight. I would have preferred just staying by the fire — it seemed so romantic, but maybe he was wary of that. I was tired and relaxed, not eager to leave the warm glow of the embers, but he seemed determined, so I went along.

Banner acted like it was perfectly normal, getting all tacked up in the middle of the night. Remarkable, how a dull and familiar setting could take on this other appearance in the moonlight — mysterious, like a woman transformed for an evening out — all made-up with a certain glow, as if the earth herself had donned a foamy taffeta shawl around her exposed shoulders.

"You warm enough?" he asked me. The temperature was dropping, and I accepted the jacket he had tied to the back of his saddle. As he handed it over, his hand stroked my arm. We rode on, and went through one of the Crown T fences, stirring up some cattle, which were wary of our passing. They put their heads down, backing up with their spooked, white faces glowing in the moonlight. In the distance I could hear a dog barking. "That's Treat's German shepherd," Sam said. "I don't know what they need a trained killer dog for, but if it comes any closer, it's going to be a dead dog."

I wanted to go back, get off of their land. I couldn't figure what drove Sam on. Wasn't it enough that he had won the race? It was as if the contest were never over for him. Or maybe he wanted me to know that he wasn't afraid, that he would protect me if it came to that. Maybe he wanted to show me the Indian way across this valley, how his people had once moved freely over all of this land — no fences, no gates, no ownership. The moon shone equally on all of it now, and it was ours at that moment as surely as I was his. Nothing recorded, except in the stars.

IT WAS A SLOW, HOT, dusty afternoon. "*When a man loves a woman,*" was coming over the bunkhouse radio. Sam turned toward me and opened his arms. We did a little slow two-step shuffle, back and forth in the shade under the canopy of the open shed, and at that moment I felt a huge sunflower opening inside of me, felt the sun-like rays of it filling me with gladness. He lowered his eyes then and seemed to soften a bit, from his face through his body, as if registering my emotion, but then he looked back up at me, and nodded, yes. *Yes, I thought, he owns it!*

I saw Sam glance toward the house — we both knew that Pedro had gone up to Tucson for supplies — and without speaking, we headed inside, and went straight to the guestroom. He shut the door behind us, and I closed the curtains before he pulled me down beside him onto the discreet single bed. He stared at the Mexican Tree of Life that hung on the wall as he undid his buckle, a silver oval, finely etched. I felt a thrill when I heard him unzip himself, and found myself dropping down the length of his body. I wanted to swamp him with adoring kisses. I wanted to sink into oblivion, as if this were my own private feast day with my own chosen saint. *Darling, darling sweetheart.*

But then he said, "Take off your pants." It seemed like we were children, and now it was his turn to do what he wanted. Looking into my eyes, he entered me with his hand, and I felt our eyes emptying into each other, as if we were attached in a never-ending circle. But I could also tell he wasn't wholly comfortable with this — and it made me say — "Let's wait." I slowed his hand — still, keeping it there, and though there was no sign of immediate remorse or frustration between us, only this stirred-up amazement, something in me didn't feel safe. I

167

felt as if he could easily disappear, that he was like some mirage on the desert, a dream of water, a drenching dream, and I could wake up parched.

WHEN I ASKED SAM IF HE WANTED to take the afternoon off, he answered — "The cows don't take a day off." But then he relented, and said he wanted to take me down to the Sonoita Creek, to show me the hummingbird gazebo. A friend of his had built this canvas and wood construction years ago, before the Nature Conservancy had bought up the land and made it into a bird sanctuary. But as far as Sam was concerned, it had always been a sacred place.

Parking the truck on the side of the road, we took an almost indiscernible trail, crawling under fallen mesquite, working our way down to the river. There it was, beneath the giant cottonwoods, a sweet little haven set close to the river in bright green grass, soothing to listen to the trickle of water, a luminous ripple over stone and cress. We sat in the warmth of the afternoon, and watched the humming-birds dart like living needles, gathering nectar. I felt a similar hum in my own veins, as if my heart were singing on its own propeller — I was just so glad to be there with him, to hold his hand, to feel the dry, rough texture of his skin. What a pleasure it was, sitting in this little homemade gazebo with the beautiful birds all supping on sweetness, to smell the odor of the air — like beeswax candles —a good place to get married, I said.

I don't know why I would deliberately break the spell by saying that, for marriage brought up everything in my life that burdened me. I wanted to live in the bliss of the moment, and marriage meant dwelling on the future and the past. All I wanted to do was to lie down with him here, on the hard dirt floor of this makeshift gazebo and to marry ourselves, but of course that didn't happen.

We decided to drive on to Sierra Vista, maybe take in a movie. Usually I loved riding in his old red pick-up with the broken leather, but that evening I felt the springs coiling beneath me and couldn't get comfortable. There was an edge to my voice that even I didn't like. I wanted him to tell me about Manuelita. I wanted to know how it had been with her, if he still went down to Nogales to watch her, but instead, I got into a mood.

Sam was certain that Ken Treat had been making passes at me. It was true, Ken had taken a liking to me for some reason, but it wasn't reciprocated, and I felt Sam should know that. If he cared about me, if he had any instincts, wouldn't he know that Ken was not a threat? I was not drawn to Ken Treat in any way — his big beefy limbs, his legs like sausages stuffed into his jeans. He had rather wide hips for a man, I thought, and his long, droopy mustache seemed strangely affected, the way he constantly pulled on it to get it perfect. I tried to assure Sam that I wasn't about to date a cowboy who took longer getting dressed than I did. Still, it had become a recurring complaint. Treat was all that Sam was not — a wealthy, white, Anglo rancher. Ken's mother had come from back east, and he had been sent off to prep school and had gone to Lake Forest College. All of this was intimidating to Sam, who would never inherit anything from anyone.

"Maggie Treat isn't local, you know," he told me. " She came out here to the Circle Z, back when you could buy a Chihuahua for a quarter."

"And a *señorita* for a dollar," I added. I was beginning to feel tired and achy, annoyed with Sam. I wanted him to want me in a way my husband never had. Was this going to be a familiar repetition? Didn't people do that, live the same scenario over and over until they finally woke up? I felt sick to my stomach. Was it emotional, hormonal, or something else? One day I felt as if my lungs were aching, and then it was my lower back, maybe my ovaries. I felt like my nerves had all but worn out — I no longer had my old resilience.

We decided on a movie that was mediocre, and halfway through I asked him if he would buy me some candy. Even if he wasn't a big, wealthy rancher, he could still afford to get me some sweets, I figured.

Sam got up and returned with a box of Milk Duds. Handing them over, he sat down, one seat away. I realized that I had offended him, but I felt self-conscious sitting there by myself. My discomfort grew as I filled my mouth, salivating on the chewy, chocolate-covered caramels. Why was he being such a *bufo*? I could barely concentrate on the film at that point, and decided if he didn't want to sit next to me, then I would leave the row and sit somewhere else.

As I got up, he demanded, "Where are you going?"

I didn't respond, so he followed me out into the lobby.

"I'm going to the ladies' room, OK?"

"I thought you wanted to leave. I thought you didn't like this stupid film."

"I don't, but I wanted you to get your money's worth."

The drive home was icy, silent. After we drove up to La Querencia he didn't make a move to get out of the truck. I left the door open, and he jerked forward so fast the side door slammed shut by itself.

I stood in the yellow kitchen, and everything looked unreal, too bright and not my own. I thought about my childhood, how the plates would rattle on the open shelves when you walked across the kitchen floor. Crying with self-pity, I wanted to go home. I wanted to get out of this relentless desert that wicked the water out of everything. I wanted my mother to bring me a washcloth with an ice cube inside it. I wanted to suck on that thin blue terry cloth, to feel her hand on my forehead.

No word from Sam on the following day, and as evening came on, I felt all bound up in my own confusion. It gnawed at me. How could I have been so insensitive. I hadn't been thinking about Treat, but from Sam's point of view, I could see it — Ken had been getting more and more familiar, calling me Little Coyote, telling dirty jokes that made me uncomfortable, bringing unexpected gifts — a flat of primroses, a sack of tangerines, a six-pack of *Dos Equis*.

Earlier that evening Ken had picked up Pedro on his way into town. They were headed for the Big Steer, where they often played poker on Thursday nights. The day had been especially hot, and it was still oppressive. All I wanted to do was put my feet up and drink a gallon of lemonade. I was constantly feeling dehydrated, and yet I had to pee about every half hour. I kept thinking I should probably have a physical, a real check-up, but I couldn't bother. I had taken care of others for so long, I wasn't in the habit of taking care of myself.

As I sat there alone, I felt another pang of homesickness. I wanted to see grass so green it would hurt my eyes, feel the amniotic warmth of our swimming hole, and hear the big mowers sweeping the hay fields, spewing out dense, rich bales of timothy — rivers rushing, rain falling, water everywhere.

An hour later, when I heard the truck pull up, I assumed it was Sam, for it was too soon for Pedro to come home. I was pleased with myself for holding out, for letting Sam make the first move. I thought, rather vaguely, that he had been drinking, because of the lag between the truck's arrival and the bang of its door, the length of time it took him to make it to the front porch, but I sat still, ignoring his approach. When I heard the knock, I yelled, "Come on in." But then I saw Ken Treat standing in the doorway, grinning with stupid assumptions. He had a rifle in his hands, and a rope looped over his shoulder. "Where's Pedro?" I asked.

"In town," he smirked. "He thinks he owns that goddamn bar."

"How's he supposed to get home?"

"Is that my job," he asked, resting the butt end of the rifle down, leaning it against the wall, "to take care of every goddamn wet-back? I thought maybe that was *your* job." He cleared his throat, but I didn't look up at him. "Maybe you lure a lot of guys out into the foothills, Little Coyote." He came a bit closer and touched my hair. "Little Dirty-Blond Coyote."

"You're drunk," I said.

"Who sent you here, Coyote Woman? Coyote *Bitch!*" He finally said the word that had been tickling the back of his brain.

I put my feet on the floor and stood up. "Would you leave," I said, without a trace of humor, but he grinned that lascivious grin and came toward me. I made the mistake of backing up. I thought maybe I could dash into the bathroom and lock the door, but as I saw him handling the rope, I tried another tactic, to make small talk — "I always thought the coyote was considered God's dog."

I hoped that might sober him, but he only said, "Bullshit. You've been stepping in that Indian bullshit again." Then in one swift movement, as I turned to bolt, he threw the rope at my foot and jerked it secure, giving a little cowboy *whoop.*

I hopped once before he snapped me off balance. Hitting the floor, I said, "Damn!" But all this seemed to excite him, as if we were enacting some peculiar cowboy ritual. "Cut it out!" I yelled. "You don't know what you're doing."

But he knew exactly what he wanted to do. Keeping the rope nice and taut, keeping me at a distance so I couldn't kick out, he dragged me down the hall — the runner burned my hand, my hip — I tried to brace myself but he yanked so hard I thought he might snap bone. The table lamp in the bedroom was on. He picked me up and flipped me onto my belly, the way he would have handled any young heifer. Taking the loose end of rope, he tied my hands together, but as he reached around to grab my shirtfront, I bit him *hard* on the hand. He mashed my head down so I had to gasp for air. Jerking at my belt, he got my jeans to open. I could feel him hunching over my ass with his bulky form — I could tell he intended to mount this little coyote like a proper house dog. Teased, he would say — *That bitch was in heat!* He began to massage my buttocks, crooning over the smooth round globes — I could feel him trying to make himself hard with his hand as he got himself into position.

I never heard Sam come into the house. I never even heard a footstep, so I was shocked when the bedroom lamp exploded, spraying splinters of glass and smoke. Looking over my shoulder, I could see Sam's form in the frame of the doorway. He had picked up the rifle in the living room and was pointing the barrel directly at Treat. "If you don't want your balls blown to the far side of the pasture, I'd advise

173

you to get your fat buckaroo ass out of here."

Treat got up in a hurry, and went stumbling past. I began to whimper, and tried to cover myself. Though Treat had not succeeded, I felt mauled, defiled. I heard the truck start up and then Sam was beside me, loosening the rope. "You all right?"

I pressed my cheek against his good, hard chest and began to sob, shaking badly. He stroked my hair, and helped me quiet down. But what if Sam hadn't appeared. What would Ken Treat have done to me? No one else was around to be a witness. I imagined Ken telling his drunken brain — *This doesn't hurt* — *She deserves it.* He could have pinned anything on Sam, for didn't Sam Harrigan Mendoza have a documented temper? Even Pedro would have to acknowledge that.

I wondered if we should call the police, but Sam said no. He knew we'd get nowhere on that score. Treat was from one of the largest ranching families in the county — too much power, and I was still considered an outsider. Who could blame a healthy young bachelor for wanting to have a little fun? It would be considered harmless, and probably a well-deserved initiation. It was hard to prove anything like that in court.

Sam led me into the bathroom. He sat me down and drew a hot tub, lighting a candle in the ceramic bird candleholder, before he helped me out of my clothes — I was still shivering — and then eased me back into the deep, warm water. I let the water cradle my head, while he put one hand under my floating back, took the pink bar of soap and slid it over my body. I was surprised that I could stand being touched after what had just happened, but Sam's hand was soothing, and so were his words. He told me how beautiful I was, moving his sure hand all over my body. I didn't want him to leave me alone.

It seemed natural for us to spend the night together, but still we didn't make love. As we fell asleep, I remembered his words, "I'm going to take care of you," and for once in my life, I began to feel safe, pulled into the tight lock of his arms.

THERE WAS NO SIGN OF A STORM that afternoon, only a few strange, greenish clouds in the distance, but it was as if the entire heavenly cup were pressing down over the valley, creating a strange electrical song. I suppose if we could hear energy in motion, there would have been a high-pitched squeal — until the goblet exploded right there in the saddle and Sam was flung aside.

After a quiet lunch, Sam and Pedro and a new man, Hank, rode out to cut a group of heifers away from their mothers, a chore I preferred to avoid. They had just split into three directions when they heard this snap, not much louder than a branch being broken, though the air around them seemed to crackle.

Pedro looked wild when he rode into the yard, yelling for me to call an ambulance. "Sam's been hit!" — waving a hand toward Picnic Tank — almost panting — "Sam — ground lightning!" I ran for the phone— then back to the corral — they would have to bring in a chopper. I grabbed Pedro's reins and jumped on *Dos*, flew in the direction of the leased land, as if the force of my love and fear and will could put Sam back together. *Just don't leave me, just don't leave.* I knew I was too happy!

Once I saw him lying there, I felt helpless. It looked as if someone had dropped him from a height and he had landed like pickup sticks. I wanted to flick all the wrong sticks away. Hank pulled the horses over to the side— they might be startled by the chopper's arrival. I took Sam by the shoulder and said, "Hey, I'm here," as if everything was going to be all right now. No response. I ripped open the pearl snap buttons of his shirt and felt for his heart — no response. His belt buckle was singed and the face of his watch had turned a strange yellow. He had the acrid, burnt smell of an electrical appliance that had blown a fuse.

175

Hank said calmly, "His tongue's turnin' blue." How could Hank just stand there? I stuffed the strange meat of Sam's tongue back in his mouth — I barely knew what I was doing, but I pounded on his chest and cupped his face and pressed gulps of air down into him until I heard the helicopter coming.

When the medics appeared, they pushed me aside, got the plastic mask over his mouth, gave him a shot of adrenaline. That seemed to bring him back with a jerk, though it was as if he had woken from a disturbing dream and couldn't quite relocate, didn't know where he was or what was happening to him. Sam looked at his hat with the hole blown out of it. Pointing a pistol finger, he said, "*Pow*," then let his head collapse back on the dirt. "Lightning can't kill a Mexican."

"Don't talk," one of the medics warned, his hands traveling over various limbs, as if searching for a broken bone, but there was none. Sam had never broken a bone in his life and was proud of that. He liked to say that he knew he looked brittle as a dried piece of mesquite, but his body always bounced back.

They lifted him onto the stretcher, and then Sam saw his horse, lying on its side. The horse didn't seem like Arivaca anymore — it had become inanimate, like a piece of wrecked furniture. They carried Sam over to the waiting helicopter. I followed, but felt as if I was in the way. I wanted to come, but they said there wasn't room. Better if I drove to Nogales, then I'd have transportation home. I could be there in an hour. Then the helicopter began the *whip whip* sound of its aerial oars, ascending like some terrible angel.

By the time it had tilted southward, Pedro had arrived on another horse. As the wind and roar of the machine veered down the valley, Pedro began a kind of sing-song prayer in Spanish, which seemed to repeat itself over and over. I wanted him to keep on praying until all was well, but then he crossed himself and said, "You go — I'll take care of things here." He told me that everything was going to be all right, and I wanted to believe him, but he didn't know how things turned out for me, how I seemed to lose everything I cared about.

Running around the house, I tossed various belongings into a brown paper bag, two oranges, a hairbrush, toothpaste, a bottle of beer. I felt like a fool collecting these objects as if I were an adult on a scavenger hunt, made to run for this and that, when unbeknownst to me the game had already been dropped. For a moment, in my stupor, I thought I could reach my hand in and find a maple leaf, a feather, a big grey stone, a label from an old tin can — I started to cry. Eight years old, and I didn't want to play. I didn't want to be the loser, coming up the hill after everyone, all of them laughing, already eating cake.

By the time I pulled into the hospital parking lot, I felt a dull foreboding. I locked my car and walked toward emergency. I told the receptionist I was looking for Sam Mendoza. "He was just brought in by helicopter." This made no impression on her.

She gave me a weary look — "You can sit over there," pointing to the severe blue couch by the magazine rack. I was willing to do whatever she told me, as if my good behavior might maintain some equilibrium in the greater scheme of things.

I closed my eyes, and said *Our Father* as my mother had taught me, but as the words filed past, I felt as if my life would now be as sterile and empty as this dumb hospital corridor, clean, blank, linoleum space, with its soundproof ceiling and burnished metal. I felt like I wanted to scream, knowing full well that the sound would be engulfed by this padded, cottony feeling, and that I'd never feel anything again.

How could I sit there! Where was Sam? My mouth was dry, almost sandy. I went down the hall with the pretense of looking for the Coke machine, but when a doctor walked past me, I asked, "Emergency? I'm looking for Sam Mendoza."

"Oh yes," he acknowledged. He had been on call, and I was just the person he wanted to find. He told me that Sam's heart had been partially singed, on the lower left ventricle. I could imagine that healthy, pumping heart of his, blackened, charred, but willing to make a comeback. Sam had a love that was like the heartbeat of the universe, mysterious and proud. "I don't believe that we'll have to operate, but in case something comes up, I wanted to make sure, because the only blood we have on hand, that matches Sam's blood type, is Mexican."

"You mean the blood you have for transfusions?"

He nodded, yes. "It's been thoroughly checked out."

"I'm sure it would be OK with Sam. He's had Mexican blood in his veins his whole life. I don't see why he'd object to it now."

The doctor marked the paper on his clipboard, and had me sign with a cheap ballpoint pen. "He's still in shock," the doctor acknowledged — "He thought Richard Nixon was the president, and that we were in Albuquerque. I'm sure he's not easy to keep down, but he should stay in bed for at least a week. I'm leaving that up to you," he winked.

I thought to question the doctor about my own symptoms, my persistent cough, the ache in my chest, the exasperating tiredness. Was it possible that I might have lupus? I had read about lupus in the Sunday paper — there were an extraordinary number of cases in Nogales, and some speculation about pollution. But this didn't seem the time to be worrying about myself.

"Sam's going to be fine," the doctor assured me. "He'll probably mostly complain about the rivets in his saddle — they burned his butt."

It seemed off-putting for this tall, grey-looking doctor to speak in such a manner. I wanted to tell him that Sam rarely complained, and that he would be riding in no time. Apparently, there was nothing I could do right now for Sam. He was under sedation, but still, I headed down the corridor in the direction of emergency — snuck into the unit — no one was on guard. Peeking behind several thin blue curtains, I found Sam on one of those high, narrow beds, a white sheet up to his chin. He was out, unconscious, but I sat down beside him and held his hand, kissed his scraped and dirty knuckles. I moistened a paper towel and gently bathed his hands, until a nurse looked in and clucked her tongue. It was time for me to go.

I went out to the car and cried from exhaustion and gratefulness, as if my own heart were courting Sam's heart on some level. My love, I knew, had been a torment to him. I would try to be easier, easier on us both.

I reached back and found the hot sudsy beer that had been rolling around on the floor in the back. I started grinning over what a little piggy I was, gulping down his *Corona*, as if he could enjoy it too, through me. I felt very sleepy and lay down in the front seat of the nice, warm car. I lay down and closed my eyes, listening to the starlings filling the cottonwoods. I was glad to be alive.

ON THE HOTTEST, MOST SWELTERING DAY of the year, the memory of my mother comes over me, a warmth I would normally want to wear, wrapping it around, but now I can not take the closeness, and have to push that fevered blanket away.

I remember her taking a wicker basket full of clothes, white ones mostly, shaking distilled water from the bottle with its sprinkler cap, tossing clothes like salad, and then the burning bleach smell of metal smoothing cotton — she was a perfectionist when it came to our clothes.

I remember her at that magical moment of stalled light when the sky became luminous and the house lamps came on. We ran wildly through the circlet of droplets spun out, having a sprinkler party — sliding, *leaping*, getting drenched, falling down. My brother dragged me by the ankle, and Mother yelled, *Stop it! Why do you always hurt your sister?* But I didn't mind, and she wasn't really angry, handing out the pink plastic bowl of potato chips, onion dip with the tennis can lid. My striped suit sagged and my brother told me with some authority that I'd never fill it properly. He put two hard oranges under his shirt, and showed me what I was supposed to look like.

I think of our mother sifting flour from a can, pure white flour made even finer as it sifted like powder. Pleasure released in the squeezing of the handle, making the curve sweep over the screen. Sifter, sprinkler, divider of things, deciding what I had outgrown, what should be given away to Pee-wee's family, though he refused to wear girl stuff, even if it was blue. I wore all of Jimmy's hand-me-downs, T-shirts, cut-offs, his black skates. Only on Sundays did we get dressed up. And then my mother looked radiant. She wore high heels and long thin skirts with a slippery feeling, a navy hat with a part-way net.

I remember her pop-bead pearls, how she let me remake them into ankle bracelets. Little pearls, big ones — on her they looked real, great big pearls from some make-believe ocean.

But when I finally found her pink leather box of costume jewelry, gold circle pins, her clip-on earrings with the pharmaceutical pads, chain-link bracelets, garish, gaudy, the pop-bead pearls had yellowed, and all of it seemed dated. The one thing I kept was the charm bracelet, a disk with *James* on one side, *Joanna* on the other, a golden bench with two seated hearts, a little pair of scissors that actually cut, an hourglass, the head of Nefertiti, a clear glass bottle containing a pearl smaller than a bead of tapioca, a miniature gold-dipped sand dollar, and a little golden book that opened and shut. Each charm must have had some significance, which I made up to give her life substance, to fill out the stories I might have heard if she'd stayed around long enough for me to listen. I would have been a good listener, as she sifted her flour, the sprinkler outside batting the window.

I remember her filling the cake pans, three equal layers, licking the spatula, the oatmeal-colored bowl, licking and listening, and when the oven door opened, the pans slid in. We had to be extra careful, quiet, until we could smell the sweetness rising, and then we took little cake steps across the speckled linoleum floor.

Mercy worked for us after Mama departed, but then I didn't hang around much to watch. She sprinkled water with her fingers from a bowl, *scat scat*, as if I was a dry piece of cloth that needed moistening. Everything she did was different. The old order gone. Store-bought Hostess Twinkies if we were lucky. Even the sprinkler changed from roundabout to back-and-forth— too easy to outrun it.

I realize now, I'd been trying to outrace my mother's death all my life, and perhaps it was finally catching up with me. I could no longer keep myself dry, away from her sprinkler, her power, her absence. Loss should let you feel what's left of your life a little more intensely, but in this heat, I knew the pieces were all coming loose in me and that I could no longer hold water. Sloshing, sloppy, dragged through the mud, I felt sopping wet as an old raggy cloth pushed over the dirt-shamed floor.

WHEN SAM CAME HOME, HE SETTLED down in the living room on the big feather sofa — he liked being in the middle of things, hearing what Pedro was talking about while he puttered around in the kitchen. Sam would sometimes get up and hobble in there, insisting that he would do better if he were up and around, but the metal trim that ran around the counters made his solar plexus tingle.

Pedro nodded for me to take him back to the couch, all the while talking about *this one time, way back when* — Pedro's manner of speech always soothed Sam, and he was willing to rest and listen if Pedro prattled on. "I was leading these ole cows one time, one on this side and one on the other, and we was going through some brush, you know, and it got to raining really bad — an' I told Shorty, cause Shorty was with me, that we better hurry up and cross that canyon before it filled with water. So we crossed over, but coming out of that brush, the thunder hit right close..."

"Thunder doesn't *hit*," I interrupted. "You only *hear* thunder."

"Well, it sounded like thunder hit something," Pedro answered. "There were sparks all over, right under those horses. My horse started pawing as if he could catch one."

I thought of how my mother always used to love a storm — she kept us from being afraid of them. She could feel a storm coming, and it made her excited. We'd make popcorn and have a Dr. Pepper party as she ran around the house. *Isn't this something? Isn't this fun!* She wouldn't shut the windows, because she wanted to smell the rain, to feel the spritz of it coming through the metal screens. I'd press my nose and make an imprint, then twirl as the curtains blew in like big ballgowns. After it was over, we'd have to sponge the moisture from the windowsills, because father always worried about water damage.

"I think lightning sort of likes me," Sam said with a grin.

But I thought of how exposed we were riding out on the range, how much we anticipated a good monsoon, and yet when rain did come, it often brought disaster — arroyos flooding, sweeping up careless cars and campers. Sam's bolt of lightning had not brought rain. It was merely a ruthless, killer bolt that had taken Arivaca.

"If only I'd let him go barefoot," Sam said, thinking the ground lightning had been drawn to the metal in Arivaca's shoes.

When I told Sam he shouldn't blame himself, he shot me a look that was pure Apache. So I got up and made him a glass of iced coffee with sugar and milk, which he claimed he wouldn't like, saying that hot drinks were better for cooling you down, but once he'd tasted the froth of it, he declared it was almost as good as ice cream. He drank it all down and started chewing on the ice cubes, crunching away.

I thought of how Jackson used to hate that, how he wouldn't let me take food or coffee in the car, nor let me sing when songs came on the radio, even if I knew the words, how he hated putting leftovers all together in a pot, how Buster's snore disturbed him, Jovey's baseball cap, not closing things, or closing them too loudly, dishes in the sink, especially the right side, which was *his* side, dancing of any kind. Why wasn't *he* hit by lightning? But worst of all, I realized that Jackson had never liked me. How he must have hated that pretense.

"You know one time I was riding about twelve miles south of here." Sam took my hand, and gently swung it back and forth. "I was following this fence line for about a mile, and there was a bull standing right next to that fence, about a hundred yards ahead of me. I could see the sparks coming off that wire — it must have hit the fence somewhere up the line, and the electric went through and just clobbered that bull — he didn't even struggle or anything. He just went — *Oonnnnn*, like that, and went down."

Maybe it was like that for Arivaca, I thought. I asked him what he was going to do, and he said he would probably have to train

183

another horse. "Life's too short to get stuck on an animal. Horses come and go."

"So do people," I answered. "That's even worse."

"Well, horses can help you get used to it."

As Sam got better, I began to feel worse, as if I'd absorbed all his aches and pains, allowing him to get up and around, while I just wanted to go to bed and rest. I tried not to let him see how I felt. I didn't want him worrying over me. Maybe I'd picked up a virus in the hospital. In any case, I was now the one trying to take it easy. Setting up a folding chair out in the yard where I wouldn't disturb him, I watched him training the new three-year-old grey he had gotten over at Hudson's.

He began with hours of preliminary groundwork, lunging the grey on a long weathered line, talking to him steadily with a low and easy tone, giving constant little tugs on the line to keep the horse's attention — everything seemed amazingly interesting to this highstrung creature, any move the cat or dog made crossing the yard, a blowing piece of paper, but Sam liked the horse's energy and alertness.

Sam's main interest seemed to be in getting the horse into a good steady jog, for that was the gait that kept a horse in shape, and the speed that was most often useful to a cowboy. After ten minutes of trotting in one direction, he'd slow the grey down to a walk, and make him walk on — he always wanted him moving forward. When Sam went, "Whoa," he expected the horse to respond to his voice, and when the horse did, he'd say, "Good boy." Then he'd pull him in and reward him with a pat on the neck, giving him lots of reassurance, before making the horse move out in the other direction — walking, trotting, loping a little. He tried to keep the two directions balanced, though a horse generally went better in one direction or the other.

Sam hadn't named the grey yet, and I thought that was a natural part of his resistance, not wanting to get too personal, protecting himself from feelings of attachment. If he named the grey, it might begin to take the place of Arivaca. Or maybe that connection would never happen again.

Sam raised his arm and brought a switch of rawhide down against his boot — the grey broke into a bucking lope. Sam jerked the line to let him know that such behavior was unacceptable, and the horse slowed down to a more collected gait, his head and neck bending a little. You didn't want a horse carrying his head up high in the air, because that hollowed out the back and created all sorts of problems.

From my chair I could see Sam was trying to get the grey used to a lot of things — not only to the saddle, but more importantly, to his voice, even to his smell. He took off his shirt and let the animal explore it. He rubbed his hat over the horse's neck and ears, letting him sniff it. At one point the grey stuck his face right into the empty bowl of the hat as if it were some new-fangled feeding apparatus.

Unlike most cowboys, Sam didn't believe in breaking a colt with force, because if you broke a horse's spirit, you lost something essential you could never regain — the horse became a mere working animal, not a partner in constant communication, responding to his master's every impulse.

Most cowboys probably couldn't tell the difference between breaking and gentling an animal, but Sam thought it worth the extra effort and time. Though he was always firm, and would reprimand with a tone of disapproval, his voice was all it took. But Sam was never soft. He was clear and sure in every gesture. I could see that the grey was coming to respect him, that they liked each other already. I imagined that Sam would make a very good father, but it was probably too late for me on that score. Still, I liked to imagine having a family with Sam. It was my experience that people who were good with dogs and horses were also good with small children.

"It might not just be love, giving you these mood swings," Donna said one night over the phone. "Everyone I know is taking estrogen. Really, you should get yourself checked out. That cough sounds bad. Summer colds are the worst."

But I had had enough of doctors for a while. Besides, I didn't like to take medicine, but Donna insisted that estrogen was not medicine—"It's more of a supplement, like vitamins."

But didn't she know that estrogen was made from pregnant mare's urine? Didn't she know about those horrible ranches, where they tied up mares in tiny stalls, deprived them of water so that the urine was more concentrated? And as soon as the mares gave birth, they impregnated them again?

Still, Donna urged me to go see a doctor. They also made estrogen out of soybeans now. Even Pedro thought I might have walking pneumonia, and I certainly didn't want to pass that on to Sam after all he'd been through. But what finally convinced me to go to a doctor was a sympathy visit from Maggie Treat. She had heard that I was under the weather.

When I saw her drive in, I felt like hitting the floor like we used to do on Beacon Hill when the Jehovah's Witnesses rang the doorbell. She arrived with her *tepizcuincle* dog, a small, nervous rat dog that was supposedly worth thousands of dollars. It ran around the yard after Hairball, the cat, tearing through my flowerbeds while Maggie plunked a frozen meatloaf on the counter and threatened to drive me to Tucson.

I lied and said I already had an appointment with Doctor Rosen that very afternoon — in fact, I had to get ready to go. She had started looking over my spice rack, as if she wanted to borrow something — what on earth did one do with star anise anyway? She had never heard of Dr. Rosen before, what kind of a doctor was he? I said I'd gotten his name from the homeopath in town. At least that part was true.

"From the sound of that cough, I think you need a specialist. When you're ready, you give me a call." And then she miraculously picked up her purse and left me to my own sorry choices. The meat loaf was a nice gesture, but it had freezer burn.

Dr. Rosen was somewhat New Age, tall and skinny, a certified

M.D. with a big galloping laugh that put me quickly at ease. He told me that we could be informal — I could call him Dr. Dan if I wanted. Huge hunks of crystals lined his bookcase, and a variety of green plants lent a breathable brightness to the office atmosphere. We talked for a full half hour, about my unhappy marriage, my difficult children, my present situation, how tired I was, always worn-out, like a rattletrap car speeding on empty, though I insisted I'd never been happier in my life.

I told him that I seemed to have trouble, more upsets, right after my periods, rather than before, as if I had *post*-menstrual syndrome. He thought that indicated a need for more estrogen. He often prescribed estrogen and progesterone in the form of Mexican wild yam. It was anti-carcinogenic, and had no bad side effects. Did I begin menstruating late as a girl? Yes, I was one of the last ones in my ninth-grade class. He nodded in confirmation. He also gave me a few bottles of a natural expectorant for the cough, and suggested I drink as much water as possible. He wanted me to begin 2 mg. of Estriol daily as soon as we received the results of my blood tests. He drew eight full tubes of blood.

Anticipating my next appointment, I let my list of Tucson errands grow. I was going to have my hair lightened, and wanted to return to Patagonia like a new woman, with wet-looking polish on trim, clean nails. That would last about an hour, but I wanted to look good. I wanted to dazzle Sam.

When I returned to Dr. Rosen's office, he didn't burst out with his jovial, welcoming laugh, but he opened his arms for a hug. I liked Dr. Dan, and felt comfortable with him. He was casual, genuine, direct — all qualities I admired. The results of my blood work were there on his desk. My hormones, apparently, were all at rock-bottom level, including the testosterone. I didn't even know that women had testosterone, but as he spoke, I felt like he wasn't getting to the heart of the matter — like a husband who is lecturing his wife on house cleaning when he has already decided to leave her. How rarely we talk about the core issue, the essential nut, but instead go around and around, talking about this or that annoyance, some pet peeve, dissatisfaction with some aspect of the partner's body, when what we really want is out.

Had I ever been a happily married woman? Was Jack ever a happily married man? Or was he only angry within the tight circumference of his double-life, never living either one fully? How I'd managed to escape and come out here was a mystery to me. It reminded me of my awesome, basic ignorance. Perhaps faith was based on a similar lack of knowledge, accepting what could never be fully known.

Facing Dr. Rosen, with his shelves of geodes and crystals, I wondered how hormonal replacement would change my life, what fate had to bring me now. Was I too old to have another baby?

In response to that question, Dr. Rosen put a hand on the papers before him. Apparently, we had something more important to discuss. Simply put, to repeat his putting — "We've done a lot of blood work here," he straightened the pile of papers before him, "and two of your tests show that you are HIV positive, strain one as well as four. I sent several test tubes to a specialty lab I've been using in California, because normally we can't even detect strain four." He paused, as if waiting for a reaction — I gave him none, but my heart was pounding like some sort of machine, punching a plasticene form out. "I'm afraid this dual infection indicates a highly active form of the disease. But we have caught this early on, and we can take aggressive action." He rifled through his papers, but my mind, like an animal, tried to flatten itself out, as if to make itself invisible. I thought of slapping Jovey across the face. He had only been a child, and I had no recollection of what he had done or why I'd been so angry. I only remembered the shock we both felt, how his eyes became dull, vacant.

I had the strongest impulse to lie down on the carpet, to get as close to the ground as possible. But at the same time I felt myself becoming very light — I held on to the arms of the chair I was sitting in. My eyes tried to hold the solidity of objects I saw in the room. The geodes and crystals had substance, density — they looked as if they would last forever, holding their hard mineral shapes throughout time, whereas I felt as if my body were falling through space like sand within an hourglass.

I was appalled by this verdict, as fair and frank as it must have seemed to him. "I was HIV negative, in Boston," I argued. "That was in February."

"I can see that." He looked down at my chart. He'd had all of my previous blood work faxed from Mass General, but then he asked the next logical question — "Have you had sexual intercourse since that time?"

I sat there in silence, suddenly thinking of that wild drunken party with Tonio, how he'd told me my body was as delicious as polenta. Now I felt spurts of black ink entering my bloodstream, squirting into the aquarium of air that I breathed, *jert jert* of black jism, sickening come, from a man I never knew and certainly never loved, the dark descending angel who had entered my body, stabbed it with his knife and fork.

When I told Dr. Rosen that Tonio was from Tunisia, he said, "That explains something. Strain four is believed to come from North Africa, and it's highly contagious. Not that anything's being contained these days."

I asked Dr. Rodent — for that's how I suddenly saw him, with his pasty skin and whiskery hair — if you could pass this strain orally. He said that would be highly unlikely. He was quick to be professional, clinical in his response, saying how the climate of the mouth was protected by all sorts of natural antibiotics, how one could always use prophylactics, but they were not always foolproof. He paused then for a moment before continuing. "I know during your last visit you spoke of a relationship, that you were in love."

"Yes," I said, surfacing, wishing Sam was there with me to fend this off. He had said — *I'm going to take care of you,* and I needed him now more than I'd ever needed anyone.

"Have you been intimate with him?" the doctor asked. There

190

was a strained pause.

"No, not yet, not completely." My open hands looked red and unrecognizable. I didn't see them as my hands, attached to my body, but as objects that were strangely colored, floating hands.

Dr. Rosen acted as if the worst were now over. We could both relax and discuss my options like adults. "If you were to consummate the relationship, it would be a risk. I'm sorry to be blunt, but you have to consider this."

I realized what he was getting at. I wasn't exactly offering Sam lifelong love and companionship.

"When he finds out I'm sick, do you think he'll just dump me?"

"I didn't say that." What he really was saying was — Will you do right by him?

Forget it, I thought. I'll never give Sam up. This was all ludicrous. He was out of his mind, if he thought I'd give up the one thing that could save me. There was no going back for either of us now. But then I had a morbid thought — I could see Sam crawling into the casket with me. I could see the lid closing on the two of us, and I had to admit, I felt some relief, imagining myself being held by his arms. I could bear this if he was beside me.

"I've seen many couples infect each other, especially through drug use. Do whatever you can to keep from spreading this thing. I'll help you as much as possible. There are very effective antiviral drugs — AZT and protease inhibitors, and we do have some new experimental —"

I held up my hand — I wanted silence, and he was kind enough to let me go down, down into the deepest well of quiet I'd ever gone into, until I touched the cold, dismal water at the bottom. "And if I don't take anything? How much time?"

He didn't want to answer specifically, but I guess he felt I'd taken the rest fairly well, so it was safe to give a sporting figure. "Will you be here in a year? Probably not. Though I'm being conservative."

I was astounded, appalled by this outrageous prediction, disgusted by this man with his scraggly beard. This was surely the office of a quack. The furniture he'd inherited from some previous M.D. was in such poor taste, I wanted Jackson to see it, to have a good laugh. Were the crystals supposed to have healing powers? Should I run out to the Gem Show and buy myself some? I laughed again, and he nodded, as if he understood the lack of gravity in my response.

Going back outside into the shocking glare, I saw cars jolting by as if they were cells on some unknown mission to self-destruct. I walked through the parking lot. A mother and her toddler got out of a yellow car. She was having trouble managing, though they were both young and healthy, and didn't have an inkling that they too had to die. Everyone on the sidewalk, under the blaze of the sun, was in such blissful ignorance, going through the motions of simple human beings, while I was separate, on a different course.

*So, what should I do?*
*Talk to him, tell him that you must leave him.*
*But he'd follow me.*
*Tell him that you don't love him.*
*He'd never believe me.*
*I know it would be a great sacrifice...*
*Oh, say no more, it's impossible, no.*

All I wanted was to go to sleep. I wanted to get home so I could crawl into bed. Sam would come find me, and I would tell him everything. I knew he would think we could beat this, but at that moment, Sam already felt other, apart, on the other side of this flayed reality. I felt my being had no substance, nothing to hold onto. For a moment I was afraid my hands might slip from the steering wheel. The tiny particles that made up the landscape were shimmering. I was no longer solid, in a solid world. More like a smoldering chemical, or a piece of dry ice — gases blowing off into the thirsty air. *I was going to make my love hate me.*

I didn't allow myself to succumb to his lanky form as he banged through the front door of the ranch house, ready for his first cold *Corona* of the evening. He was still limping slightly from the accident, and it made me want to reach out and hold him. Usually the mere sight of him made me slide like a hunk of butter on a cast-iron pan, but now I turned my ice-cold smoke screen on him. "Oh, it's you. I didn't hear you drive up," I lied.

"You going out? You're looking pretty fancy."

"Maybe," I answered. "Maybe not."

Sam opened the refrigerator, and pulled out a beer, looking around for the opener. He tried to kiss me, but I turned my head.

"What's wrong?" he asked.

"Nothing," I responded, dull, lackluster, turning my attention to the window. "I guess it's true what they've been saying about your little Lochiel *chiquita*."

"What are you talking about?"

"Life is more than kisses and promises in the moonlight, Sam. Even you must know that. We really have to look this thing square in the face."

He took me by the shoulders and turned me around, so that he could focus on me. "What do you mean?" Pushing forward with the question, and yet withdrawing back into some inner cave, as if he could feel the blow coming and wanted to be ready to defend himself.

"I mean, we're coming from two very different worlds, and when the fun wears off, you're going to find yourself with a pampered easterner, and I'll be looking at a worn-out cowboy and wondering how to have a real discussion."

"Is this a real discussion? What's wrong with you? What did that doctor guy say?" He tried to pull me to him, but I shrugged him off as if he bored me.

"You just don't get it, do you." I was feeling cruel now, capable of cruelty. "I want to see other guys. I've got someone waiting for me right now. Someone who can afford to take me out to dinner."

"What are you talking about? Who?"

"Maybe Ken Treat," I said coyly, hating myself. "Don't get on your high horse, but I guess you should know — he took me down to see Manuelita. Pretty hot ticket, Sam. I invited him out here that night you broke up our party, when you blew out the lamp and supposedly saved me. Did you ever once think I might be enjoying myself?"

Sam didn't say a thing, but I knew it was working.

"I'm not in love with him, if that's what you think, but he *is* a good lover. I don't mean to be making comparisons here, because we don't really know much about that, do we."

I was afraid I had said too much, that Sam might try to force himself on me, to punish me for the dry-ice hatred of my words.

"You bitch," he said, grabbing the collar of my shirt, dragging me toward the door. The material cut at my throat, and I was afraid of him. He knew where Treat was, at the Big Steer, and he was going to take me straight to him.

We didn't speak on the drive into town, though on one sharp curve a young heifer appeared on the road, its white face shining, and he had to swerve. I sat as far away from Sam as possible, removing myself from the situation. I thought of my mother, how she had said that she'd be gone for just a little while, that she needed to have a vacation. All the time she was acting a part. The *Isle of Capri* sounded so lovely, even the mention of its name seemed to light up her face — at the time she was hiding her illness, but was her secrecy such a benefit to anyone? Could I have coped with her death without all the pretty stories? I think it was worse finding out that she was never coming home, but now I understood her wanting to go away, like an animal slipping off into the forest.

We pulled up in front of the bar, and I got out slowly. As we approached the door, he gave me a shove and I almost stumbled into the smoky, liquored atmosphere. Everyone there seemed dulled by a common stupor. Treat was leaning forward at the bar, his long legs stuffed into some tight-fitting jeans. I felt like I was going to gag, but instead, I sidled up next to him, and slipped an arm around his shoulder. He was drunk enough to act like he'd been expecting me — "You look kind of thirsty, Little Coyote. How about a *Naked On The Beach?*" — a horrible blue drink that was currently popular.

"Fine," I responded, but then whispered in his ear. He hooted and glanced to the left and the right as if to alert his audience. Sam was standing somewhere back behind us where he could be a witness. I was only performing for Sam. Treat swung himself around on the stool and pulled at his mustache. I let him draw me up beside him, instantly repelled by the smell of his deodorant — it reminded me of Jovey's dorm. I was afraid to look toward Sam, but I could feel his heat, his darkness behind me.

Suddenly Sam grabbed me by the arm and jerked me away. "You whore," he said, taking out his wallet. He had just cashed his monthly paycheck, and he had a handful of bills. Everyone in the bar was watching now. Even the jukebox music seemed to stall. Cigarette smoke was drifting up to the lanterns. No one touched a pool ball. "Why don't you go buy yourself a dress." He threw the money at my face and it slid down my body onto the floor. "Something nice and short for easy access."

The bar girl ran around the counter and grabbed a handful of the money, shaking a fistful at him. "Who do you think you are, anyway? Throwing money at a good girl like that — she's no more a whore than I am." Everyone thought this amusing, but she quickly scooted back behind the bar where she could have the last word — "I tell you, these ignorant, black Mexicans."

THE NEXT DAY, I LEFT SAM'S BELONGINGS in a box on the step to the bunkhouse. I even pried the rusted, metal cross from the bunkhouse wall and laid it on top of everything. I wasn't sure if he would come, but I was hoping I could catch a glimpse of him. Maybe I'd run out and apologize, and he would know the truth. I told Pedro to take the day off, I wanted to be alone, and then I paced around the kitchen, obsessively cleaning, every surface, each bottle, every single drawer.

Around two, I heard Sam's truck. He pulled up and parked over by the corral. He didn't have to go into the bunkhouse. I had written his name in magic marker on top of the box. He opened the lid, as if to check the contents, and then he went into the tack room and got his saddle and bridle, threw them in the back of the truck.

I stood in the shaded corner of the kitchen, and could see that he wasn't wearing his hat for some reason, and it made him look vulnerable. I was desperate to run out and tell him not to go, but then he picked up his box of belongings and put it on the passenger side of the cab. He didn't once glance toward the house. I watched him get in, and felt dazed, numb. I wanted to cry out — *Don't leave me, Sam* — but I just stood there and watched him pull out, leaving a height of dust that would never really settle. Sometimes I think I'm still choking on it.

After Sam left, it was the oddest sensation, as if I believed my own story, my total lack of feeling. I became cold, as cold as I had pretended to be. The sky itself became flat at that moment. I felt no love for anything. It was as if I had welcomed death into my body. No part of me wanted to live anymore. All I knew, was that it was over — the door was closed, and I was trapped in the tightest space of all, my own soul.

196

Pedro came into the house that evening, having heard the news in town — "So now you've gone an' done it," he scolded. "Lost me my one good ranch hand." He probably thought that we'd just had a lovers' spat, that it could be mended like some barbed wire fence.

"Did you hear where he went?" I asked Pedro, but he shook his head, no.

"You never can tell with Mendoza — he's like some kind a crazy roadrunner, that kid — you don't know which way he been, which way he gonna go." Somehow, after everything else I couldn't take this, and burst into tears. Pedro felt bad for having upset me. He sat down, and put his hand on the back of my chair, patted my shoulder until I told him everything—how sick I was, what the doctor had predicted.

Pedro shook his head, and said he didn't believe that — no one should say such a thing. Then he made it clear that he would stay with me, take care of me, as he had intended to care for Aunt Carla, but he looked so stricken, my heart went out to him.

"You know, once I had a little dog," I said to him, "and he always looked sad when I was sad, and I loved him so."

WORD GOT BACK TO US THROUGH ELEAZAR that Sam had taken a job in the Chiricahuas, over near Portal, New Mexico, and though I knew it was for the best, it was another door closed.

I didn't regret anything, really. Maybe now he'd have a future. It all seemed as if this were supposed to happen, as if my life were but one tiny piece in a great big puzzle, and though it wasn't my plan, what I would have chosen for myself, I found myself yielding to some greater will as I put my affairs in order.

I was grateful to be where I was, not in some hospital in downtown Boston with the best medical care in the country, everyone making heroic efforts to save me, a guinea pig on experimental drugs. I wasn't afraid of death. In fact, I had this notion that when I died, everything would be revealed to me. It was a bit like waiting to go on a trip — I just didn't know where I was going, or when it would begin. I felt sure that somehow I'd be reunited with my mother. I wondered if I would recognize her, if she would be waiting for me. I was certain that death wasn't any more frightening or terrible than birth — I was just waiting for that first contraction.

The ranch work was getting to be too much for Pedro alone now, especially since I wouldn't allow Ken Treat on the place. We didn't have the kind of money most men expected. Even Eleazar had moved on. After talking it over with Pedro, I decided it would be best to sell the cattle in late fall. Pedro didn't like it, but he quietly agreed.

Without Sam there to fill my days, I discovered a new kind of existence, a milder form of love, more diaphanous, that gathered everything together — it gave me the sensation of being held. Sometimes I felt like I was holding God's finger under the door crack, and He kept telling me to *just hold on*. I thought of the simplest flower, the unfolding of its radiant parts, like a perfect dahlia, each petal connected to the scintillating whole. I pictured myself so small, I could stretch out on that glistening flower and float downstream. I imagined the rays of the sun up above, and my brain seemed to dilate.

It became easier to experience awe — not in the grand sense, but the minuscule. I realized all you had to do was stop, and contemplate the thing at hand — a coppery feather that Pedro had brought me, glinting in the afternoon light, turned between two fingers — an iridescent bug, pale translucent green, as if it had been born out of the fresh shoots of grass that were now beginning to appear, for at last the rain had begun to fall, another gift that had come too late, though the blissful rhythm on the metal roof made my little nest a haven.

I realized now why they called the Huachucas, "the thunder mountains," as a storm came barreling down those craggy slopes, bending the yucca and ocotillo to the ground. I lay for hours in my warm, white bed, holding my pillow close to me. At last our cattle could eat to their hearts' content, though I knew their pleasure would be short-lived.

As I lay there I drifted into daydreams, as if I were falling into a big pile of leaves — I thought of the game we played sometimes at birthdays — a tangle of strings called the Spider Web. Each child got a stick with a different colored string — and winding, you made your way, bit by bit, as if you were gathering your whole life in, working forward until you came upon your treasure. The Treasure, I realized now, must be death.

As I wound my life toward me, I saw my dark-haired mother in her pink quilted robe, holding a warm rubber bottle to my lips, then Jimmy and me sitting on our big white horse, Rosie. I remembered a tall plastic clown with a weight in its bottom —you could knock him and knock him and he'd always spring back — a white patent-leather purse with a brass twist closure, three different scents from my starter perfume kit. I wondered why I would think of my favorite rubber doll with her sockets exposed, her limbs lying elsewhere, why the warm sickening scent of cotton candy — fresh sharpened pencils, bite marks on those pencils, the little hollow scoop in my wooden desk. Out of nowhere I'd think of some meaningless scene — walking down a driveway, or those wobbly TV dinner trays. I could almost feel the texture of the crunchy excelsior packed around the Hummel figurines my mother collected — being punished with the backside of a hairbrush. I remembered molding eggs out of colored Play-Doh, crawling beneath the house until the hard-packed earth became incredibly smooth — taking a pack of Juicy Fruit from the IGA and having to return to give the grocer a nickel — swallowing a hornet in a can of Dr. Pepper, rushed to emergency, the clammy feeling of a wet life preserver buckled on. I remembered being sent off to Whispering Pines, where we had a BM chart — I was dying to come home and drew a circle that showed my father how much I missed him. I remembered pouring mud pies onto hot cement, dissecting bleeding hearts to find the lady in the bathtub, staring at the painting of waves smashing rocks above our living room fireplace, saying *ding* when it was time to turn the page. I remembered taking a drag from Jackson's cigarette as we sat writing postcards by a bright shining wall. I remembered trumpet vines in profusion.

THE DAY BEFORE THE TRUCK CAME to collect our herd was a sad day for Pedro and me. A chill was in the air, and the cows were all humped up and shaken. Pedro said — "It seems those cows know where they're goin'. Normally, we'd be cutting out keepers. It's kind a strange not to be cutting any keepers." We were going to leave the cattle in the big corral overnight, to help settle them down, but their bawling was getting to Pedro.

"They say they ride better if they're not full a water. Some buyers they can tell if you water your cattle— they get a little puffy, but they always charge shrink." Pedro said how he usually tried to keep the cows away from water, because that was how the buyers generally liked it. He told me how usually a buyer went through the whole lot and looked for anything he might not like, but Pedro usually cut out what wasn't good to begin with — "That way you keep on their good side. But tomorrow they're taking everything anyway — Well, the price is right, I guess. But it seems kind a strange letting some of those cows go." He paused, as if trying to picture it — how when the truck arrived on the following day, they would run them all through the scales and load them up. "The only trouble is," he frowned, as if he weren't reconciled to what he knew was going to happen, "I let some of those cows get into me."

At dawn I woke early and watched the sun rise through my bedroom window. I could hear the truck in the yard, but I just lay there and listened to the lowing of the cattle. I felt as if I were a person without religion, as if I were being buried under a dump load of dirt.

After the actual loading began, it sounded like animal agony, as if they were being torn from each other. Most ranchers would say I was being sentimental, but I knew they had feelings, instincts so strong it could break down fences. I was vulnerable to their sounds of confusion, separation, that old familiar knife come down from heaven, driven back into my gut.

The quietness that followed was more like a shudder, the empty feeling after a funeral when everyone has gone. I got up and got dressed, went out to see Banner, but even the horses looked vagrant.

Pedro seemed resigned when he sat down with his coffee. He stirred his cup around and around, waiting for me to make small talk, but I had nothing to say.

"They got a doctor in Nogales, you know," he began. "Maybe you should go down and see him. That doctor, he told me — you eat one green chili a day, you'll stay young forever."

"And how old are you now, fifty-one?"

"Me? I'm sixty-seven years old!" he laughed. "One chili a day, I tell you." But then suddenly he looked like an old man. "You know, this is the first day my entire life, I been out a work. I don't think I'm gonna get used to it."

You can get used to anything, I thought to myself. You can get used to damn near anything.

*Hi Mom,*

*How are you and things down there? I hope their good.
I'm done with work for today and I thought I'd write you a
letter. I've thought about writing you just about everyday but
I never really got around to doing it. Sorry! You have been in
my thoughts every day. Things are going well for me. This
weekend I was working and trying to write a new song while
everyone else was partying. I'm pretty proud of myself. I've
been making some really good friends. Our band has the best
drummer and keyboard guy around. We're layin down some
funky tracks. I sure hope everything is all right with you. I lost
the number again and the address so I feel bad about not calling you more often. I love you so much its hard to say, its
easyer to write. I'll try to call dad and get the number from
him. Jen and I are talking about coming out for Christmas, if
you want us that is. I'm writing you a song. I love you very
much,*

*Your son,*

*Jovis Hawkins*

GOOCH GOODELL, A COWBOY JEWELER from down the valley, showed up at our door one afternoon. I could tell he was a little wary about coming into the house, as if he might catch something. He refused a drink and stood in the doorway, until Pedro walked over and held out his hand for whatever it was he was holding. Gooch gave him a folded up piece of white paper, and Pedro took it in the palm of his hand, weighing it as he walked it over to me. I opened the paper, fold by fold, mystified by what it could be, until I saw the ring. It was perfect, a solid silver band with three small diamonds bezelled in a row.

"Like Orion's belt," Gooch repeated what Sam must have told him.

I put the ring on my left fourth finger, and knew we were wed on some level now. Perhaps time and space didn't mean so much — superficial dimensions that simply helped us keep our lives in order. We'd see everything more clearly someday — life but a piece of ribbon floating in the universe, twisting and combining what we thought were loose ends, beginnings and endings, births and deaths, an endless curve of experience.

"It's just what he wanted. And it's all paid up."

Somehow I doubted this last part, but I said, "Thank you, Gooch. It's beautiful. A real work of art."

He seemed a little sheepish standing there, tall and sweet and awkward, but then he remembered something else. Turning to Pedro he announced, "I've got some antelope meat in the truck." I could tell he wanted to get going, this emotional business was not for him. He mustered his courage and walked across the room, held out his hand and I took it. But I felt the effort in just lifting my arm.

Symptoms came and went — sometimes I felt as if I might be

in remission, and then the rug would be jerked out from under me.

"You take care of yourself," he told me.

"Yes," I answered, letting those words sink in, feeling their isolating effect.

I was no longer comfortable going into town, because I knew I'd see a familiar face and wouldn't be able to say, *Hi Marcia.* I would just stand there trying to swallow, going through the blank Filofax in my mind. I didn't like people looking at me, assessing my weight, or my lack of it. They inevitably asked, "How *are* you?" with too much enthusiasm, or — "You're looking so *good!*" but when I began to cough, I could see the horror, their disgust.

I turned the ring around and around, bringing up the triple diamond constellation, as if that were the only reality — the stars in the heavens, this ring on my hand. Sam seemed so close, I wondered if he were thinking about me at that moment. I hoped that he was.

JEN AND JOVEY ARRIVED like the two best gifts in the toe of my stocking. They came in with an armful of presents and an evergreen tree, which they had hauled all the way from Tucson. They insisted they wanted to do it themselves — "With popcorn and cranberries and everything."

I flashed on a scene when they were still young and made their own presents, how we cut up tin cans to make Christmas tree ornaments, sprinkling them with glue and glitter, building tiny wreaths out of miniature pine cones. They had loved spraying white flock on the windowpanes over stencils of reindeer and holly, setting up the crèche with its manger of hay. Jen would place the wise men at just the right distance, and Jovey would tend to the plaster animals. I remembered how excited they always were about hanging their stockings, setting out a snack for Santa, how Jackson and I gobbled up the cookies later, leaving crumbs and splashing milk on the saucer. For a moment I realized I actually missed Jack, missed being a family together.

Pedro shook Jovey's hand and gave Jennifer a rather formal hug. He was amazed at how much they had grown — "So *big*!" he insisted.

"Last time I saw you, you were a little fella — red cowboy boots!" Now Jovey wore dirty, torn grey Adidas.

Pedro had cooked up *posole*, a pork and hominy dish with lime juice and shredded lettuce on top, very festive, though I didn't think Jen would be able to handle that, so I'd asked him to make *calabacitas* too, with onion, sliced zucchini, *queso fresco,* and corn.

The kids said they had something more for me out in the car. I let them run out together while I sat in the living room. I couldn't figure out what was going on, though I could hear them whispering, giggling to each other. I heard a jingle bell sound, and then standing there in the doorway — I saw Buster in Jovey's arms, wearing a bright red bow and a grumpy expression. My heart clapped out with such happiness I nearly died laughing. Jovey put Buster on the floor, and the pug turned around and around, trying to figure out how to get the damn bow off. He approached me, stopped — a moment of recognition — then he barked and scolded for a good five minutes — *How dare you leave me in Boston.*

"What a grumpy old Santa you are," I said to him, and he gave me one last piece of his mind before I patted the sofa and he jumped up beside me, licking my face as if I were delicious. He then curled up, settling down right next to me. I had almost forgotten what a comfort he was.

We ate too much and stayed up late talking. I tried to ignore the waves of exhaustion. The kids avoided any talk about my illness. They were making an extraordinary effort to act normal, which felt abnormal, but it was so wonderful having them with me.

Jovey's band had made a demo for a New York producer, and he was trying not to be too optimistic, but Jen was full of enthusiasm. "Wouldn't it be a shocker, to just turn on the radio and hear *Jovey Hawkins?*"

She had decided to become a physical therapist, and she wanted, at some point, to give me a massage. They had brought a box of marzipan from Donna — the quintessential taste of Christmas. I started right in on a frosty peach with its crystalline glow, grateful that I wasn't on some dreadful diet. "She also sent this." Jen handed me a small, unremarkable package, but when I unwrapped the tissue, and saw the fetish, a smooth black mole with a turquoise arrow embedded in its back, I felt as if Donna was there in the room with us.

I asked if Donna was still seeing that lawyer, and Jen said no. "She's going out with a stone mason now. She thinks he might be the one, but she didn't want to jinx it. She'll call as soon as she knows." Jen glanced at my ring but didn't comment. Roberta Bricker, apparently, had run off to Barbados after delivering half-black twins. For a second I thought Jen meant that one was black and one was white, like salt and pepper shakers, but then I thought of that Christmas party — eggnog, mummers, and basketball players, and wondered how Bill was taking it.

"I've got some news of my own," Jen added, warily. "Didn't you wonder why I went from being a vegetarian to eating almost everything?"

"He's in training to be a chef," Jovey supplied.

"The Culinary Institute. I'll probably get fat."

"*Ooo scary*," Jovey added, and it felt like old times.

"So what's his name?" I asked, bracing myself.

"Tom," she beamed.

"Thank God," I said, and we all laughed. Both kids were in such good humor, I didn't feel I had to try very hard. I didn't have to perform or do anything special. I just sat back and actually watched *them* decorate the tree for a change, inhaling the fresh balsam scent of it.

I had written to both of them about my illness, assuring them that their father had nothing to do with it. I had told them how I hoped they would always remain friends, how I loved them both more than anything. All of that was understood, but we had not gotten around to talking about the big subject yet — that somehow seemed off-limits.

Jovey was eager to do chores, wanting to remain active. Pedro had him chopping mesquite, stacking it up on the side porch. We had a continual fire going in the living room, and it felt very cozy, sitting around together, doing nothing much. Jen was knitting me socks, of all things, using caramel-colored alpaca yarn. "You've got to take care of your feet, Mom." It was peculiar having her mother me. Maybe that was something I'd resisted before.

On the second day, Pedro took the kids out for a ride. I let Jen ride Banner, and Jovey wanted to try out the new grey. Pedro had been working Sam's gelding since the cattle had been sold, mostly to give himself something to do, and he thought the horse was safe to ride now. Besides, Jovey had always had a good seat.

But Jovey was bothered by the fact that no one had named the grey — he thought it made the horse seem like an orphan. I hadn't told the children about Sam, about Arivaca and the lightning, how we bought the grey as a replacement. I didn't mean to keep all this a secret from them, though much of my life since I'd left Beacon Hill seemed to be private, my own. It felt natural to keep the details of my love life to myself. I thought it would only confuse them.

Banging back into the house after the ride, Jovey was exuberant. "I've got a name!" he announced. He was obviously bursting to tell us, but instead of blurting it out, he filled the kettle for hot chocolate. We all waited until he came into the living room with a tray of steaming cups, whipped cream squirted on top of each one. Presenting them to us, he said, "Redondo."

We all listened to that, and let it sink in. "I like that," I nodded, "Redondo." Pedro agreed and so did Jen, though she scooped the whipped cream off the top of her cup and discarded it on the tray. *Redondo* meant round, and I thought of Sam lunging the little grey, around and around, first in one direction, then the other, how he patted the horse's neck and praised him. Sam would have liked the name.

"I wrote you a song, Mom," Jovey told me, but he didn't get up to go for his guitar.

Jen had to urge him — Well, come on, come on. She thought maybe she would be his manager someday, not a bad idea, for she was so organized, while he tended to list to the side, distracted.

I took Buster up on my lap as Jovey tuned his guitar. I could tell his feelings were as tightly strung as the metal strings, but finally he looked into the fire and began.

> *I've stood alongside of your holy fountain*
> *I've carried torches for your fire*
> *I've waited down on the steps of your dark temple*
> *I was commanded not to tire*

*Walking out on the mesa grande*
*just to hold myself right there*
*I called to you with an echo in a canyon*
*And heard my answer there—*

*Joanna, Joanna*
*Mama your name sounds so clear*
*Joanna, Joanna*
*Mama your name brings me near*

*You have a heart like a* GEYSER *in the desert*
*First oasis of my soul*
*You answered prayers & hopes & dreams to last a lifetime*
*You have a heart that won't grow old*

*I know it must be hard for you to slow way down*
*to hold so still in your slight frame*
*There is nothing that I would lay before you*
*except to sing your lovely name*

*Joanna, Joanna*
*Mama, your name sounds so clear*
*Joanna, Joanna*
*Mama, your name draws me near*

*But every year brings a transformation*
*I got some creases in my sleeve*
*I cross my fingers and begin to whisper*
*You got to dance when the waters freeze*

*If we could gather every single power*
*Hold it steady in our hand*
*We'd know enough of love to light up the heavens*
*Let it all collapse to stand*

*For Joanna, Joanna*
*Mama your name's a holy place*
*Joanna, Joanna*
*Mama you've showered our lives with grace*

When he was finished singing, we all sat there in silence. I looked up at my son, and wondered if I was dreaming — how could I be so lucky? Jen was wiping her eyes, but Jovey just nodded, looking down at the carpet. Finally he broke the silence and said, "I went to see Aunt Carla, you know. Before she died."

"You did?" I tried to sit up a bit. "Why didn't you tell me?"

"Because," he shrugged. "You were doubting me and everything. Aunt Carla thought it was good I dropped out of school, that I was pursuing my music."

"Is that why you ran away?"

"I wasn't running away, Mom. I never thought *you* were ditching *us*."

"I did," Jen said.

Jovey got up then and said he was going out to check on Redondo. Buster followed, and that left Jen and me alone together. She said how she wanted to give me a footrub, and I said I'd be delighted. We had slept so late that morning, the day was slipping away too fast. Going into the bedroom, I didn't turn on the light, but took Jennifer over to the window. The Huachucas were covered with a dusting of snow, and the sunset was turning the peaks a luminous opal. On the other side of the valley, the ragged Patagonias were etched with a golden light, as if someone had taken a gold magic marker and run it along the outline. Jen stood there and absorbed the scene while I watched the light pass over her face. I realized how beautiful she was, how she was this separate person, not something I was fighting against, within myself. "Can you forgive me?" I asked her.

She nodded, yes, but didn't want to talk. She heated up a pan of warm water for a lavender footbath. It was very soothing. She patted my feet dry, and helped me lie down, arranging the comforter over me. Then, sitting at the foot of the bed, she began massaging my feet all over, before concentrating on each small area. I winced at one point, and she said that spot related to the lungs. Another area, just above my heel on the inside of the foot, was also extremely painful, and she said that was connected to the uterus.

Jen said how she had convinced Jovey to give up smoking, and her protectiveness pleased me somehow. "He was smoking a lot of dope, but I made him record some songs while he was stoned, and he found out they were actually better when he wasn't."

I said that I was worried I would fall asleep, that this was making me so relaxed.

She said that was fine — it was good to let go — "It's really nice being able to do something for you. You always took care of everything — it didn't give me much of a chance."

I realized then that I was just now learning how to receive — you'd think that would be so easy, but actually, for me, it was the hardest part. I explained how it probably had something to do with my mother, because she was the one who'd always given to me, and when she disappeared, I had to protect myself.

"Protect yourself from what?" Jen asked, and without even thinking I said —

"From love." At last I knew, *from love.*

"Did you ever feel like you had to take her place?"

"In a way." I sounded a bit like a girl, a weary little girl, who didn't want to be in charge anymore.

As Jen worked I could feel my whole body giving in. I began to drop onto a deeper level. Her hands felt so sure, I gave myself over. I was in her hands, allowing for that.

"I'm afraid of losing you too," she told me. I could hear the emotion catch in her voice. "I'm afraid I'll spend the rest of my life thinking I was such a little shit."

I listened to what she said, then responded, "I was never a very good mother to you. I guess I was unhappy, and just didn't know it. You've got the best hands," I told her.

212

"I think it was great you came out here. We didn't get it at first — but now I see why. Dad can't hide all his junk behind you anymore. He does all this stuff with Granny Hawkins, the dutiful son trip, but it's driving him nuts. And you should see the basement — he's turned it into this whole environment for model trains — towns and tunnels and everything. Weird."

"It sounds like he's going to be a good grandfather, anyway."

"Yeah, I've been thinking about that. Tom would be great with kids."

"So would you," I added. "That's one thing I'm going to really miss." I could feel the grief coming, flooding my heart, and I didn't want to hold back now. Jen's hands had stopped moving, and when I glanced up, I could see she was crying quietly to herself as if she didn't dare show it. I opened my arms to her and said, "Sweetie, come here —" Jovey was in the doorway, and I reached for him too — they both climbed onto the bed and tried to cuddle up until all three of us were bawling, holding onto each other. Jen was sobbing as if her whole being might shatter, and Jovey was gripping me, saying — "Why? Why!" and when I turned to kiss him on the cheek, both cheeks, rubbing his hair back, he looked at me fiercely and made a sound that was somewhere between a groan and a growl, and then he put his head down on my shoulder and *bit* me — "Ow!" I yelled, and we all laughed together. They were trying to comfort me, to comfort themselves — but they were still kids and they were losing their mother.

Finally, exhausted, they both fell asleep — Jovey was upside down by my legs, with an arm slung over my ankles, and Jen, face flushed, was curled at my side. I breathed their sleeping essence.

PEDRO SAID THE VISIT HAD WEAKENED ME, but I didn't care. I didn't have to be strong anymore. I was just glad that I'd seen my children. I wanted to let the wind blow over me now. I wanted to empty out. Everything took such an effort.

Pedro asked if I'd talk to a priest he had heard about — he was from some Italian order of Franciscan missionaries who traveled all over, healing sick people. I thanked him but said I wasn't ready for that. I was discovering a new kind of existence that only wanted to rest. I felt open, like a brown paper bag full of wind. But sometimes the emptiness frightened me. I'd wake up with my heart crashing in my chest. *If anyone's up there, please help me!*

When I opened the door to Father Raphie, I thought I heard him gasp, as if he were taken aback by something — as if he were responding to the aura of disease, or perhaps he found me beautiful. That seemed unlikely. Father Raphie himself was not very alarming, of medium height and build. As he followed me into the living room, wearing his plain brown robe cinched loosely at the waist, I asked him what part of Italy he was from, and he answered with a thick Italian accent, that he was from Enna, in *Sicilia*. It made me think of Donna Marie — she always said that Enna was the bellybutton of Sicily. Her father's people had come from this central region, with its bountiful rolling countryside filled with gangsters and priests.

Father Raphie moved a chair closer to the sofa where I sat down, and he looked at me with such compassion I felt I was looking into the face of Christ. I could feel my sitbones even as I rested on the soft feather cushions — my wrists looked so thin, like bird bones, I thought. I wondered what he saw — a house finch, turned upside down in a glass of water?

As Father Raphie spoke, he half-closed his eyes and let the words flow through him — let the water of his words surge through his hands, like tributaries, articulate. "We are not so much human beings trying to lead a spiritual life —" he breathed out with a sigh — "as spiritual beings, trying to lead a human life." He then opened his eyes and looked at me, and I did feel I was registering more than his physical presence. "I make myself a receptacle, you see. God's energy is everywhere, and it flows into you. That is the important thing. We Catholics believe that God sends disease as a form of purification, does that make sense?"

Yes, I thought, like a childhood disease can make a child stronger, if it doesn't kill him first.

"Each person I come to is worthy to receive. You are an artist, yes?" I nodded, though I imagined he perceived everyone that way. "Every impression you take in, that does not find expression, becomes a kind of hardening. Breathe in divinity — exhale creativity. *Breathe in divinity, breathe out creativity,*" he repeated.

I thought of the two intertwining doves I'd carved for the children's Christmas — the image had come to me in a waking dream — two perfect doves above my bed, curving together — spaceless. The carving had seemed a crude representation, but it still had that mysterious combination of parts, the charm of any puzzle when the pieces fit together. Each of them had received one half.

But my tools were now too heavy, too cumbersome to lift, and I had put them away thinking, that was commendable, letting things go, releasing my hold on life, bit by bit.

But Father Raphie indicated that I should stay in touch with this creative part of myself — perhaps I could draw, or do watercolors. I did have oil pastels, and the thought of putting color on paper filled me with eagerness. I wanted to go straight outside to catch the rhythm of the mountains in the distance. I could feel this little spark igniting inside of me — I could feel it spring into a brighter flame, kindling a future I had been willing to deny.

He then placed his hands on my shoulders, and I bent forward. He seemed to enter a meditative mood. I could feel the warmth of his hands passing over me, but it also felt tingly, as if it gave me the chills. He told me that I wasn't a fighter, that I was used to losing, giving things up, but that I didn't really let things go — "That is your secret, yes?"

Yes, I nodded, for I did try to hold onto everything that had ever been precious or hurtful to me, kept it in my pink leather jewelry box. He could see a dark crescent, like a scythe over my heart, and he wondered if I were willing to change this. "God can only do fifty percent of the work. You have to meet Him halfway."

I had thought there was nothing I could do at this point. I wasn't taking medication, and this was the first time I felt there was something I could do to participate in what was happening to me.

"There is so much strife now, conflict of power — that battle is taking place inside you, too."

I told him about my fling with Tonio in Boston, and he didn't look as shocked as I thought he might be. He only said, "Some might say that's a very bad sin, but all I can tell you is cleansing is needed, purification is needed."

He went on as if he could see my entire life — "There is no one to blame. Do you believe that?" Not my brother who'd hurt me, not my mother who had left, not my husband, not Tonio, not Sam. He could sense all of the experiences I held inside my little pink box with the blade of death curving over it, as if these characters of the past were figurines I'd shrunken into idols for my own cult purposes. I had taken them out of the stream of life and let them harden and dry. I felt another tingle of energy wafting over my body as if there were some other-worldly breeze coming in. He repeated that I should forgive all I could, that I too needed God's compassion.

"Christ was only on the cross three hours!" he said with a vehemence that startled me. "Why do we always want to keep him there? Let Him come down, and live with us, *here*." As he said this, I could feel old resentments loosening, especially toward Jack and his moth-

216

er, who I felt had controlled him, contorting his nature, damaging us — but now blame was moving out, passing out through my fingers — I could almost feel it sliding away from me.

He asked if I felt hatred for anyone, and I immediately thought of Ken Treat. "Let go of that now," he instructed with such authority, that I opened my box and let that hatefulness go — then I felt a broad colorful spectrum of love washing over me, like water streaming over the windshield at a car wash, as if a golden-pink shower of peacefulness arched over my brain through rain-filled light.

He told me that it didn't matter to him if I were a Catholic or a Protestant, if my husband were gay or a Buddhist, or a Pygmy. We laughed over that. There was only One God, One Power, *One Life* — "Remember the first commandment and all the rest follows. God loves each one of us. We are the ones who make divisions, not Him."

At gut level, I was sure this was true, but what did it mean for me. He returned to the sickle that was over my heart. He said it was tempered by a very great sadness. I told him about my mother, who had died when I was eight. "How would you feel," he asked, "if you knew you hadn't lost her, that she was still right there for you. Just as you are there for your children." I started to cry. "Your mother has never forgotten you. We are all born, and we each have our moment, our time to move on — we do not know what is waiting, exactly. What's important is how you live right now, and how you choose to die." He told me I could take this sickle, this scythe, and make it into a circle — I could bend it around, and when the two ends met, I would see a ring of light.

In my mind's eye, I pictured my self-wounding weapon coming full circle, making a silvery moon, a shining ring, a hula hoop!

"Good," he laughed, as if he could see a softening — I was standing in my old backyard, working my hips, whipping that pink plastic ring around and around — *back and forth, back and forth,* a sexual movement. Ashamed of moving my body in that motion, I let it drop. He must have seen my face fall, for then he said — "Pick the ring back up — lift it over your head."

I closed my eyes and imagined stepping inside the hula hoop. It was shimmering now, and I lifted the circle and then tossed it up into the air — the circle expanded into a halo that went out into wider and wider circles, rippling outward into concentric rings, moving further and further away, until the universe seemed to make a kind of music that was more like chords of light than sound.

I imagined myself in the woods back home, coming down the path that ran through the forest when the leaves were uncluttered — that young, citrus green that delights the eye — myrtle warblers and the veery's high watery song, rolling through the treetops, lifting me up — my heart felt weightless, and Father Raphie said, "Good, give yourself this time."

Then he asked if he could pray over me. I said yes, and he put a hand on my forehead. I felt myself falling back, as if a breath of air had just pushed me over. I could feel my own breathing going in and out, and I said to myself — *Whatever God Wills, Whatever He Wants* — I just lay there while he kept his fingers pressed on my forehead — his other hand cupped, as if receiving rain. He moved this hand over various parts of my body as if he sensed hot or cold springs, and when he took his hand away, I could still feel the impression of his fingers on my forehead. I felt dazed, as if I'd been flung back in years and had awakened with innocent eyes.

He told me to stay there, to just lie still, and I felt a deep, utter calmness. He took my two hands and opened them, unstopped a little bottle of oil, and said some words in Italian, marking the palm of each hand and my forehead. "I am wrapping you in a blanket now. It is for comfort, protection, a glowing warm blanket all around you. You can put this same blanket around your children. You carry those children in your womb nine months, but you also carry them in your soul. They are still inside you. Your love will continue, even when you are gone. We Italians like to go home to die, and if that happens, you will have peacefulness. God bless you," he said then, though I was falling asleep and barely whispered, thank you. I felt very small, like a tiny newborn all wrapped up — it was as if he had scooped me out of dangerous water and wrapped me in flannel swaddling cloth, rested me in the arms of my mother, who still cared for me, who loved me so — I could almost hear her singing, as she rocked me back and forth.

"I ALWAYS GIVE UP SMOKING FOR LENT," Pedro confessed. "But it sure can make me want some sweets." He set a bag of supplies down on the kitchen table and pulled out two packs of hotdog buns. I wondered if he were planning a picnic, but no, the buns were for *capirotada*. He raised his eyebrows and licked his lips, explaining how Mexicans always made this dessert right before Easter. "It might not look pretty, but it's better than anything."

I remained skeptical as he melted a hunk of butter and proceeded to slather it over the opened buns, which he then toasted on trays in a slow oven. Meanwhile, he began opening bags of dried fruit — figs, prunes, apricots, pears, raisins, dates, even dried blueberries, chopping them up, tossing them together in a stainless steel bowl. He then melted down a big brick of Mexican sugar, diluting it in water with vanilla, adding cinnamon and clove, letting it simmer into a dark brown syrup. After spreading the mixed fruit over two layers of buns, he poured the syrup over all of it, covered the top with aluminum foil and slid the baking pan into the oven.

The smell of cooking fruit permeated the house. The anticipation of sweetness made us hungry for nothing else. But when Pedro pulled the *capirotada* out, he said — "Now we've got to let it cool some, otherwise it melts the ice cream too fast."

I was patient for almost half an hour, and then pleaded with him to serve it up. I hadn't been eating much lately. Still, I took a good helping of the warm bread pudding, and he scooped vanilla ice cream on top. Sitting across from each other, I lit a candle, and Pedro bowed his head. I bowed mine too, but snuck a peak at the pooling ice cream. Pedro crossed himself, and then we both dug in. I had never tasted anything so delicious.

Pedro said that he'd take me into Patagonia on the following morning for Easter Mass, though he usually went down to Nogales where the service was in Spanish. I had called the priest the week before, and had asked him if I could take Holy Communion at Easter. I knew that wasn't normally acceptable, but Father Anthony had said yes.

On Easter morning both Pedro and I decided to fast. I still felt full on the *capirotada* from the night before, but Pedro didn't even make coffee for himself, and he looked a little groggy driving into town. On the way down Harshaw Creek Road he remembered that Father Anthony was known for the length of his sermons. Maybe he should have made coffee after all.

The church was practically full, but we found a place about half way in. As we settled down, I saw Pedro nod to a beautiful *Chicana* across the aisle. She wore a black lace mantilla over her head, a garish pink dress with matching shoes. She was even wearing black lace gloves. She turned to smile, and her eyes glittered — I was shocked. It was Manuelita. My whole body flushed with an indescribable emotion of horror or shame mixed in with a desire to stare at her, to speak to her, to know everything she knew about Sam. Why had they broken? Was she in touch with him? Had they been in love?

She turned her attention back to her prayer book. Pedro confirmed it was Manuelita Hermosa, daughter of Betty and Rudolpho Hermosa, "from over near Lochiel." Pedro never mentioned Sam anymore, as if he thought that would only upset me, but I longed to talk to someone about him. Where was he? What was he doing? Was he healthy, happy, riding a new horse? Was he getting along on the job? Did he ever think about coming to see me? I prayed for him, that he would forgive me, that I could see him once more and explain.

Father Anthony came down the aisle with two altar boys dressed in spotless white. The church was relatively modern, with yellow stained glass windows. There was an airy, full feeling in the room. Perhaps it was the mood of Easter — after all the darkness and suffering — an elevated feeling, a lifting up. It was a relatively poor town, mostly Hispanic, but the altar was covered with an abundance of lilies, and their scent drifted toward us.

Father Anthony told the congregation how he had just been up north in Montana doing missionary work, and how terrifying it had been for him commuting between these two small towns, mainly because of the way this other priest drove, braking and pumping the accelerator, talking as he sped over the icy roads. Father Anthony spared no histrionics, imitating the braking and speeding motion, bobbing back and forth.

But then one day as they were driving, Father Anthony said, they skidded on black ice and went right off the highway, down an embankment. He was amazed that he felt totally unprepared, not ready for the end. "All was a blank," he said. "I didn't even pray, or have time to call on God." Father Anthony asked himself what he had learned from the experience, and he had to admit — "It's good to have a big, heavy car!"

We all laughed, but I wondered — was anyone prepared when it came to death? The surprise of that first contraction. Was I getting ready now, or would I get better, despite the doctor's prediction? I seemed to be in some kind of holding pattern — or was I fooling myself? I was especially grateful that I had seen my children. I felt more at peace about them now. I believed they would do well. They were leading their own lives, and felt good about themselves. I would not have to mourn my children, as I had mourned my mother. They would outlive me. They would move on. They were protected by something far greater than anything I could provide.

Father Anthony scolded his congregation, saying that he thought more of them should have been there the night before, at the Easter Vigil, when the church was bare, and only one candle burned. But I could also sense the love he felt for these people, urging them to bring their children to church, especially the teenagers, imploring the parents, saying over and over how important it was.

As we were called forward for Communion, our row filed out at the same time as Manuelita's, and our eyes met for a moment before we turned, walking up to the front together. I lifted my hands to receive the host. I could see that almost everybody else simply opened their mouths to receive the wafer directly onto their tongues, but Father Anthony placed the small white wafer in my cupped hands and said the same words he said for everyone — "The Body of Christ," and I said, "Amen," taking the host to my mouth, letting it dissolve, and then I received a sip of wine from the goblet, and crossed myself, "Amen."

As we sat back down, Pedro checked his watch, and then whispered, "If he sees anyone looking at the clock, he adds on another ten minutes."

The service lasted close to two hours, but I felt good, strangely happy. Right after the processional, I saw that Manuelita had slipped out ahead of us, and that Father Anthony was giving her an Easter embrace as he did with everyone who passed, taking each person's hand, blessing the babies. One mother insisted that he kiss each one of her children. He shook Pedro's hand, and spoke to him in Spanish, before turning to me, saying how glad he was that I'd come.

Manuelita had paused and was waiting for us. She seemed breathless, nervous when she greeted Pedro. She must have known him from her days with Sam. But then she turned to me, and said hello. I realized that she knew who I was, and that she knew that I knew about her. Pedro moved on to speak to someone else, and I could tell she had something she wanted to say to me. I walked with her out to the parking lot, to her vintage copper-colored Ventura. It was in perfect condition. Even the interior looked pristine. She kept her gaze down on the cement as we moved, as if she were afraid to speak to me. I thought she wanted to tell me something about Sam, something about his character. Maybe they shared some awful secret. Did she still love him? Was she jealous of me? Did she know where he was? Did they speak?

But then stopping by her car she looked up and said, "I've been lighting candles for you." I was taken aback. All of my questions flew from my head. None of them seemed to matter. She didn't want news about Sam, but she was there with me because of him. It was as if our meeting had evoked him, and he was with us there in the parking lot. He was all around us, in the texture of the air. He existed, I was sure, like *all love* existed, in every direction — he was a part of our love, and in that sense he was everywhere. Which was almost like being nowhere.

FOR ALL THOSE MONTHS I felt I was waiting. I had said his name like a mantra or prayer — Samuel Harrigan Sixkiller Mendoza, each word like a point in a constellation, lighting the night sky above my house. I was waiting for him to appear, to come stand in the turquoise doorframe with the sunlight behind him, shaking his head. I would reach out a hand and he would come take it. Practicing this now, the gesture leaked out of me, yet my life was strangely full, full of all we'd held, which hadn't died inside me, which wasn't dying, would never die, though I hated to think of his bitterness.

At certain moments that trap door, hope, would suddenly open and I'd be falling through space — there was nothing to stop me from falling, blank dark waters without resistance, sinking, until I had lost my breath. Then I thought of those pulsating jellyfish and tried not to panic, but slowed myself down, as if I could breathe like a plant underwater.

Lack of sleep perhaps changed my waking hours, for even inanimate objects seemed to take on this vivid, articulate quality, so that the dots between the numbers on the clock on the wall had a kind of perfection about them. Sam still seemed to penetrate my world, perhaps the way Christ fills the life of a nun, making each moment significant, her heart bereft. The memory of his words often rose to the surface like a figurine released underwater. *Fancy,* he'd say, or— *Lightning can't kill a Mexican.* I felt the righteousness of his warrior blood urging me not to give in, but I also heard a blind giant's booming footsteps sounding in the heavens above me.

I imagined him riding his paint, Arivaca, over the San Rafael, whooping and raising his voice to the moon, just as the sun put a glow on the Huachucas. I imagined him building me a simple cross, decorating it with ribbons that would ripple in the wind, colorful flowers that would quickly catch dust. Maybe he'd carve a hummingbird in a heart where the pieces met — it is what I would have done for him. Maybe he would sit halfway up the foothills and wait for the poppies to all twist shut, as the Patagonia Mountains took on that jigsaw outline. I imagined his eye traveling over it, as if he were feeling his way toward my pain.

But when I realized that I was only fooling myself, about his warrior blood and how it would cure me, that he would not be able to honor my grave, that it would be too late to call and explain, too far for him to come, then I was as mad as a swarm of killer bees, mad at God for allowing us our moment, only to snatch it away. *Ha*, I thought, what an Indian giver, taking and expecting the bounty to remain. But maybe God gave life and then took it back again because He knew it was all One Nation. Those luminous jellies in the darkness of their tank, contracting in order to move themselves forward.

I gathered my relics around me, wanting to make my own holy niche — colorful bottles and pools of wax, Jovey's round face on the baby medallion key chain they'd given us at the hospital, the little yard-sale pin Jen bought me for Mother's Day, back when she could still say, *I love you.* It was a basket of flowers — the blossoms were jewels — half of them were gone and there was no pin to attach it, but I kept it propped on the windowsill — the lucky sixpence from my Aunt Carla, the postcard of a peacock from a Roman wall, and Sam's yellow-faced watch, the one he'd been wearing when he got struck by lightning, 2:10, both hands pointing in the same direction like hands in childish prayer. Maybe time itself had saved him. So, why did it have to be my turn, now? I thought perhaps I should mail the watch back to him, tell him it was time to come, that I had only been trying to spare him. But I could imagine him stomping on the face of it, discarding the past — over and done with — behind him.

I couldn't bring myself to tack up his photo, the one with the corner creased from my wallet. He was wearing no shirt, hands on his hips, looking down in the dirt for something. I didn't want to limit my memory, as if contemplating that pose would seal his fate too, like the photos in the Catholic cemetery marking each tomb, but he was not a dead man, and I wanted to remember the living, loving man who liked to sneak up behind me with his sinewy arms — it didn't take much to set off that kindling heart of his or to get his blood rushing in his veins. Often he would just walk away from his nature, and with me he had such maddening, admirable control, sleeping together with most of our clothes on, pulled tight into the safe lock of his arms, bending before the curve of his body, snapped into place, wanting to get closer, skin against skin — thank God he had never come into me.

My joints ached, and I couldn't seem to get enough liquids. Pedro was there, resolved to stay by me, though I felt I was wasting away. He brought lemons from Tubac, made vegetable broth. His presence was calming. He didn't get alarmed, even when I cried out, even when I swore — *Jesus, I want my life back!* He would go and sit in the rocker on the porch and roll his Bugler tobacco. The sound of his chair was a comfort to me — it took me to another time.

I was swimming and my hands were making a pathway, moving through the dots of algae on the surface — when I sat in the car the blue leather was hot — my skin stuck onto it — pulling lilies of the valley up to hear them squeak, making a crunchy handful, the pole she used to prop up the clothesline, those punty boats of milkweed pod, the tissue-thin material of my summer pajamas, how I'd swoon on the ground beneath the deep purple lilacs. I could feel the cool of our secret club in the spring house with its moist sand floor, the root-beer taste of the sarsaparilla saplings — and then the weight of her bracelet, picking out the charms — the gold bench where the two hearts sat. Was my life but an accumulation, *jingle jangle?* The wrought iron lamp with the stick figure girl, the bright yellow bulb that kept away bugs and the face of a witch in the bathroom marble at school, the red handprint from my father's hand, the pink and white stuffed dog that took up a corner of my room — I didn't even care much about it, but it was the only thing I'd ever won — dragging up the dented, metal, flying saucer, the red mitten wool that stuck to my hands — the smell of the wreath, between the storm door and the front door, that luxurious feeling of tiredness, finally, coming home.

Last week I had a day when I thought I felt better. I told Pedro that I wanted to ride. He had to lift me up onto the saddle, and then tied me on with a rope. Banner seemed to know to take it easy and didn't even jog. We just walked down the dirt road in the direction of Lochiel, heading south to where the sky seemed to open — the clouds in continual soft rearrangement. The sun slashing through made the grandiose scene appear personal, mine, almost intimate. But by the time I got home I was slumped forward in the saddle. Pedro only said, "OK, maybe that's enough now."

That same night I heard the trumpets of a heavenly host and yet there was also deep silence, deep and hollow as a giant bell. And when the formation came close — golden beings composed of light, almost without outline — the sound of vibration became sweeter still, and yet I did not really see or hear them, but sensed a warm wind, pushing me forward, caressing like my mother's hand, flowers littered in a pool of light at the doorway — *Avanti avanti* — I heard. There was the taste of little apples in the rain-moistened air and I was carried in a hammock made of strands, but as I flowed out into luminous space, I was reminded of a moment from my childhood when the catkins hung like slender dancers from the birch trees and the shad tree bloomed in the forest — it was as if all the beauty of the world held its breath, and then I saw my son, riding up beside me — reaching out to take my hand —

I ask Pedro to drive me down to the Sonoita Creek, to stay in the pick-up while I make my way down to where the water bends. I rest there amidst the bright green grass along the river and wait to see a heron lifting from a cottonwood like an apparition, following it with my eye to where it lights upon a tree further downstream. My eye follows for as long as it can, from limb to limb, progressing, the heron with its wide wingspan, blue-grey, like the color of wood smoke. It shouldn't be so difficult to follow.

The creekside path is crowded with mesquite. I wonder how much longer I'll be able to do this. My awareness of my limitation makes the moment lit, like a candle burning in an alcove. I imagine both children beside me now, Jackson too. My father is there, grey and solemn as Berkshire granite. I want to hold his hand, but he is cold, unyielding. I remind him of the time he saved my life, and he looks up. I say, You know if it hadn't been for you, coming to the pasture when Pee-wee dared me — chased by that mean mare — if it hadn't been for you, picking up that two-by-four, I'm sure she would have kicked my brains out. Now I want him to hold me, not to let go — then I see her standing in the distance, like a welcoming presence, as if time were nothing but the briefest moment and she were just opening the door — I look through and see the heron flying further downstream — I follow its flight — it is pulling me along, and then I am alone with Sam. He is saying that this is all a mistake, that he never should have believed me, throwing him out, that he would take care of me now. He would make me live, and I would get better. I would do it for him.

> *And I'll be fine again, won't I?*
> *Of course, of course.*
> *It's just my heart. It's not used to being so happy.*
> *I've been everywhere, trying to forget I ever loved you.*
>     *Can you forgive me?*
> *Forgive you?*
> *You'll live, you have to — you've got to live!*

His heart, so mysterious and proud. His arms like the dry gnarly branches of the mesquite, that good, smart tree, worthless on the range, snapping hot in the cookstove, but my fire has settled into ashes now with no more embers, rain down the chimney and remnants of wood smoke drifting downstream, for I am no longer fighting it — *easily easily*, stroking the side of my mare, telling her that she is a good girl, and I want to tell Sam that I am at peace now, at peace inside myself, at home in my own diminutive kingdom. It is our quietest glory.

*And Lord a soul's been realized,*
*the most deeply kept secret of your ends.*
— Marina Tsvetaeva